ADRIANA PRIDEMORE

Thank you to the other half of my heart.
To my wonderful husband, Frank. You keep me going.
Also, thank you to Stacy and Michael for always being my
cheerleaders and my lab rats.

CONTENTS

REVELATIONS

"Hurry up!" Malcolm glanced back at Madraeus and Rami. "The secondary tunnel is down here."

Farther up the tunnel behind them, they could hear the elevator. It had almost reached the bottom of the mine shaft, bringing the police with it.

"Why are the police even here?" Malcolm muttered.

"Cecelia must have tipped them off," Rami answered.

"She knew we'd have to stay and clean up after the battle." Madraeus scowled. "She set us up."

Madraeus mentally kicked himself. *I should have found Cecelia sooner. I shouldn't have been distracted by hunting down Whitney's ex-boyfriend. I should have noticed Cecelia was building an army. I have been dealing with Cecelia's insanity for more than 1,200 years. I should have known better!*

The three vampires ran past the cells filled with the smoking remains of Cecelia's prisoners. She had used them as human cattle to feed her army. As the smell of burnt flesh filled his nose, he knew those smoldering bodies had cut him off from Whitney forever.

Madraeus shook his head and followed Malcolm as the younger vampire led them to the secondary exit. Malcolm had found it during the battle while chasing one of Cecelia's vampire minions.

Rage surged up in Madraeus. *That vampire had attacked Whitney and nearly killed her. Even now she might be—* Madraeus stamped down that thought. He couldn't think like that. *Whitney has to live.*

Up ahead, shouts echoed out of their would-be escape route.

"We can't go that way. They must have found the second entrance."

"What now?" Malcolm looked at the other two.

"We go deeper into the mountain and wait."

"Oh, that sounds fun." Malcolm threw his hands up.

"We don't have a choice," Madraeus said. He turned and led them back to the main tunnel.

They turned at the first branch and then dodged down another tunnel. The sounds of the police faded as they ran deeper and deeper into the darkness of the mine. After about an hour, they stopped to rest in a side tunnel.

"Let me see that disk," Madraeus said.

Rami dug in his pocket and handed Madraeus the disk he had found in Cecelia's abandoned paperwork.

Madraeus sat down next to him and pulled out his cell phone. He flipped it open. The dim light from the screen reflected off the small piece of metal. He studied the image of three rabbits chasing each other around a circle, their ears forming a triangle in the center.

The giant sank to the floor and looked over Madraeus' shoulder. "Thoughts?" Rami asked.

"I think we've been chasing the wrong rabbit," Madraeus mused. "It's the symbol of the Three Hares."

"What do you know about these Hares?" Malcolm asked as he squatted against the opposite tunnel wall.

"They are not our friends!" Rami's deep voice rumbled in the darkness. "They have been hunting down members of the Races for centuries."

"They fancy themselves the protectors of humanity," Madraeus added.

"I've never heard of them," Malcolm said.

"They have not openly hunted in many years." Rami sighed. "Many of the younger members of the Races have never had to deal with them."

"Why?" Malcolm asked. "Not that I'm complaining, but why did they stop?"

"Not sure." Madraeus sighed. "Last time I had dealings with them was during the French Revolution. A large group of them were hunting in Paris, but then they just went quiet."

"Do you know who they were after?" Malcolm asked.

"No." Madraeus turned the coin over and over. "Why would she have this? What is Cecelia's interest in the Hares?"

"Unkhabami said that many of the Old Sources were imprisoned by the Hares," Rami reminded him. "I have seen this symbol in nearly all the texts I studied about the Old Sources."

"Maybe they marked the prisons with the bunny thing," Malcolm offered.

"It is possible," Rami agreed. "We need to get back to the office, reexamine those texts, and compare them to the Dreaded Filing Project. There may be a connection."

"But first we have to get out of here," Madraeus growled in frustration, snapping his phone shut.

"Rest," Rami cautioned him. "Then we can try backtracking the tunnels. Maybe we missed a hidden exit."

"By the time we do that, it'll be dawn," Malcolm grumbled.

Madraeus sighed. "Cecelia would never have used this as a hideout if there was only one entrance and exit. She loves to have escape routes."

"Me too!" Malcolm chuckled, making Rami and Madraeus smile.

The three men lapsed into silence. The only sound was a slight echo coming from somewhere in the mountain above where the police were discovering horrifying evidence of monsters.

They listened for a while.

"Whitney's right, you know." Madraeus let his head rest against the rock wall.

Rami turned to look at him. "About what?"

"She said that I should have killed Cecelia years ago."

"I agree!" Malcolm snorted from across the tunnel.

"It is complicated," Rami said to Malcolm.

"I don't see why." The younger vampire gestured helplessly into the blackness. "She's a pain in the ass, always has been. Would have saved a lot of time and trouble if someone had offed her a long time ago."

Rami sighed. "It has to do with honor."

"Whose honor?"

"Mine," Madraeus said. "I made a vow a long time ago. I always thought honoring that vow was…"

They heard him shift his feet in the dirt. They waited for him to continue.

After a moment, he said, "It doesn't matter."

"But it does matter," Rami chided. "You have kept that vow for centuries."

"What kind of vow was it?" Malcolm asked.

Madraeus shifted again, trying to find a more comfortable spot against the icy rock. The bite marks on his arms and legs still ached. He hadn't consumed nearly enough blood to heal them completely.

"I made a promise to someone very dear to me that I would look out for Cecelia, no matter for how long, and no matter what happened."

"Why would you do that? She's horrid!" Malcolm cried.

"Shhh!" Rami hissed. They froze, listening for any sign that they had been heard by the police. Fortunately, only silence filled the darkness.

"So, what's the deal? Why would you want to look out for her?" Malcolm whispered.

"It's a long story."

"We have lots of time."

"All right." Madraeus began, "A long time ago—"

"In a galaxy far, far away?" Malcolm chuckled.

Madraeus couldn't help it, he smiled. "No. In a monastery, on a far, far away shore."

"A monastery?"

"Yes." Madraeus pulled his knees up and draped his elbows over them. "In the late 700s, I found myself on the doorstep of the St. Cuthbert Monastery on the island of Lindisfarne. I was taken in by a monk and shown considerable mercy, considering what I was."

"A vampire in a Holy House of God?" Malcolm grinned. "What could possibly go wrong?"

"Brother Edwin helped me when I was lost. I studied with him for years, learning the art of illumination and how to live with myself after all I had done." Madraeus smiled sadly as he remembered. "I owed him a lot. That's when I met Cecelia. Her father was one of the Viking chieftains who had come to the island to trade. She was wild and mischievous."

"I'll bet," Malcolm murmured.

"Even her father couldn't control her." Madraeus frowned as he thought back. "I'm still not sure how she became a vampire. I didn't turn her. I had tried to stay away from her, but I found her bleeding in the corridor outside my chamber. Her father went insane. He blamed the monks for turning his daughter into a demon. His men sacked the monastery. They destroyed everything. All those illuminated pages, years of work, all that knowledge was gone. They killed the brothers and took anyone else they could find for slaves. As he was dying, Brother Edwin made me vow to take care of Cecelia. I couldn't say no. He knew what I was, and he thought I could help her."

Brother Edwin had tried so hard to save his soul. He had given Madraeus purpose and hope when he'd had none. Madraeus laughed unpleasantly. "If only he had known."

"Known what?"

"Cecelia was half mad already. She was impossible to control. Becoming a vampire only made her more dangerous. Sometimes it was like she was being driven by demons in her head. Instead of me helping Cecelia, she took me down with her."

Madraeus fell silent. After Lindisfarne, he had chased Cecelia across Europe, trying to influence her, but it was like she had taken over his mind instead. He had succumbed to her ways. Wielding that much power and terror had intoxicated him. He had started to enjoy it. Her demons seemed to be in his head too, as a slithering voice that wound through his thoughts. He shivered, remembering that hissing voice reasserting itself recently.

Then he'd met Mary. His first real love. His wife. And with her, sanity returned, and he remembered all that Brother Edwin had taught him. He was ashamed of what he had become. Madraeus left his life of destruction and built a new one with Mary. He had been happy until the day he'd come home and found Mary's body. Cecelia had murdered her and massacred their entire village.

" Then why did you keep your vow?" Malcolm asked. His voice was filled with awe.

"Why indeed?" Madraeus muttered.

He had wanted to kill her. All that destructive power Cecelia had awakened inside of him called for revenge. He wanted to destroy her for what she had done. Her demon hissed in his head, tempting him, urging him on.

But then, he remembered Brother Edwin and Mary's faith in him. He would not betray them; he could not become that monster again. He knew he had to stay away from Cecelia; if he went after her, they would leave a path of destruction across the continent.

To honor their memory, he buried himself until he could control his raging pain. For centuries, he stayed as far away from Cecelia as he could. By the time he had been named the head of the Council of Races, it had been a little over 800 years since he'd had any dealings with Cecelia. By that time, he had become numb.

Over the subsequent years, Cecelia had surfaced and tried various schemes to take over the Council. By then, he had come to see her antics as more of an annoyance than anything else, and it had been easy enough to shut her down without breaking his vow.

But this time, something was different. She had never moved against the Council on such a grand scale before. And the hissing voice of her demon had slithered into his head again.

He had to get out of this mine and stop her once and for all.

PHILTZER'S CHASE

She was running for her life.

Hot on her heels, Philtzer could hear her crashing through the underbrush just ahead of him. Even if he hadn't been a werewolf, it would have been easy for him to track her. She wasn't trying to hide her trail. She was just trying to escape.

On and on, he chased her through the mountain wilderness. Although their pace had slowed a little, she showed no signs of stopping. He knew it was probably adrenaline keeping her going. She was terrified and wasn't stopping to find out that he was actually nice.

She has to be getting tired by now, he thought. *I know I am.*

It had been nearly twenty-four hours since Philtzer and Madraeus had come up into the mountains looking for their kidnapped receptionist, Whitney. Less than a day since enemy werewolves had jumped them and captured Madraeus. Less than a day since they stormed the abandoned mine to save

Madraeus and Whitney. And less than a day since Philtzer had first seen her, the cute little werewolf he was chasing.

She had been magnificent, facing off against a huge, white werewolf. It had stirred his blood watching them fight. The little brown wolf with the white paw had been fighting in any way she could against the well-trained fighting techniques of her albino opponent. She had been losing, but the passion with which she fought! Philtzer couldn't wait to catch her.

Philtzer wondered where the white werewolf had gone and thought, *Probably should have gone after that one instead. If she was fighting against this cute little wolf, then she was probably working for Cecelia, and I should've tried to catch her for questioning. Too late now.*

His tongue lolled out of his mouth as he panted. He needed a drink.

And a nap. And a sandwich, no, three or four sandwiches. Or maybe a pizza, he whined.

He could smell water just ahead of them. He slowed his pace. He wanted the little wolf to stop for a drink. She needed it as much as he did.

Philtzer slowed a little more. He wasn't worried about losing her. He could still hear her crashing through the trees ahead of him. Dropping to a walk, he picked his way carefully along her trail. The volume of her flight lessened and then stopped.

Philtzer smiled. *She must have noticed that I'm not on her tail anymore.*

He stood still, waiting with his ears pricked for any sound she might make. He raised his nose to the air and tried to detect the exact location of the water source. Then slowly, trying to be stealthy, he moved forward.

The moon was just beginning to rise as he neared the stream. For a moment, he watched from the shelter of a pine tree. She had indeed stopped to drink. Her ribs heaved as she tried to catch her breath. Philtzer ran an appreciative eye over her. She was delicate to the point of looking fragile.

Her head shot up, and she looked around.

Philtzer faded back behind the tree.

After a long moment, she picked her way along the bank of the stream, sniffing the ground. Then, cautiously, she stepped into the water. When all four feet were in, she turned and stepped carefully upstream.

Philtzer had to smile again. She was smart. She was trying to mask her scent and throw him off the trail. *Good try, girlfriend.*

He waited until she was almost out of sight then stepped out to get a drink himself. The icy mountain stream was like a shot of espresso, filling him with renewed energy. With his thirst quenched, he moved back into the shadows and followed her upstream.

Nearly an hour later, she stepped out of the freezing water onto the opposite bank. She stopped and scanned the trees behind her. Her ears flicked backward and then forward again. After a moment, she started down the mountain.

He followed sedately, often losing sight of her and tracking by scent alone. He hoped she would think herself safe enough to stop for the night and get some sleep. They both needed it.

The hours seemed to drag by as he continued to trail her. Periodically, Philtzer could hear the echo of car engines. They must be nearing a road. He wondered if she planned on finding a house or flagging down a car.

Philtzer chuckled to himself. *Would be a hell of a sight, driving along a mountain road at night and seeing a naked woman hitchhiking.*

The trees began to thin as they neared the highway. He could see her more often now. She wasn't turning to look behind her as much.

She must think she lost me, he smiled.

She began to run parallel along the road. In the distance, a faint glow lit up the low-hanging clouds.

Civilization. That'll complicate things, he thought.

He followed her until they could see the buildings. Then she stopped. For a long time, she stood staring down at the town. She finally flopped down on the ground, and he caught the sound of a quiet whine.

Philtzer crept a little closer until he was almost parallel to her. He didn't want her to bolt again. With a tree between them, he shifted into human form.

"Makes it complicated, huh?" he said.

The little wolf jumped to her feet and ran.

"Wait! I can help you!"

She stopped about twenty feet away. Standing on three legs and ready to run again, she watched him. Still squatting next to the tree, he held up his hands.

"I don't want to hurt you! I just wanna talk."

She didn't move.

"I saw you fighting against that white wolf."

Still, she didn't move.

"We're on the same side."

She took two steps away from him.

"Wait!" Philtzer spread his hands and gave his most charming grin. "Come on, at least let me get you off the mountain. Let me call for a ride?"

She looked around for a moment and then paced a wide circle around him until she was behind a large tree about ten feet away from him. She shifted into her human shape.

She peeped at him from behind the tree. "You don't have a phone."

Philtzer laughed. "Nope."

"So, how would you call anyone?"

"Well," he nodded at the lights below, "I don't mind trotting down into that town naked. You willing to do that?"

"No."

He grinned. "Then I guess you need me."

"I could just run as a wolf until I'm home."

"You could." He nodded, picking up a stick and poking the ground. "But my way is faster and will get us food a lot sooner."

She was quiet for a long time. Philtzer glanced over to see if she was still there. The moonlight illuminated her face. From what he could see, she was just as cute as a human as she was in wolf form.

"How do I know I can trust you?"

"Oh, come on, babe!" He shrugged, pointing to himself. "Nobody this good-looking could be bad. Am I right?"

He heard a snort.

"Seriously, honey, I'm the real deal: cute, heroic, and sweet." She snorted again.

"OK, think of it this way. I'm the other side of the coin," Philtzer said almost seriously. "If I'm the enemy of that old white wolf, and you obviously had a difference of opinion with her, then I must be okay. Why not let me tell you my side of the story?"

She stared at him from behind the tree for a long time. She nodded. "K. Talk."

"That's it?" Philtzer laughed. "Just talk?"

"You wanted the chance, take it. Who are you?"

CRAZY NAKED GUY

PHILTZER SAT BACK ON the grass and stretched his legs out in front of him. "My name is Philtzer. I work for the head of the Council of Races. We try to keep lovely people, like us, out of harm's way and give a hand to those members of the Races that are struggling with the mortal world."

"That's not what I heard."

"What did you hear then?" Philtzer heard her settle onto the ground behind the tree. He took it as a good sign. Maybe she was becoming less afraid of him.

"I was told that the Council wanted to subjugate all supernatural beings."

Philtzer laughed. "That's totally bogus! Let me guess... Cecelia told you that."

"No. Spark." She crossed her arms and shivered. It was nearing the chilliest part of the night. Even though it was late spring, it still got cold in the mountains, especially when there were no clothes or fur to keep a person warm.

"Who's Spark?"

"The white wolf I was fighting with."

"Ah. She works for Cecelia." Philtzer nodded and rocked his feet back and forth. "Well, she's a big fat liar."

"Spark found me and helped me when I didn't even know what I was. Where was your precious council then?"

"We would have found you."

"Yeah? When?" she snarled. "After I'd killed someone else?"

"Maybe."

She went silent. Philtzer waited.

"I don't want to be a werewolf."

"How long has it been?" he asked.

"A little over a week and a half."

"Damn, girl!" Philtzer laughed. "You're just a puppy!"

"Screw you!" She started to stand but remembered she was naked and pushed herself farther back behind the tree.

"I'm sorry! I was just surprised." Philtzer shook his head. "A week? So, what happened?"

"What do you mean?"

"Well, you were born with werewolf genes. It's a dormant gene." Philtzer sat up and rubbed his hands together, then stuck them between his knees. "Most of us don't become full-blown werewolves unless there is a traumatic event that triggers the instincts. Otherwise, you stay a perfectly normal human. So, what happened?"

When she didn't answer, Philtzer took a guess. "Car wreck?"

Still, she didn't answer.

"Were you attacked?"

"Yes," she whispered.

"I'm sorry." Philtzer nodded and stared off into the darkness. "It's scary as Hell when it first happens."

She scooted forward and looked at him around the tree. "How did it happen…?"

"To me?" Philtzer looked over at her. "I was shot."

"Were you a soldier?"

"No." Philtzer looked down at his hands. "It's actually kind of embarrassing."

"Getting shot is embarrassing?"

"No…" He grinned in spite of himself. "I was fifteen," he shook his head and looked around sheepishly, "and I was kind of sleeping with a married woman."

"15?" Sophia gaped. "With a married woman? That's messed up!"

Philtzer looked everywhere but at her. "Yeah, well, anyway, her husband caught us and took after me with a gun. I was scared shitless at first, but when he took that first shot at me, I got angry. I started to shake all over, you know, like right before you shift? Then that second bullet hit me, and I don't remember what happened after that. I woke up in the hospital. Found out later that the chick's husband was dead. They thought he'd been killed by some wild dog. But he wasn't. It was me."

"What did you do?"

"I ran." Philtzer shrugged. "After a while of living on the streets, Madraeus found me. Sorted me out."

"Madraeus? Isn't he the head of this Council you're so fond of?"

"Yep. Good guy. He was up at the mine." He looked at her, hoping for some recognition, "Kinda beat up. Had a sword."

"He was the one in the cell." She frowned as if trying to fit together a puzzle without the picture.

"Yep, Cecelia locked him up." Philtzer pulled his knees up and hooked his elbows around them. "They captured him when we were searching for Whitney."

"Who's Whitney?"

"Oh, she's this walking catastrophe that works for us as a receptionist." He shrugged and shook his head. "I've never seen anyone get into trouble faster than that girl."

"Is she a werewolf?"

"Nah, she's human."

"Human," she said longingly. She shivered again. "So, you came up to the mine to rescue this Whitney person, not kill her?"

"Yeah, definitely to rescue her! There is no way that we would kill her! Madraeus would go berserk!" Philtzer didn't want to imagine the explosion if anything happened to Whitney.

"Seriously?" she asked. "He actually cares about what happens to her? Even though she's human?"

"Yep, it's a long story." Philtzer shuddered as a wave of goosebumps raced across his skin. "Damn, it's getting cold! You wanna finish this conversation somewhere warm?"

"That would be nice, but I'm still not sure I wanna trust you."

"That's fine, but it's just as easy not to trust me where it's warm." Philtzer shoved to his feet. She scooted back behind the tree again. "You comin'?"

"Um. I'm naked."

"So am I!"

"Yeah, but you don't seem to care. I do."

"So, change into a wolf and follow me." He shrugged. "I'll slip down, make a call, and get us out of here. You can stay a wolf until we get somewhere with clothes."

Her teeth started to chatter. "I don't know."

"You'll be perfectly safe, I promise."

He sounded so sincere that she finally nodded. "All right, but if I don't like what's happening even for a moment, I'm gone."

"That's fair enough." He smiled. "What's your name?"

She hesitated.

"You can tell me your name." His smile went a little lopsided. "Come on, we've already been naked together!"

"Oh! Eww!"

"Come on... Come on..." he coaxed. "You know you wanna tell me."

"Fine. It's Sophia."

"Sophia...?"

"Sinclair."

Philtzer stopped grinning and gaped at her. "Wait. Sinclair?"

She watched him warily. "Yeah."

"You related to Regina Sinclair?"

Sophia looked as if he had slapped her. "How do you know my mother's name?"

"Ha!" Philtzer bounced around for a moment and cackled. "Dude! That's awesome!"

"Hey!" She scrambled to her feet, forgetting her nakedness. "Hey! Crazy naked guy! How do you know my mother?"

"I can't believe it! Regina had puppies!"

"I'm not a puppy!"

"She was always dead set against reproducin'!" He bounced over and grabbed her by the shoulders.

"Stop it!" Sophia shoved his hands away.

"I should have seen it! You look just like her!"

"Hey!" She punched him in the shoulder. "I asked you a question!"

"What?" He rubbed his shoulder, pretending that it hurt.

"How do you know my mother?"

"She taught me about being a werewolf!"

Sophia stumbled backward, shaking her head.

"What?" Philtzer sobered. "Sophia? What's wrong? Regina's okay, isn't she?"

"I wouldn't know!" Sophia wrapped her arms around her waist and turned away. "She ditched me when I was two!"

Philtzer stared at her back. He hadn't expected that. Regina had never been a 'family' kind of girl, but he wouldn't have thought she would abandon her kid if she'd had one.

"Sophia, I'm sorry." He stepped forward and placed his hand lightly on her shoulder. "There must be a reason."

"Doubt it." Sophia shrugged his hand off. "You just said she was always against kids."

"That doesn't mean that she would just abandon you. Regina's not like that."

"Whatever." Sophia turned away. "You coming?" She shifted into a wolf and started walking down the mountain toward the town below.

Philtzer followed her down the slope. He knew that Regina wouldn't just ditch her; there had to be more to it than that.

Philtzer shook his head and thought, *This poor girl is getting the raw end of the deal all around. Who knows what that wolf, Spark, filled her head with, and now her mom?* He sighed. *It's going to take me a while to get this one sorted out.*

STILL ALIVE

A SIGH WAS ALL Whitney could manage. She was so tired, so bone weary, so want-to-sit-down-and-give-up tired. Fuzzy memories of Mrs. Myers and Dr. Kirkland hovering over her mixed with nightmares about the mine and made her head hurt.

All those people in the mine had suffered as food for an army of vampires. Victims, like her. Terrorized and abused, locked in darkness, and half-starved. Their ghostly faces haunted her dreams. Their screams woke her again and again. When she opened her eyes, she expected to see nothing but the darkness of her prison cell. Instead, it was the cozy, rose-covered room at Mrs. Myers' house, but the darkness still wouldn't go away.

The blood that had been stolen from her by a nameless vampire in a mountain mine had been replaced. But her will to live hadn't come back yet.

"Hey there," a familiar voice said, "you awake?"

Whitney turned toward the voice. Sandra Conners was sitting next to her bed.

"Sandra?" Seeing her friend again pulled Whitney a little closer to the land of the living.

Sandra was no longer the straggly, gaunt prisoner Whitney had shared a cell with. A shower and clean clothes had made her look human again. Although after being held in the mine for three months, malnourishment still made her look like a blonde skeleton.

Whitney struggled to lift her weakened body. Sandra leaned forward and slid a hand under Whitney's back. Together, they managed to prop her up against the pillowed headboard.

"You're here? How did you get out?"

"Your boss let me out." Sandra shrugged.

"Madraeus?"

"I'm not gonna lie." Sandra sat down again. "He's scary."

"He can be." Whitney shuddered, remembering eyes as black as night, snarling fangs, and blood covering her apartment after Madraeus' fight with Justin. But she also remembered how resistant Madraeus had been to the idea of feeding off of her to stay alive.

On the last day down in the mine, she had been locked in the cell with Madraeus. Cecelia knew that he had lost so much blood from his wounds that he would be forced to feed off Whitney to survive, hopefully killing her in the process. But he had repeatedly refused until Whitney had goaded him into feeding so they could escape.

When Cecelia's vampires had fed off her, it had been a violation. But with Madraeus, his touch had been gentle. Seductive.

It felt like he... Whitney shook her head, unwilling to finish her thought. She tried to focus on what Sandra was saying.

"I wasn't sure what would happen when they brought me here," Sandra looked around, "but they're nothing like those bastards in the mine."

Whitney thought about her new friend's assessment of the people she worked for. Most were good deep down, but they were still monsters, and it didn't take much for their scary side to come out.

"You're okay though?"

Sandra shrugged. "So far. Just been a lot of trying to get me to the 'still alive' stage, same as you."

"Have you contacted your family?"

Sandra looked down. "Not yet."

Sandra was the most practical person that Whitney had ever met. She had never failed to say what she thought, regardless of what it was. Whitney hadn't known her for more than a week, but she had the feeling that Sandra wasn't telling her something.

"Sandra?" Whitney prompted.

She glanced up, met Whitney's questioning gaze, and looked away again. "Whitney, there's something that you should know, but I don't think—"

The door burst open, cutting her off. Elizabeth Martindale bustled into the room and landed on Whitney, enveloping her in a breath-stealing hug. "Oh! My poor Whitney. You've had a rough time of it." She sat back and went straight to fussing with Whitney's blankets and pillows.

"Grammy?" Whitney gasped as she was jostled by her grandmother's rearrangement of the bedding. "How are you here?"

Whitney's mind raced. *Does she know about the Races, or is it just that I've been missing and Mrs. Myers called her?*

"Whit? You okay?" Elizabeth sat forward and brushed Whitney's dark hair away from her face.

"I'm okay," she lied. She tried to smile for her grandmother's sake. "I'm just really tired, Grammy."

She had no idea what to say. She wished again that there was some kind of script to follow with this whole 'don't tell mortals about the Races' thing.

"I'm not surprised after what you've been through." Elizabeth sat back and shook her head. "I'm still not sure about all this vampire, werewolf, witch nonsense."

"It's not nonsense. They are very real." Sandra raised her hand. "I can vouch for that."

"Wait!" Whitney stared at her grandmother. "You know about them?"

"Yes, I know about them."

"How?" Whitney searched her grandmother's face for signs of distress.

"I came to that 'office' you work at looking for you."

"You came to InfiniCorp?" Whitney squeaked, imagining all the ways that could have gone wrong.

"Yes." Elizabeth pursed her lips. "It was an eye-opening experience."

Sandra laughed, drawing Elizabeth's attention.

"You find this funny, missy?" Elizabeth stopped as she took in Sandra's emaciated appearance. "Who are you? What happened to you?"

"This is Sandra," Whitney explained. "We were in the mine together."

Elizabeth looked from Sandra to Whitney and back again. Elizabeth sighed. "I wish you hadn't gotten involved with all this."

"I didn't mean to."

"I know it wasn't your fault, honey."

"Yes, it was," Whitney murmured.

"Whit, you didn't make all this happen. You were just in the wrong place at the wrong time."

Whitney shook her head. "That's not true, Grammy."

"Yes, it is. Your temp agency assigned you to the Infini-Corp office. I don't call that a choice."

"It's more complicated than that, Grammy. I was singled out. I was picked to be harassed and hunted."

"You're confused and not thinking right. No one picked you out for this."

"Yes, they did!" Whitney's frustration bubbled over. "Cecelia did all this!"

"Whitney, I don't—"

"No! You're not listening!" Whitney cried. "In the mine, Cecelia told me!"

"Calm down and tell me what you're talking about."

Whitney sniffled and swiped at her nose. She took a calming breath.

"When I was in the mine, Cecelia told me that she had planned all this from the beginning. She bought the recording studio so she could put me out of work. She turned my boyfriend into a vampire so he could hunt me and put me in danger. All to make me pathetic enough that Madraeus would hire me and try to protect me."

"That sounds a bit far-fetched."

"It's true."

"Why would she do that?"

"I don't know!" Whitney sniffled again. "She told me that she picked me because I was so pathetic that Madraeus couldn't help but come to my rescue, and that would keep him distracted."

"Hey, at least you were important." Sandra chuckled. "I was just dinner!"

Elizabeth glared at her. "You're not helping."

"Sorry."

Elizabeth returned her attention to her granddaughter. "Why would she want Madraeus distracted?"

"I don't know." Whitney shrugged. "Maybe she didn't want him to notice the army she was building."

Elizabeth frowned. "Seems like an awful lot of trouble if you ask me."

"Why not just kill Madraeus?" Sandra asked.

"What?" Whitney stared at her friend.

"Well, I was thinking. If she's so worried about him finding out what she's doing, why not just skip to the end and kill Madraeus instead of all this elaborate distraction crap? It gets him out of the picture once and for all. That's what I would've done."

"Well, you're practical and she's nuts!"

"That may be, but it seems to me that she is wasting time and energy screwing with Madraeus. Why not just boot him out of the picture altogether?"

Whitney thought about it. Cecelia had made a point of using her to torture Madraeus, but she had never tried to kill him.

"I think their relationship is really complicated."

"Complicated?" Sandra laughed. "It sounds downright sadistic!"

Whitney thought back to the conversation she had had with Madraeus in the mine. She had asked him the very same thing. 'It's complicated,' he'd said. When she'd pushed him for an explanation, he'd snarled at her with his fangs out. Whitney shuddered at the memory.

Her grandmother saw her shiver and stood. "This will keep for another day. It's time you got some sleep."

Whitney did feel exhausted, but there was one thing nagging at her. "Wait, Sandra, what were you going to tell me?"

"Ah," Sandra glanced at Elizabeth, "we can talk about it later."

"But..." Whitney started to protest, but her grandmother was already pushing Sandra out the door.

"Get some sleep, Whit, I'll check on you later."

"What aren't you telling me?" she asked, but the closed door couldn't answer.

MOONLIGHT STROLL

PHILTZER MADE HIS WAY down to the town. He had shifted into a wolf because, despite his protestations that he didn't mind being naked, it was cold. Behind him, Sophia waited just inside the tree line. It was far enough into the night that most of the houses were dark. Only the barflies were awake.

He padded cautiously down one alley and up another. He was looking for the perfect house. Not one with toys in the yard. Not one with cars parked outside, or with home security signs.

He moved out of the nicer area of town and over to the poorer side. Three more alleys finally brought him to the perfect house. The porch light was on, but there was no car out front, and no lights on in the house. Three or four newspapers were disintegrating on the sidewalk, and the weeds weren't mowed.

Philtzer crept closer. His black fur helped him blend into the shadows. He crept up to the back door and glanced around. Everything was quiet. He shifted to human form and peered through the dirty glass window next to the door. Nothing moved. He tried the door. It was locked, but the house hadn't been painted in so long that the wood looked half-rotted from the weather. He scanned the area one more time, stepped back, and threw his shoulder against the door. It cracked and popped open easily.

Cautiously he stepped inside, shifting back to wolf. He let his ears and nose scope out the house. It stunk like old cigarettes and stale beer. No one was home. He padded through the rooms looking for a phone but couldn't find one.

In the bedroom, Philtzer rummaged through the closet and found pants and shirts for each of them. He grabbed a hoodie and a jacket. He looked for shoes. Although this guy's feet were too small for him, he grabbed a pair of flip-flops for Sophia. He piled everything together and wrapped the hoodie around it, tying the sleeves to hold it.

Philtzer carried the bundle to the back door and then went back to the kitchen. He grabbed the towel and returned to the bedroom. He wiped off everything he had touched in the room and then went to do the same for the back door. Tossing the towel back into the kitchen, he shifted back into wolf form.

Philtzer stuck his head out the door and sniffed. Everything was still quiet. He pulled back inside, picked up the bundle in his jaws, and slipped out the door. He loped back through the alleys toward the edge of town where he had left Sophia.

As he approached the trees, his eyes searched the shadows. He ran along the edge of the tree line; suddenly, she stepped out. He dropped the bundle in front of her.

She lowered her head and sniffed at it. She sneezed.

"Sorry, it's not the best," Philtzer said after he shifted. She backed up and averted her gaze from the naked man in front of her. He crouched down to untie the bundle.

"It's alright, babe, we've been naked together before!" He laughed and started to pull on the jeans. They were a bit big. He should have looked for a belt. He dug out a shirt and sweatpants, set them in front of her, and then turned his back to pull on the other shirt.

"This guy didn't have a phone, so we'll have to go down to the bar I saw on Main Street and call from there." Philtzer reached over and pulled the hoodie out of the pile. He yanked the string out of the hood and laced it through his belt loops, cinching it tight enough to keep the jeans from falling off.

"I can't believe you stole these clothes," Sophia said as she folded the top of the sweatpants over a few times to try and make them smaller.

"Desperate times, sweetheart." Philtzer grinned as he pulled on the jacket and reached down to pick up the flip-flops. "Here. You wear these."

She took the sandals from him and leaned against the tree for balance while she slipped them on. She glanced down. "I hope no one will be looking at your feet."

He followed her gaze and then shrugged. "His feet were too small for me."

Philtzer bent over to pick up the hoodie. He gave it a shake and handed it to her. She pulled it on and zipped it up. He stood with his hands on his hips and grinned at the picture they made in their oversized clothes.

"All warmed up?"

Sophia nodded. He started checking the pockets of the stolen jacket, hoping the guy had left some money, but they were empty.

"Right." He reached out and grabbed her hand. She jumped back, trying to pull her hand away. "Come on now. I won't hurt you." He tugged on her hand and started down the mountain. "We're just two people out for a stroll."

She followed him, but only because he wouldn't let go of her hand.

They worked their way over the uneven ground carefully since it was a lot harder to see the way without the benefit of wolf eyes. Finally, they reached the road.

"So, tell me what this Spark chick told you about being a werewolf."

"Well," Sophia hesitated, "not much really. She said that we were a superior species and we should be the dominant force on the planet, but the Council kept everyone under their boot heel. She said the time had come for a rebellion against the unjust control of the Council."

"And what did you think of that?"

"I thought she was right at first." Sophia looked off down the street.

"But..."

"But then I started listening and watching." They crossed an intersection to the main road. "I saw them bring up this..." Sophia shuddered, "man."

"What man?"

"I didn't know who he was, but he looked awful." She reached up and rubbed her forehead. "He was dirty and looked half-starved. And he was raving like a lunatic. They took him outside and let him go. He ran off into the trees." She started walking slower as she remembered. "A bunch of the wolves chased after him and..."

She stopped walking.

Philtzer turned toward her and prompted quietly, "And..."

"And," Sophia took a deep breath, "I heard screaming from the woods."

"I'm sorry."

"I asked Spark about it and she just shrugged and said, 'It happens'." Sophia started walking again. "That's when I started to doubt."

"Natural reaction."

"A few days later, something happened. I don't know what. Everyone was supposed to leave. They were loading everything into the back of semi-trucks. They were so busy carrying stuff and packing up that they didn't notice me slip away. I went looking and found a bunch of people locked up in cells down in the mine. They were all starved and half-crazy. Just like that guy they had…" She shook her head, trying to dispel the memory. "It turned my stomach. I didn't know what to do."

They walked a few steps in silence.

"That's when I saw your friend. He was in a cell with a woman. I didn't get why a vampire would be locked up since we were supposed to be," she made air quotes with her fingers, "in this together." She shrugged and said, "So, I brought him the keys."

"Thank you for that."

"I couldn't just leave them there, but I didn't want to be there when they got out. So, I ran. That's when I found Spark."

"And you confronted her?"

Sophia shrugged. "You saw the fight."

They walked in silence for a moment. The only sound was the distant music from the bar just ahead.

"Do you hunt people?" she asked quietly.

"Not like that." Philtzer shrugged. "But sometimes we have to hunt down our own kind if they get out of control and hurt people they shouldn't."

They walked a little farther in silence.

"How did it happen? You said you were attacked, but what happened?"

"My friend and I were on our way back to our apartment after a party. Four guys jumped us. They pulled us into the alley and," Sophia wrapped her arms around her waist again, "they were… um…"

Philtzer stopped and turned toward her again. "They tried to rape you?"

Sophia nodded. "We tried to fight back but... they... they had a knife and..."

"Hey," Philtzer lifted her chin with one finger so she would look him in the eye, "it's okay. I get it. You don't have to talk about it."

She looked away from him and started walking again. When she spoke again, her voice was almost steady.

"I just... I woke up in the hospital, all bandaged up." She glanced at him. "There was this detective there. He asked me all these questions about what had happened and if I'd seen some guy."

"What guy?"

Sophia frowned as she tried to remember. Finally, she gave up. "I don't know. I think it started with a J."

"What about the detective? What was his name?"

"Uh, I think it was Sa...Son..."

"Sanders?" Philtzer supplied.

"Yeah, that's it! You know him?"

Detective Sanders, thought Philtzer. *The same detective asking questions at InfiniCorp.* "I've heard the name." He shrugged, thinking that the detective was getting a little too close for comfort. "Go on. What happened next?"

"Well, I didn't know what he was talking about, and he finally left. I spent a few days in the hospital having nightmares about what had happened. Then this white-haired woman comes in and says she can help me."

"Spark?"

"Yeah," Sophia sighed and shook her head as they stepped up to the door of the bar, "I don't want to be a werewolf."

"Well," Philtzer held the door for her, "if it helps, you make a really cute wolf."

"It doesn't," she frowned at him, "but thanks, I think."

Philtzer moved over to the bar and motioned to the bartender. "Hey, can we use your phone?"

WANNA PRETEND

SOPHIA HUNG BACK AS Philtzer stepped up to the bar. She looked around and shifted nervously. A handful of die-hard barflies were the only ones left in the bar. The one on the nearest stool watched her through bleary eyes.

"Need a ride?" the bartender asked Philtzer as he handed him the phone.

"Sort of." Philtzer grinned sheepishly. "Actually, it's kind of a funny story."

The bartender stood back and crossed his arms expectantly.

"You see, my girlfriend and I were up camping and we got a little, you know," Philtzer glanced at Sophia, leaned forward, and said quietly, "frisky."

"Frisky?" The big man behind the bar raised his eyebrows but started to smile.

"Yeah, you know. Well, anyway, she got all excited and kinda kicked the door closed on the truck and," Philtzer looked sheepish again, "well, the doors locked and the keys were in it along with my wallet and our phones and everything."

"Really?" The bartender grinned at Sophia. She wrapped her arms around her waist. She wasn't close enough to hear what they were saying.

"I gotta call my buddy to bring my spare keys." Philtzer picked up the phone and dialed Thomas' number. "Is it okay if we get a couple of drinks while we wait? I can pay when they get here."

The bartender looked at him and then at Sophia. He chuckled. "Yeah. Sure."

"Beer for me and—" He turned to Sophia, making a drinking motion with his hand. "Drink?"

"Coke," she said as she joined him at the bar.

"Right." The bartender moved down the counter to get their drinks as Thomas answered.

"Hey, Thomas, can you come get us? Yeah, us." Philtzer paused for a moment, grinning at Sophia. "A town called Alma. Yeah. And bring the stuff."

"The stuff?" Sophia frowned as he hung up.

"Yeah, the stuff." Philtzer poked her on the end of the nose with one finger. She swiped at his hand. Just then, the bartender set down a bottle and a fizzing glass next to the phone.

"Can we grab a couple bags of chips too?"

The bartender popped two bags off the little rack next to the register and tossed them up next to the drinks.

"Thanks." Philtzer picked them up and nodded toward the back of the bar. "We'll just hang out back here if that's okay?"

"That's fine." The bartender grinned at Sophia. "Just keep your friskiness to a minimum."

Sophia tugged on Philtzer's sleeve as she followed him to the back of the bar. "What was he talking about?"

"Oh, nothing," Philtzer shrugged, "just my little explanation for why we're," he gestured at their borrowed clothes, "you know."

"You didn't tell him you stole our clothes!" She glanced back at the bartender in alarm.

"No." Philtzer slid into a chair in the corner. "Just that you got over-excited and accidentally locked our keys and wallet in the car."

"Over-excited?" Sophia looked back at Philtzer. He waggled his eyebrows suggestively and winked.

"You didn't!" She practically shouted, causing the bartender to glance their way. Her face turned red, and she looked around the bar in horror. "Oh no." She saw the bartender looking and pulled her hood up. She buried her face in her elbows on the table.

Philtzer saluted him with his bottle. The bartender shook his head, grinned, and turned back to what he had been doing.

"What's the matter?" Philtzer sipped his beer.

"Everyone is staring at me now," she moaned. Her voice was muffled.

"Sorry. What? Can't hear you."

She knew he heard her just fine. Sophia raised her head a little and looked up at him accusingly. "You're enjoying this."

"Honey, I enjoy everything." Philtzer grinned at her. He opened his bag of chips and started munching. She buried her face again, but he nudged her with his foot. "Come on. Sit up and drink your Coke, or they really will be staring at you."

Slowly, Sophia sat up. She glanced behind her at the barflies again.

"See? No one is staring." He chuckled. Most of them were absorbed in their drinks, except for the one near the door who had been staring at her since they had come in.

"He is."

"Who?" Philtzer let his eyes wander over the crowd.

"That guy by the door." She took a drink of her Coke.

"Him? He's just trying to figure out why we look familiar." Philtzer shrugged and took a drink but didn't take his eyes off the man.

"What do you mean?" Sophia tensed.

"Relax." Philtzer smiled. "He just recognizes his clothes, not us."

"You stole our clothes from him?"

"Shh." He sat forward and glanced at the bartender, but he either hadn't heard or had given up being curious about them.

"Sorry, but it makes me uncomfortable." She shifted in her seat nervously.

"Would you rather be sitting here naked?" Philtzer sat back. "I wouldn't mind. If that would make you more comfortable…" He shrugged.

She kicked him under the table.

"Oww!"

"Oh, don't act like that hurt!" she snapped and picked up her bag of chips.

"But it did!" He made a big show of rubbing his leg. "You're a big meanie."

"Whatever." She couldn't help it; she smiled.

Philtzer gave her a big, toothy grin and tilted his head back to shake the last of the chip crumbs out of the bag and into his mouth.

"So, how long will it take your friend to get here?"

"Depends on where they are."

"They?" She squirmed. "How many is 'they'?"

"Thomas and Hamilton at least."

"Maybe I should go." Sophia moved to stand, but Philtzer stopped her with a hand on her arm.

"You don't have to run." He searched her face. "We're not going to hurt you."

She stared at him silently.

"Look, I understand. You don't want to be outnumbered by a bunch of strange guys." Philtzer said gently. "But I promise you, we're the good guys."

She was still staring at him when a commotion at the door drew everyone's attention. Three boisterous men tumbled through the door, laughing.

Philtzer grinned and jumped up. "Thomas!"

The trio looked toward their table and plowed their way to the back of the bar like a frat party on wheels. Sophia shrank away from them, moving so that the table was between her and them.

"That didn't take long!" Philtzer came forward and shook hands with Hamilton, Thomas, and Cody.

"We were just over the mountain." Thomas grinned. "Stuff's in the Jeep." Thomas jerked a thumb over his shoulder and then looked down at the tiny girl behind Philtzer. His smile faded.

Philtzer glanced back at her. Sophia's eyes were wild. She was starting to shimmer and blur slightly.

"Hey!" He sat down, pulling her down into a chair. "Hey!" He grabbed her hands. "Calm down." Philtzer pulled her around so she could see only him. "Take a breath."

The other three quickly positioned themselves to form a screen to shield her from the rest of the bar.

"Come on. Breathe. It's just a stress response." Philtzer rubbed her hands between his. "You have to control it or you'll shift." Sophia's eyes never left his as she tried to slow her breathing. "You can do this. There's nothing to be afraid of. We're here to help, remember?"

After a moment, her breathing slowed down. She stopped shimmering, but she was still shaking. Sophia's eyes fluttered. She lowered her head onto her knees.

Philtzer reached out and rubbed her back. "Attagirl!"

"We should go," Thomas said.

"Yeah." Philtzer nodded, still watching Sophia. "You wanna pay our tab?" Philtzer looked up at Cody, who nodded and headed to the bar.

"Come on, babe." Philtzer scooped a hand under Sophia's elbow and pulled her to her feet. "Let's get you outta here."

Hamilton led the way. Thomas moved back to let them by and then followed them out of the bar.

Once outside in the cool air, Sophia began to stand a little straighter. She stepped away from Philtzer. They followed Hamilton down the street to where Thomas' Jeep was parked.

"You alright?"

"Yeah." She rubbed her forehead. "I don't know what happened."

"You started to shift," Thomas said, "but it's okay, you controlled it."

"You know how stress causes Fight or Flight?" Philtzer said. "Werewolves tend to shift first, then Fight or Flight kicks in."

"Spark never mentioned that."

"No doubt there's a lot she didn't mention," Philtzer muttered under his breath.

Hamilton unlocked the back hatch.

Philtzer tried to steer Sophia to the back of the Jeep.

She put the brakes on. "Whoa, wait a minute."

"Would you rather keep wearing that guy's stolen clothes?" Philtzer cocked his head like a puppy, gesturing to the bag sitting in the back. A large red cooler sat next to the bag.

Sophia glanced at the huge duffel and then at Philtzer. He dug in the cooler and found a package of beef jerky. Stuffing a couple of pieces in his mouth, he looked back at Sophia and offered her the bag. "Want some?"

She took it from him and wolfed down a few pieces. "This is The Stuff?" she asked, watching him pull clothes out of the duffel.

Hamilton, Thomas, and Cody once again formed a line, this time with their backs to her.

"Yep. This sort of thing happened to all of us at one time or another, so we started keeping an emergency kit. You know, food, clothes for each of us, money. Stuff." He pulled out some pants and looked over at Hamilton. "Hey? Do you care if she wears your stuff? You're about the same size."

"Nah, go ahead. That's fine. "Hamilton glanced over at Philtzer. "Wait. Is that a short joke?"

"Hamy, he didn't say anything about height." Thomas grinned. "He said you were the size of a girl."

"I'll make you the size of a girl." Hamilton playfully lunged at Thomas. They wrestled, nearly falling.

Sophia pressed herself against the side of the Jeep. Philtzer continued to sort out clothes for a minute, then leaned over and kicked the closest hind end.

"Hey! You're gonna get us noticed!"

Immediately, the men stopped wrestling but continued to laugh and punch each other playfully.

Sophia shifted from one flip-flopped foot to the other.

"Don't mind them," Philtzer said. "Here." He handed her a pile of clothes and pointed to the back of the Jeep.

Hesitantly, she took his offering. Glancing at the others, she crawled into the back of the Jeep to change. Philtzer grabbed his clothes and stepped back to shut the hatch so she would have some privacy.

"She's cute." Thomas glanced at Philtzer.

"I know, right?" Philtzer grinned. He discarded the stolen, oversized pants and pulled on his own jeans, and slipped his shirt on over his head.

At that moment, Sophia climbed out of the Jeep dressed in Hamilton's clothes. She stayed back, trying to keep as much distance between her and them as possible.

"Better?" Philtzer grinned at her. "Allow me to introduce my compatriots. That's Thomas." He pointed to the tall, thin one with dark hair.

Thomas did a little chin thrust toward her. "What's up?"

"That's Hamilton." Philtzer gestured toward the short guy with glasses and a tan leather jacket and then pointed to the one wearing a Western shirt and boots. "And Cody." Cody tipped his cowboy hat to her. "Guys, this is Sophia Sinclair."

They all stopped and stared at her, then looked at Philtzer in surprise.

"Like Regina Sinclair?" Thomas asked.

"Yep." Philtzer stepped over and put his arm around Sophia's shoulders. "Freaky, huh?"

Sophia pushed his arm away and glared at him. "Why does everyone know my mom but me?"

"Don't take it personally," Thomas said as he walked around to the driver's door. "She's just that way."

"Now that we're all friends," Philtzer said as he held the door and gestured for Sophia to get in. "Your chariot, my lady."

Thomas started the Jeep. The radio blasted out the news, reporting sixty-six people found dead at the Mount Sherman Mine.

"What the hell happened after I left?" Philtzer whispered.

Behind him, Hamilton was already dialing his phone. "What do you mean they still haven't come back?" He exchanged a worried look with Philtzer. "Yeah, we'll go there now."

"Madraeus is still there, isn't he?" Philtzer asked.

"And Rami and Malcolm." Hamilton rubbed his forehead. "Looks like we need another rescue plan."

Philtzer sighed and looked at Sophia. "Sorry, sweetheart, your ride home is gonna be a little delayed."

NEWS TO ME

WHITNEY COULDN'T STAND IT anymore. Whether her body wanted to or not, she had to get up. She had been in bed so long her feet couldn't remember what the floor felt like. It had only been a day since they'd been rescued from the mine, but it felt like a lifetime. She was tired of feeling imprisoned.

It took ages to get from the bed to the dresser so she could find her clothes. Her arms shook as she pulled her jeans on. She flopped backward on the bed and panted.

"Getting dressed used to be easy," she grumbled.

When her breathing finally evened out, she reached down and fumbled with the button of her jeans. She felt like she had lost all strength in her fingers. After a few tries, the button was done and the zip was up. She slowly sat up and reached a shaking hand for the T-shirt she had found. Awkwardly, she pulled it over her head but had to stop to catch her breath.

"Oh, come on, toddlers can do this!" she snarled.

One final effort and she was dressed. She looked down at her bare feet and shook her head. "I don't care."

She heaved herself off of the bed and started toward the door. Her progress felt ridiculously slow. With every step, she had to lean on the wall or furniture for support.

"Five years later…" she mumbled as she finally reached the top of the stairs. For a moment, she contemplated sliding down the banister just because it would be quicker than hobbling down each and every step. But sense won out. "Knowing my luck, I'd fall off and end up breaking my neck."

As she started the slow process of descending the stairs, she could hear a TV chattering somewhere below her. Step by step, she descended. Halfway down, she had to stop and sit. Her legs shook and her heart raced. She leaned her head against the banister.

"Maybe I should take my chances sliding," she puffed, glancing at the railing again.

As she sat waiting for her body to regain its strength, noise from the TV intruded into her thoughts. It sounded like the news. She could hear little snippets of the reporter's words and her grandmother's voice, but Whitney couldn't tell what they had said.

Curiosity prodded Whitney to pull herself up and renew her descent. She focused all of her concentration on just making it down the steps. Finally, she reached the ground floor. She clung to the newel post, resting her forehead on the cool wood.

"—have found more bodies this morning—" the TV reported.

"How could they have done this?" Whitney's head lifted at her grandmother's words. She pushed away from the post and shuffled forward, drawn on by the snatches of conversation floating out of the living room.

"I don't blame them." Came Sandra's matter-of-fact voice.

"How can you say that? You were down there with them! Whitney was down there!" Elizabeth's voice drowned out the news reporter.

Sandra's response sounded flat. "That's why I can say it."

"Sandra's right," Mrs. Myers said quietly.

"No! This was wrong!" Elizabeth said just as Whitney made it to the doorway.

Whitney leaned against the door frame unnoticed. Her attention was riveted to the TV.

A reporter stood in front of the shaft house that served as the entrance to a mine. The very mine that she and Sandra had been held prisoner in for a week. Cecelia's lair. The camera showed a cluster of uniformed personnel milling around a long line of black body bags, in the background were emergency vehicles with their lights flashing.

"Less than 24 hours ago, police were given an anonymous tip that a cult was holding people hostage in the Mount Sherman Mine. When authorities arrived and searched the area, they found evidence of recent occupation. After a more thorough search, K-9 units found what authorities are now calling the most gruesome mass murder in Colorado's recent history." Footage from the night before popped up on the screen. Emergency lights glared, illuminating row upon row of black body bags that lined the parking area outside the shaft house. "The death toll has now reached sixty-six." The picture changed back to the reporter. "In a press conference earlier this morning, a representative from the Colorado Bureau of Investigation issued a statement that they have taken over the investigation and their forensic team is going to be studying the evidence very carefully."

The news commentator back in the studio came on and asked, "So, Barbara, do they believe that the alleged cult responsible for this is still in the area?"

"Yes, actually, the police are searching the surrounding area, and there are still K-9 teams down in the mine looking for any clues as to who may have done this terrible deed. Police are asking for anyone with information to call the Crime Stoppers Hotline."

Whitney sagged to the floor.

"Whitney!" Mrs. Myers jumped up. "What are you doing down here?"

"Why didn't you tell me?" Whitney croaked.

"I'm sorry, Whitney." Mrs. Myers reached down to help her up. Between her grandmother and Mrs. Myers, they managed to help her to the couch.

"Why didn't you tell me?" Whitney stared at the TV. Her face was pale, and the shaking had started again. "All those people!"

Elizabeth picked up the remote and shut off the TV.

"We didn't think that in your weakened state it was safe to give you a shock like this," Mrs. Myers said.

Whitney looked at Sandra. The truth slowly pieced itself together. Sandra was here. Everyone else was dead.

"It was him, wasn't it?" Whitney continued to stare. "Sixty-six people. Madraeus killed sixty-six people."

"Yes." Elizabeth sat next to Whitney and put her arm around her granddaughter's shoulders.

Mrs. Myers sat down on the other side of Whitney. "He didn't murder them. He did what had to be done."

In disbelief, Whitney turned to stare at her boss: the sweet, kind, gentle Mrs. Myers.

"You can justify it any way you want, but it was still murder!" Elizabeth snapped.

"No, it was mercy." Mrs. Myers shook her head. "What kind of a life could those people have had if they had been allowed to leave?"

"They could have had a life!" Elizabeth hissed.

Whitney let her gaze drift away from the two arguing women. Their words washed over her, but she didn't hear them anymore. She wanted to cry. The pain of betrayal spread through her torso. She wanted to lie down and stop. They were right, she wasn't ready for this kind of shock.

Sandra moved around the couch to sit in the armchair next to the TV. Whitney looked up and was surprised to see that Sandra's face was completely devoid of expression, watching her.

Why aren't you upset? Whitney's mind screamed, but then she stopped and thought about it.

This was Sandra. Sandra, who had been with her in the mine and had helped taunt Cecelia. Sandra, who had been a meal for vampires for three months. Sandra, the slightly insane, practical one.

"Tell me," Whitney whispered, halting the argument. "Tell me why you're alive. Why did he kill them and let you go?"

"Because of you."

"Me? Why?" Whitney trembled as she waited for the answer. "What happened?"

"Madraeus came to the cell and let me out. Just me. For a long time, he just stared at me. So, I told him to hurry up and kill me if he was going to, but instead he asked me what I thought should be done with all those people." She paused for a moment and then looked at each of the three women watching her. "I told him that they should be put out of their misery."

"You what?" Elizabeth gasped.

"I know it sounds bad, and I'm sorry, but like I said, I was down there. I'm not even sure that I am happy that he didn't include me in the body count. He left me alive because of my friendship with you, and I'm grateful. But I have had constant nightmares and flashbacks about what happened in that damn mine. I wouldn't want to curse anyone with these memories." Sandra looked at Whitney. "You know what I mean."

Whitney couldn't hold her gaze. She'd had her fill of nightmares since she had started this job. There were times when the nightmares clutched at her, and the screaming in her head wouldn't stop, and she wished Justin or Cecelia had finished the job.

"But still, sixty-six people, surely there was someone who could have helped them!" Elizabeth protested.

"There's no help for the damned." Sandra stood and walked out of the room.

MINE SHAFT HIDE AND SEEK

From the shadows, Madraeus watched the two police-men approach. He motioned to Rami and Malcolm to move farther back into the darkness of the tunnel. Madraeus' mouth began to water. His nostrils flared as he caught the scent of live prey.

He was starving.

Unfortunately, his body was still trying to repair the wounds from the fight with the werewolves two days ago. He had been stupid to go into that fight without feeding first, but he couldn't stand the accusations in Elizabeth Martindale's eyes and he had gone off half-cocked. The only reason that he had lasted this long was the small amount of blood that Whitney had harassed him into taking. But the days had stretched on, and without an intake of fresh blood, his body was starting to consume itself. Now, with food so close, hunger was taking over his brain.

The police edged closer, shining their lights to the left and the right. They stopped to check their map.

A few more sssteppsss... the voice in his mind hissed, *clossser...* Madraeus felt his fangs elongate.

He stepped forward only to feel Rami's hand on his chest. The giant pushed him back against the rock wall and held him there. In Madraeus' weakened state, Rami barely had to exert any effort to hold him still.

Rami pinned him until the police moved off down the tunnel. Madraeus reached up and patted Rami's hand in thanks. Shame flooded through Madraeus. It was getting harder to control his instinct to attack every time they saw someone.

Cecelia had effectively trapped them. Playing hide and seek in the darkness and dodging the searching police force was starting to seem like a hopeless cause.

At least Whitney is safe, he thought.

He closed his eyes and conjured up her image. He could still taste her. The sweetness of her blood and the softness of her lips. Pain stabbed through his chest as he thought about how close she had come to death again. It was his fault. He had allowed her into his world. The pain spread as he realized that once she found out what he had done with all those prisoners, he would lose her forever. She would never want him after this.

The voice in his head whispered, *Embrace your darknesss!*

Suddenly, he didn't care if they caught him. He pushed away from the wall and started for the tunnel where the police had been. Malcolm grabbed his arm and spun him back toward Rami. The giant grabbed Madraeus and pushed him against the wall again.

"Are you insane?" Rami hissed.

"Let me go."

"No. You can do this. Just hold on a little longer. They will not keep searching forever."

"It doesn't matter anymore, Rami."

"Do not say that!" the giant pleaded. "We have to make it out of here and stop Cecelia, you know that. You have dedicated your life to keeping the Races safe. Do not tell me you are going to give up now!"

"You don't understand." Madraeus groaned. "I saw how many have gone over to her side. I don't think the Races want to be saved anymore."

Rami sighed. "They are like teenagers. They do not know what is good for them!"

"Don't they? I don't know anymore. Perhaps Cecelia is right. Perhaps we should just run wild over the mortal world." He looked down the tunnel.

"You're just saying that because you're so hungry," Malcolm said, glancing back over his shoulder. He stood at the mouth of the tunnel, watching for the police.

They hunt usss... the slithering voice hissed in Madraeus' head.

"They just hunt us like dogs and force us to hide. Why shouldn't we be free to do what we like?" Madraeus hissed.

We are sssuperior in ssso many waysss...

"We are superior in so many ways."

Rami let go of his friend as if he were made of fire. He stepped back. "This is not the Madraeus that I know!"

Madraeus looked away. They didn't understand. He had been a monster for almost two thousand years.

Monsssster...

It was so much easier to take what he wanted.

Yesss, take it...

He was exhausted from following the rules.

Ssso tired! And what do you get?

Hiding in the background. Skulking around trying not to be seen. Only during the years with Cecelia had he been truly free.

Free...

But then... Mary. The memory of her mangled and lifeless body nailed to a post outside their door flashed through his mind.

Madraeus sank to the floor. He buried his face in his hands. Guilt and regret warred for domination. He couldn't breathe. The weight of his life was crushing him. He longed for death once more. He needed to quit feeling.

"Rami, they're coming back." Malcolm retreated from the tunnel junction. Together, he and Rami picked up their trembling friend and hauled him farther back into the tunnel in case the searchers turned in their direction.

"We need to get him out of here," Rami whispered.

"I know," Malcolm sighed. "I've never seen him like this."

"Did you hear that FBI guy?" The voice of one of the cops echoed from the adjacent tunnel. "He said this isn't the first mass grave they've found."

"Really?" his companion asked.

"Yeah, he was saying that they found one similar to this in Utah, but the bodies hadn't been burned. Every one of them had starved to death." A light flashed down the tunnel in the direction of the fugitives. "Have we been this way?"

"I don't know." The voices stopped for a moment. "It's not marked on my map yet."

"So, how do they know it's the same group?"

"Forensics, I guess."

"Well, it's creepy either way." The voices sounded nearer.

Malcolm and Rami hefted Madraeus' arms over their shoulders and hauled him off down the tunnel in the opposite direction. The two men's continuing conversation drowned out the sound of their retreat.

"I know I don't feel safe letting my kids out to play, even if it's just in the backyard."

"That's why I never had kids. After all the scary crap I've seen on the force, there's no way I'm bringing a kid into this world."

"Nah, you can't just stop living because of stuff like that. No matter how bad things seem, there's a lot more good in the world."

The man's words chased them down the tunnel. Madraeus couldn't shake the last comment made by the optimistic cop.

Years ago, Brother Edwin had expressed similar sentiments. Mary, too, had urged him to live for the good times. Whitney had been looking for silver linings despite her imprisonment in the mine. Even if Whitney was lost to him forever, he didn't want to disappoint her. Or to dishonor Edwin and Mary's memories.

"I'm sorry." Madraeus raised his head slightly. "You're right, Rami. We have to make it out of here and stop Cecelia."

"Especially if there are other pockets of people starving to death in abandoned holes all over the place!" Malcolm glanced over his shoulder to gauge how close the police were.

"I think I have a way of tracking that," Rami whispered. "All those discrepancies I found in Whitney's Dreaded Filing Project must be connected. I thought it looked like someone was moving a large group around. It must have been her army."

"And there is probably a cache of people in every location," Malcolm groaned.

"Damn."

"This is going to get a lot more gruesome before it gets better," Madraeus snarled as he stumbled along between his two friends.

"Well, we can't get any of it sorted out until we get out of this damn mine!" Malcolm huffed.

DECISIONS, DECISIONS

WHITNEY STARED AT HER reflection. The face was hers, but it was thinner than it had ever been, and her color was still off. The hair was hers too, but the eyes were different. She still had big green eyes, but now they were old. She had grown old in only a few weeks. This job had aged her. Her friends had died, she had come face to face with death repeatedly, and everything she had believed had been turned inside out at least twice.

She could get past the near-death brushes. At least that's what she was telling herself. Truth was she couldn't sleep at night because she relived each harrowing moment over and over in her dreams.

She could face the death of her friends. Everyone has to die sometime. It was a natural part of life. Her parents had died in a car accident when she was still young. Accidents happened all the time, and there was generally nothing that anyone could do about it. But murder? Justin had murdered Lisa. Cecelia had murdered Justin. Somehow that wasn't as bad as what Madraeus had done.

She couldn't seem to get past that.

How could he be so good and yet so evil? She wondered.

Madraeus had saved her life over and over. He had come looking for her even when she had been stupid and asinine. Whitney touched her lips. He had kissed her and made it sound like he loved her.

"No." She shook her head and stared down her reflection. "He never said that! He said I drove him crazy," she lectured herself. "That's not the same thing."

The image of all those body bags flashed into her mind. She shuddered.

"How could he say that to me, kiss me, and then murder sixty-six people?" she asked her reflection.

"You never told me he kissed you," Sandra said from the door.

"You should've knocked." Whitney turned away, pretending to look for her hairbrush. She had just finished a shower.

"Door was open, so it doesn't count."

Whitney picked up her hairbrush and moved toward the door, but Sandra stood in her way.

"Excuse me, please."

Sandra continued to stand in her way. "You gonna start being straight with me?"

Whitney didn't look up. "I don't know what you mean."

"Look, Whit, we shared the Vamp Hotel Hell experience. I'm still alive because I was with you. You can talk to me."

Whitney finally looked up. "I don't know if I can."

Sandra stepped back to let her out of the bathroom and then followed her. She plopped down on the bed in the middle of the clothes Whitney had laid out to wear. She crossed her legs, grabbed a pillow to hug, and looked up at Whitney.

"You can trust me. I'm insanely practical, remember?"

Whitney smiled. "You are that."

"Dude, you can't talk to Myers or your grandma. They can't agree on anything. It's like watching Ping Pong and you're the ball."

"Thanks."

"Just sayin'." Sandra shrugged. "Anyway, I don't have a side. I'm totally on my own. One hundred percent unbiased. Logic only."

"I don't think logic has anything to do with my life." Whitney ran the brush through her hair, wincing as she hit a knot.

Sandra unfolded and refolded Whitney's shirt. "It does. It's just supernatural logic."

Whitney rolled her eyes.

"So, here's what I know so far." Sandra started when Whitney continued brushing her hair without speaking. "Madraeus, King of the Good Vampires—"

"He's not the king of anything," Whitney interrupted.

"Then what would you call him?"

"Madraeus Nicoteles Peltrasius Ravilla, Head of the Council of Races, a one thousand seven hundred and sixty-seven-year-old pain in the ass." Whitney ripped her brush through the rats in her hair with more and more force. "Hypocrite. Moody. Snarly."

"Good use of synonyms!" Sandra smirked.

"Grumpy, distant, emotionally impaired, snarky, demanding, arrogant, offensive," Whitney continued angrily.

"A good kisser? Handsome?" Sandra offered.

Whitney paused, and in her mind, finished Sandra's list: *Gentle, passionate, caring, fiercely loyal.* She sank onto the bed. Anger drained out of her as sadness washed over her. Tears filled her eyes.

"Oh, honey!" Sandra threw the shirt aside and scooched over. She put her arms around Whitney.

"I know he's not a bad person, deep down," Whitney whispered. "I just can't seem to get past this pain. This betrayal."

"It's hard," Sandra agreed.

"I just don't see how he can be so..." Whitney shrugged, trying to find the right word.

"Complicated?"

"Yeah."

Sandra sat rubbing Whitney's back for a little while, then said, "Maybe think of it like this: a vet has a sick animal and to let it live would be crueler than killing it, so he puts it to sleep. That's kind of what your boss did."

"Those weren't animals," Whitney said. "Those were people."

"You weren't down there as long as I was." Sandra's voice turned bitter. "We were all becoming animals."

Whitney looked up at her, surprised at the menace that laced her words. Seeing the look on her face, Sandra took a deep breath and tried to smile.

Whitney leaned her head against Sandra's. "I'm sorry."

"It's okay. We're out now."

They sat silently for a while.

"You know you're going to have to talk to him sometime," Sandra said.

"I can't."

"You still work for him."

"Maybe Mrs. Myers will let me change assignments." She tried to sound hopeful, but it just came out sounding flat.

"Do you really think that will make it better?"

"I don't know." Whitney shook her head.

"You told me once that you really liked making a difference. That this was the first job that made you feel really useful. You gonna give that up because you are too chicken to talk to your boss?"

"I'm not chicken! I just don't know what to say. I don't know how I'm gonna react to seeing him and knowing..." Whitney shivered. "I just need more time."

"I understand."

Whitney bumped into Sandra with her shoulder. "What are you going to do?"

"Don't know. I officially don't exist anymore. I've been gone for three months, and Vivian told me that your little Council had me declared dead, so I can't go back to my life. I think they are trying to keep me from telling their secret."

"That was nice of them!" Whitney scoffed.

"They obviously don't have as much faith in my discretion as Madraeus does."

"Obviously." Whitney rolled her eyes. "You could always take a page from my book and just do what you want anyway. That always gets them going."

"Umm, no, thank you. I've seen your boss mad. I'm not crossing him."

"Now who's chicken?" Whitney elbowed Sandra. "I do it all the time."

"Well, I think he's a lot more forgiving when it comes to you than he would be with me."

"Maybe." Whitney picked at the scab covering a bite mark on her wrist. She didn't have the courage yet to examine how Madraeus felt about her.

"So, are you going back to work?"

Whitney gave a short laugh. "It's weird to think of work and schedules."

"It's weird to sit on chairs and sleep on beds," Sandra laughed, "but you didn't answer my question."

"Ask me again tomorrow."

SLIGHTLY ILLEGAL

"Morning, sugar pop!" Philtzer opened the door and grinned at her. The growing light of the sunrise gilded him with gold. "Sleep good?"

Sophia sat up and scowled at him. "In what world? You drag me up here instead of taking me home like you promised and then keep me prisoner in the Jeep by surrounding me with four snoring werewolves."

"So, well rested then?" Philtzer beamed.

She wanted to hit him.

"Come on, sweet cheeks. You weren't a prisoner." He held a hand out to help her out of the Jeep. "The Jeep was the warmest place. Besides, we've got more practice at this. We're just keeping you safe."

She wanted to believe him. Deep down she wanted to believe that there were good people in this new world of monsters.

Last night Thomas had parked a little below the mine in a cluster of trees that hid them from the patrolling authorities. They spent the day watching the mine and taking turns running reconnaissance. Sometimes they sat in the Jeep and argued about how best to rescue their comrades. When they were in the Jeep, they listened to the radio's minute-to-minute updates on the tragedy at the mine.

The more Sophia listened, the more she felt sick. Guilt flooded her. She could have helped those people. She could have let them out. She'd had the keys in her teeth. She should have unlocked all the cells instead of running away.

This was her fault.

Images of the gaunt faces staring out at her from the cells flashed across her mind.

Sophia scrambled out of the Jeep and ran into the trees. Stumbling to a stop, she sank to her knees.

She didn't want this, she didn't want to be a werewolf or to be anywhere near people who could treat others so horribly or kill so easily. Spark and her twisted boss had tainted her life.

A scruffy gray wolf trotted out of the woods and sat down beside her. Sophia looked at the wolf. He stared back at her with sympathetic eyes.

"I could have helped them," she whispered.

The wolf shimmered and shifted into Cody. "What's done is done. We have all been through things and done things that we shouldn't have. You can let it eat you up, or you can learn to live with it. Personally, I say you can't change the past, so let it go."

Sophia straightened up and stared out at the trees. "That simple, huh?"

"Hell no!" Cody snorted. "It ain't simple at all, but it's the reality of the situation."

Sophia looked at him, trying to decide if he was being helpful or condescending.

"Come on, it's almost sunset," Cody said gently. "Let's look to the living."

"I think we have a plan," Thomas said as they returned to the Jeep.

Sophia sat in the open door of the Jeep with her chin braced on her hands as she listened to them explain their brilliant plan.

"Well?" Philtzer asked. "Will you do it?"

She stared at the crazy group of men standing in front of her. They were all grinning like idiots.

"Aw, come on, Sophia! It'll be fun," Thomas begged.

"I don't see this as fun!" She shook her head. "I see this as illegal!"

"Desperate times, pudding pop!" Philtzer grinned at her.

"I'm not that desperate."

"You're the only one of us that has been in the mine," Hamilton added.

"You don't even know if your friends are still in there!" She gestured toward the mine.

Thomas crossed his arms. "If Madraeus hasn't made contact, then he is still in the mine."

"Come on, please... pretty please... with ice cream? Pretty please with ice cream and cherries," Philtzer pleaded grinning, "and me on top?"

"Eww!" Hamilton groaned.

"Dude!" Thomas shook his head.

"Seriously!" Cody shoved Philtzer.

"I don't care what you put on top!" Sophia cried. "I'm not going back in there!"

"But, Soph, if you come with us, then there's a chance we won't get caught." Hamilton tried again for logic. "If you don't, then we'll be blundering around forever."

"That may be, but I don't think I can lie to cops."

"You won't have to." Philtzer knew he was gaining ground. "You don't even have to talk."

"That won't help!" Sophia cried. "Just looking at my face, they'll know!"

"What if you went as the police dog instead?" Hamilton shrugged.

"Then if I have to shift, I'll be naked!" She shook her head.

"Don't worry," Philtzer grinned, "we won't mind."

"I will!"

"We promise not to look," Hamilton said while punching Philtzer.

Sophia felt cornered. She was running out of arguments, but then she had a sudden thought. "You don't have a police uniform!"

"Ah ha!" Thomas grinned and bounded to the back of the Jeep. He dug around for a moment and produced a police uniform.

"Where did you get that?"

Thomas blushed. "Don't ask."

"Come on," Philtzer prodded one more time, "it'll save a life."

"A couple of lives," Hamilton added.

"It'll ease the guilt," Cody said quietly.

Sophia glanced at him sharply, knowing he was right but still hesitant to go back into that nightmare. Sophia looked from face to face. She rubbed her forehead. "All right."

"Yes!" Philtzer bounced forward and kissed the top of her head. "Thank you!"

"So, who gets to wear the uniform?" she asked as she stood.

"Either Phil or Hamy." Thomas tossed the uniform to Philtzer.

Philtzer shook out the shirt and pulled it on. "It's a little tight," he complained, trying to close the buttons.

"Give it here." Hamilton held out a hand. He pulled the shirt on and fastened it with no trouble.

"See," Thomas grinned, "you are the size of a girl."

"Shut up," Hamilton growled, pulling on the pants.

"Flashlight," Cody said, tossing it to Hamilton.

He flicked it on and off again to make sure it worked.

"Right." Philtzer pulled his shirt off. Thomas and Cody followed suit. "We'll stick to the trees around the edges and be ready for you. Sophia, if you wanna shift, we'll put a leash on you. Then you and Hamy can walk up to the shaft house."

She looked around awkwardly.

Philtzer grinned. She was still shy around them. "Come on, boys. Give the lady some privacy." He herded the guys to the back of the Jeep to finish stripping.

After a few moments, Sophia appeared at the back of the Jeep in wolf form.

Thomas whistled appreciatively when he saw her. Sophia's ears flattened against her head.

"Sorry," he apologized.

Philtzer held out the collar and leash he had gotten out of the Jeep. Reluctantly, she stepped forward. Sophia's soft brown eyes stared up at him.

"It's only for a little while," he murmured, buckling it around her neck. "You'll be back and free before you know it."

Hamilton picked up the leash and looped it around his wrist. He straightened his borrowed uniform. "How do I look?"

"Here put this on." Cody handed him a jacket. "It'll hide the fact that you don't have a gun belt."

"That better?" Hamilton asked, pulling the jacket down.

"Good enough, I hope." Philtzer shook his head as he shifted.

"Ladies first." Hamilton bowed and gestured toward the shaft house.

Sophia and Hamilton picked their way down the mountain in the fading light. Philtzer, Cody, and Thomas followed in wolf form. As they neared the clearing in front of the shaft house, the three wolves faded into the trees.

Hamilton hesitated. Sophia looked up at him and then back at the police cars parked around the building.

Sophia whined softly.

"Sorry. Don't tell Thomas," Hamilton whispered, "but I'm as nervous as you are."

Together they stepped out into the yard. They slipped under the police tape and moved out into the open. She took a winding route around the cars to avoid most of the officers. A couple of men glanced up as they approached the building, but otherwise, no one seemed to be paying attention to them. She led him to the elevator and they descended into the darkness below.

At the bottom of the elevator shaft, Hamilton flipped on the flashlight. "So far, so good."

Sophia led him down a series of tunnels to where she remembered finding the cells full of prisoners. People in forensic clean suits worked in the tunnel outside the cells. Quietly they moved past them, trying to act as if they belonged there. Sophia started sniffing the floor of the tunnel searching for a scent she barely remembered. She stopped for a moment and glanced at Hamilton. He was watching her closely.

"Can't find his scent?"

Sophia whined.

"Right." Hamilton looked around and walked her a little farther down the tunnel. When they were out of sight, he shifted into wolf form.

If she wasn't so terrified, Sophia might have found the image of a wolf in a police uniform funny. But all she could do was watch him run back and forth across the tunnel until he picked up their trail. He looked at Sophia and growled softly. She trotted forward and sniffed the place he had indicated. She had it now.

Hamilton shifted back into human form and quickly tidied his uniform. He picked up her leash, and they ran down the tunnel.

Sophia and Hamilton followed Madraeus' scent down a series of tunnels. Periodically, they had to slow down and pretend to be a K-9 unit again when they met other officers searching the passageways. As the hours dragged on, they crisscrossed back over their own tracks several times.

Sophia shook her head and growled softly when they started back along a tunnel they had already been down twice.

"Are we lost?" Hamilton shined the light around.

Sophia sat down and looked up at him. She whined.

"You're gonna have to be a little more specific." He aimed the light at her.

She snorted and cocked her head.

"I know you're annoyed with me, but I only speak wolf when I'm a wolf."

Sophia stood and paced around behind him. He watched her, but she growled at him until he turned away from her.

"I said," she whispered from behind him, "I have never tracked someone like this, and I'm not even sure about their scent."

"Oh." Hamilton fidgeted, feeling embarrassed. "You wanna switch? I know who we're looking for."

"I guess." Sophia huffed and started to unbuckle the collar. "Otherwise, we're going to be at this for the rest of our lives."

Hamilton started to unbutton his shirt but froze when they heard someone coming down the tunnel.

WHICH WAY DO WE GO

"BACK UP!" HAMILTON HISSED.

Keeping her behind him, he stepped backward until they were hidden from the approaching officers. He glanced back to see that she had shifted back to a wolf. He pressed back against the wall, waiting for the men to pass by, not even daring to breathe.

Seconds ticked by. Finally, the officers walked past and continued down the tunnel. Hamilton waited a few more seconds, then looked at Sophia.

"Hurry and switch." He pulled off the jacket, dropped it to the tunnel floor, and started to unbutton his shirt. "Sorry, but you're gonna have to get over your modesty just for a minute." He tossed the shirt at her. It landed over her head. He started on the pants. "I'm more concerned with getting the hell out of here."

She shifted and quickly pulled the shirt on, trying to keep her back to him. He handed her the pants and reached over to unbuckle the collar. She winced away from him.

"Just put the pants on and let me get this!" Hamilton growled.

She did as he asked, holding her chin up while she zipped up the pants. Hamilton was taller than Sophia, so she had to roll up the cuffs. He strapped the collar on and shifted. While she slipped on his shoes, Hamilton was already zig-zagging back and forth across the tunnel looking for the right scent. She pulled on the jacket and grabbed for the leash.

He found the scent and dashed off, almost pulling Sophia off her feet. He loped down one tunnel, turned, and dashed down another. He stopped, sniffed, and took off down a side tunnel.

Sophia desperately tried to keep up. She was panting when he finally stopped at the mouth of yet another side tunnel and stared into the darkness.

Hamilton's ears swiveled forward, then back, and then forward again. His whole body tensed into a crouch. Sophia stared into the darkness. They heard a low growl that raised the hair on the back of her neck. Sophia backed up but stopped when Hamilton wouldn't move. She tugged on the leash.

The growl came again.

She slowly lifted the flashlight and aimed it into the black abyss ahead of them. Light reflected off a pair of eyes and a set of sharp fangs.

The thing in the tunnel rushed forward. Sophia turned to run but was brought up short by the leash wrapped around her wrist. She spun around, her fingers pulled at the leash, trying to get loose.

Suddenly, Hamilton dodged in front of her, bracing his hands against Madraeus' shoulders. She stumbled backward, aiming the flashlight into Madraeus' face, blinding him momentarily. He snarled and tried again to reach Sophia.

"Boss!" Hamilton struggled to hold the vampire back as Rami and Malcolm rushed out from the darkness.

Rami clamped a hand down on Madraeus' arm and pulled him back. Madraeus frowned in confusion as coherence slowly returned.

"Hamilton?"

The werewolf grinned in relief. "Hey, Boss."

Sophia stared at Madraeus. He looked nothing like the calm and confident man she had brought the keys to and freed from his cell. That man had been kind despite his ragged appearance. This man, however, was terrifying. He had lost a lot of weight, leaving his features sharp and dangerous, as if he had lost some of his humanity along with his body mass.

Hamilton pulled her forward. "This is Sophia."

Madraeus looked at her closely. She tried to stay back. She was still wary of him.

"She's the one who let you out of your cage."

"You're the little tan wolf?"

She nodded.

"I take it Philtzer is around then?" Rami asked.

"Yep, he's with Cody and Thomas out in the woods waiting for us to come out." Hamilton glanced back down the tunnel.

"How did you get in?" Malcolm was watching the tunnel too.

Hamilton jerked a thumb at Sophia's uniform. "We played dress up."

"I don't think that'll work to get us out." Malcolm looked back and caught the look Sophia shot at Hamilton. "Did you have an exit plan?"

Hamilton squirmed. "No, this was as far as we'd gotten."

"Oh great, that helps!" Malcolm snapped.

"At least we found you," Hamilton growled.

"Yay," Malcolm snorted.

"Look, we—" Hamilton started, but a voice down the tunnel cut him off.

"Is there someone down there?"

"Back!" Rami hissed, pushing everyone back toward their hiding place.

Sophia clamped her hand over the end of the flashlight, leaving only a dim glow. She looked around the alcove where the vampires had been hiding. It was a dead end.

"Hello?" the voice called again. This time it was closer.

Sophia glanced at Hamilton and then at the three vampires. Their faces glowed in the faint light of her flashlight. They were going to be found.

Hamilton tugged on the leash to get her attention. He jiggled the collar and then pointed toward the voice.

She shook her head.

He nodded with a look on his face that said he was going to do it whether she agreed or not. She shook her head again, but he had already shifted. He lurched forward into the tunnel, pulling her along with him.

"Who's there?" the voice called as a light from a flashlight shone down the tunnel. It illuminated Hamilton first, then Sophia. "Who are you?"

"K-K-9," Sophia stuttered. Hamilton stepped closer to the officer, dragging her with him. He shined his light on the wolf again.

"Damn!" The officer whistled. "That's a big dog!"

"Yeah." Sophia floundered. She started to shake and blur slightly.

Hamilton bounced sideways and then shook his whole body, nearly pulling Sophia off her feet. His distraction kept her from shifting.

"He's...a handful!" She choked out.

"Looks like it," the officer chuckled. "I'm glad they finally brought you guys in. It's like a maze in here. Maybe you'll have more luck."

"Maybe." Sophia tried to pull the still-bouncing Hamilton back. He kept trying to drag her down an adjacent tunnel.

"Well, looks like he's onto something, so I'll let you get to it." The officer flashed his light down the tunnel behind Sophia and then turned back the way he had come.

As soon as he was gone, Hamilton stopped bouncing and came to stand next to Sophia's leg. His tongue flopped out of his mouth like he was laughing. He glanced up at Sophia. She scowled down at him.

"That wasn't funny."

"Yes, it was," he said after he shifted back to a man.

"No, it wasn't."

"Is he gone?" Rami whispered.

"Yeah." Hamilton glanced back at the giant.

"We have to get out of here." Rami towered over Hamilton. "It has been days since we have eaten, and Madraeus is not himself."

"What's wrong with him?" Hamilton asked.

"I am not sure." Rami looked over his shoulder as Madraeus and Malcolm emerged from the darkness.

"There has to be some other way out of here." Hamilton shook his head.

"There was a tunnel that led into the woods," Malcolm said.

"I know the one you mean," Sophia said softly. All four men turned and looked at her. She took a step back. "It's by the cells. Right by where all those forensic guys are working."

"There are cops all over that tunnel." Hamilton scratched his head. "We'd never get you past them without some sort of distraction."

"Like what?" Malcolm asked. "You gonna run through there naked yelling, 'Look at me!'?"

"You know, that might work!" Hamilton grinned at Sophia.

She rolled her eyes. "Seriously!"

"Doesn't matter," Madraeus growled, leaning against the wall. "We'll think of something. Let's at least get close enough to the tunnel to see what we're up against."

"Madraeus is right." Rami sighed. "Night is moving on, and if we do not make it out of here while it is still dark, it will not matter."

"Right." Hamilton shifted and started up the tunnel, pulling Sophia along behind him. Malcolm and Rami followed, chaperoning Madraeus between them.

RUN YOUR LIFE

Slowly, they worked their way back through the tunnels, stopping periodically to wait for patrolling search parties to pass by before moving on. Finally, they huddled at the corner of the tunnel across from the archway that led to the outside.

Fresher air wafted in from the shaft, teasing them with freedom that was just out of reach. Hamilton stuck his furry nose around the corner and sniffed. Once he was satisfied that no one was close enough, he poked his head out a little farther to survey the area.

Sophia stood over him, peeking around the corner. The tunnel was full of police and forensic investigators moving in and out of Cecelia's homemade prison cells. The crews were making enough noise to cover their escape, but there was no way that the three men behind her could cross the tunnel without being seen.

Hamilton pulled back and shifted into a man. He looked at Sophia. "What if you and I were the distraction?"

"How?" She glanced at him.

"What if we do the unruly dog thing like earlier, and I pretend to get away from you? You can make a lot of noise chasing me, and they'll all watch us while these guys sneak out."

Before she could answer, Sophia heard a familiar voice. She poked her head around the corner again.

"Shit!" She pulled back, nearly falling over Malcolm in her haste.

"What's wrong?" Malcolm hissed as he reached out to steady her.

"I know that cop!" Sophia began to tremble and blur.

"Hey," Hamilton grabbed her arms, "calm down. Remember what Philtzer said. Breathe."

Sophia concentrated on breathing and slowly stopped shaking. Hamilton glanced around the corner to see if they'd been heard then looked back at her.

"Which cop?" Rami moved over switching places with Hamilton and carefully peeked around the corner.

"The one in the old-man jacket," Sophia whispered as she pressed herself back against the wall. "Detective Sanders."

"Sanders?" Madraeus hissed.

"You know him?" Hamilton looked over his shoulder at his boss.

"He's the one that was pestering Whitney."

"Great."

"I can't go out there!" Sophia shook her head. "He'll recognize me."

Hamilton watched her for a moment. He shrugged. "All right, switch with me again." He started to unbuckle his collar. "Same plan, but you take off and I'll chase you."

Discretely the men turned away as Sophia started to undress.

"I swear," she grumbled, "I've never been naked this often my whole life."

"You'll get used to it," Hamilton chuckled as he put on what she took off.

After they had changed places again, Hamilton turned back to Madraeus, Rami, and Malcolm.

"Get ready to run for your lives. Philtzer is in the woods waiting, just keep running and he'll find you. Thomas' Jeep is parked down the mountain in a clump of trees." He turned to Sophia. "You ready?"

She shook her head and whined.

"Let's do it." He gestured for her to run. "Go!" He had to shove her again to get her to move. "Go!"

"Hey! Come back here!" Hamilton shouted after Sophia had dashed around the corner. He turned back to his friends once more. "Good luck." Then he ran around the corner, yelling to anyone who would listen to catch his dog.

Rami peeked around the corner for a moment. Once everyone was watching Sophia run in circles with Hamilton chasing her, he motioned Malcolm to go. The younger vampire dodged across the tunnel, disappearing into the darkness of the exit. Rami pushed Madraeus toward the exit and then quickly followed. Sophia and Hamilton' commotion faded behind them as they ran.

"I don't remember it being this long of a tunnel," Malcolm complained as the tunnel sloped downward.

The air became colder and sweeter as they neared the tunnel opening. They could hear the sound of the wind whistling through the exit long before they reached it. Rami skidded to a stop about thirty feet from the tunnel exit. He put his arms out to stop Madraeus and Malcolm from continuing.

"What?" Malcolm hissed.

"Shh." Rami pointed to the archway ahead. Silhouetted in the predawn light were two men, talking quietly. One smoked a cigarette and the other leaned against the massive wooden beam that framed the exit.

The three vampires faded back a little. Madraeus sagged against the wall.

Malcolm whispered, "We'll have the whole mountain chasing us if they see us."

Rami watched the men, trying to decide what to do. "We must wait."

Long minutes passed. The smoker lit another cigarette.

"I think they're on guard duty," Malcolm muttered.

Madraeus' fangs elongated. He started forward.

"No!" Rami warned, "We cannot let them find any more evidence." He turned to watch them again. "We must knock them out."

Slowly, the three vampires crept forward. Inch-by-inch they closed the distance between them and the guards. They were only an arm's length from the closest one when two more men came up the little incline to the entrance.

"We're supposed to relieve you guys," said one of the newcomers.

"Nice." The smoker dropped his cigarette butt and smashed out the ember with his toe.

One of the new guards looked past the smoker and caught a glimpse of Rami. "What the Hell?"

As the others turned to see what he was looking at, Madraeus and Malcolm burst from the shadows. Madraeus punched the closest man while Malcolm tackled another. Rami backhanded the third, knocking him against the support beam. He crumpled to the ground.

The last man shouted for help as he stumbled backward. The answering response came from farther up the mountain near the shaft house.

"Run!" Rami caught Madraeus' elbow and hauled him away from the fight. With his other hand, he shoved Malcolm toward the trees. "Go!"

As they dodged and crashed through the underbrush, they could hear shouting behind them. It sounded like the entire police force was coming after them. To the east, the sky was beginning to lighten.

"Where the Hell is Philtzer?" Malcolm shouted.

They cut across the slope, away from the men pursuing them. The sky turned a bright shade of orange.

"We're not going to make it!" Malcolm glanced up. "It's too close to sunrise!"

The top of the mountain began to glow.

"Do we go back?" Rami shouted to Madraeus.

Madraeus had just opened his mouth to answer when a black furry body shot out in front of him. He stumbled and landed hard on one knee.

"Philtzer!" Malcolm cried.

"Go!" Madraeus roared.

Philtzer sprang ahead, leading them across an open meadow. They could see the red of Thomas' Jeep through the trees on the far side. With the sun in pursuit, they raced toward it.

Malcolm, Rami, and Madraeus piled into the Jeep. Philtzer shifted into his human form. He grabbed blankets from the back, shoving them at Rami across the back of the seat. The sun blazed across the tips of the trees above them.

Frantically, they pulled the blankets open, trying to spread them out enough to cover all three men. Malcolm and Madraeus huddled down onto the floor. Rami struggled to flatten himself across the back seat. Philtzer pushed and shoved until the blankets were shielding them from the sun. He slammed the door shut, jumped into the front, and fired up the engine.

Tires spun. Gravel shot at the trees. The Jeep shot forward. In the rearview mirror, Philtzer saw the police flooding into the little grove. The Jeep bounced down the rutted trail. The vampires cursed and snarled as they scrambled to keep the blankets in place.

"Shit!" Philtzer slammed on the brakes.

Thomas and Cody, in wolf form, stood on the trail in front of him.

"Get in!" Philtzer shouted, leaning across the seat and throwing the passenger door open.

The two wolves bounded over to the Jeep and jumped in. Thomas tried to jump over the seat, only to land on Rami.

"Oomph!" Rami grunted. "Get off!"

"Sorry, boys!" Philtzer grinned as he reached across to pull the door shut. "Lots of passengers, little room!"

"Get us somewhere dark!" snarled Malcolm.

"I am!" Philtzer started driving again. "Where's Sophia and Hamy?"

"They provided a distraction." Rami rumbled. "They are still in the mine."

Cody whined.

Philtzer shook his head. "We'll have to come back for them." He glanced in the mirror again. "If they saw our plates, they'll be looking for the Jeep."

Thomas growled.

"Sorry, bud." Philtzer glanced at his friend. "We gotta ditch your ride."

Home Sweet Home

Philtzer drove as quickly as he could while still obeying the traffic laws. The last thing they needed was to get stopped for speeding. Although it was entirely possible that the police had identified the Jeep and were already on the lookout, there was no reason to attract any more attention than was absolutely necessary. Unfortunately, it seemed like every traffic light was red, and everyone seemed to notice the Jeep with a naked man and two large wolves sitting in the front seat.

The sun was already high in the sky, and moods were unpleasant by the time they reached downtown Denver.

"Home sweet home." Philtzer breathed a sigh of relief as he pulled into the underground parking garage below their building. He parked as close to the back elevator as he could and glanced around to make sure the area was empty. "Right. Coast is clear."

Rami threw off the blanket and climbed out first. Malcolm and Madraeus unfolded themselves from the floor of the Jeep and crawled out stiffly. Madraeus stumbled and fell to his knees. Rami picked him up and hauled him toward the elevator. Malcolm hurried after them, desperate to get out of the light.

Rami held Madraeus up with one arm and leaned against the elevator wall. Madraeus suppressed a groan. He had gone too long without blood. The exertion of the escape and the exposure to daylight, even though it was through a blanket, had been the last straw. His body was nearing shutdown. He could feel his heart pulsating in his half-healed wounds.

"Come on!" Malcolm pushed the button again, impatient for food and relative safety.

The back elevator opened directly into the private section of InfiniCorp's offices. As soon as the doors opened, Malcolm raced out and down the hallway to the kitchen. Rami and Madraeus followed much slower.

By the time they staggered into the kitchen, Malcolm had already downed a full bottle of blood. He turned to the open refrigerator and grabbed two more bottles, holding them out to Madraeus and Rami.

Madraeus tried to take one, but his arm wouldn't cooperate. Rami handed one of the bottles back to Malcolm and then held the other one so Madraeus could drink.

Madraeus groaned. Bites and cuts flared to life painfully as the blood began to work its way through Madraeus' body, repairing his damaged cells. His body spasmed. His knees buckled, and he sank to the floor in front of the open refrigerator. He squeezed his eyes shut.

Rami glanced at him in concern. Malcolm reached for a second bottle and handed it to Rami. Once again, he helped Madraeus drink. Slowly, the shaking started to subside.

"Thank you," Madraeus rasped. "Healing hasn't hurt this much in a long time."

"Not surprising," Rami rumbled quietly. "You are almost dead from starvation."

"Night, guys, pleasure being stuck under a mountain with ya!" Malcolm gave them a small salute with the bottle of blood he was holding before trudging up the spiral stairs at the edge of the kitchen.

"Come on, we need sleep before trying to decide what our next step is."

Madraeus groaned as Rami helped him struggle to his feet.

Rami grunted and steered Madraeus around the counter.

"It's been a long time since we've been this bad off," Madraeus muttered.

The giant steadied him. "Yes, it has, my friend, yes it has."

LOST SHEEP

"Well, that's three lost sheep back home, now we need to get the rest of the herd," Philtzer said after the elevator doors closed.

Thomas hopped over the seat, shifted, and started digging for his clothes. "I'm gonna tell Hamy that you called him a sheep," Thomas said as he pulled on his jeans and then threw Philtzer his pants.

"Hey, where's mine?" Cody hung over the seat.

Thomas grinned. "You have to stay naked."

"You wish!" Cody growled as he started to climb over the seat, intent on retrieving his clothes, but a pair of jeans to the face stopped him. "Thanks."

Thomas threw a shirt at Philtzer and then a license plate.

The plate bounced off Philtzer's arm. "Ow."

"Sorry." Thomas' muffled voice came through the shirt he was pulling over his head.

Philtzer grabbed the license plate and went around to the back of the Jeep. He opened the rear hatch and looked at Thomas.

"You couldn't wait 'til I came back here? You had to throw it at me?"

"All doggies like catching Frisbees." Thomas grinned, climbing out.

"This," Philtzer held up the plate, "is not a Frisbee."

"Here." Thomas handed him a screwdriver. "Be glad I didn't throw this at you." He took the second plate around to the front of the Jeep.

Philtzer shut the hatch and started to work on changing the plate. It was only a temporary fix, but it would keep the cops at bay long enough for them to split town.

"How we gonna get Hamy?" Cody asked, coming around the back of the Jeep.

"Well..." Philtzer handed Cody the old plate and then screwed the new plate in place. "I guess we'll head back up there and see if we can find them." They joined Thomas at the front of the Jeep and watched him work on the other plate. "I told Hamy to head back toward Alma if we were separated."

"We're gonna need a different vehicle," Thomas warned as he stood and leaned on the hood. "They'll be looking for a red Jeep."

"Don't look at me!" Philtzer shook his head. "My bike can't carry three people."

"Guess that leaves your pick-up." Thomas looked at Cody.

"Ah man, I just got it!"

"So?" Thomas frowned. "It's not like we're gonna wreck it."

"Yeah. Right." Cody gestured to the numerous dents in the body of the old Cherokee. "I've seen your Jeep."

"Hey, don't insult my baby." Thomas patted the hood. "I've had her a long time."

"Yeah, we can tell!" Philtzer grinned at Cody.

"Shut up." Thomas kicked Philtzer. "Come on. The sooner we get everyone back where they belong the better. Then we can blow this town."

They raided the Jeep for the rest of their clothing and shoes then headed across the garage to Cody's pick-up.

"Hey, can we grab breakfast on the way?" Philtzer asked as he climbed into the cramped back seat of the crew cab.

"You mean lunch?" Cody smiled.

Armed with burritos and energy drinks, the three wolves drove back into the mountains.

"Oh man, I missed food!" Philtzer groaned around a mouthful.

"You ate just last night!" Thomas punctuated his exclamation with a belch. "You nearly emptied the cooler all by yourself."

"That was forever ago!"

"I don't know how someone so short can eat so much." Thomas shook his head and dug into another burrito.

"Yeah, like you can talk," Cody laughed.

"I'm a lot taller." Thomas slapped Cody in the chest.

"Hey! Don't abuse the driver!" He reached over and banged the back of his hand into Thomas' chest.

Philtzer hung over the seat and pointed. "Look, there's the turn-off."

"I see it." Cody took the exit and turned onto CO-9.

"I hope they made it out of there."

"Well, with most of the cops chasing us, they should have been able to slip away with no problems." Philtzer scanned the tree-lined road.

Cody crumbled the wrapper from his lunch. "I hope so."

Eventually, they turned into the tiny town of Alma. Passing store after store, Philtzer kept looking for the little bar they had been to before. Then he saw it. It was hard to miss. The building was bright purple.

Cody parked out front and they looked around before getting out. The town was quiet. Only a few cars and semis were coming and going.

Cody got out first and walked around the front of the pick-up. He turned toward the café that sat next to the bar. "I'll check inside."

Philtzer and Thomas hopped out of the cab and looked around. Just as Cody was about to open the door, they heard a voice coming from around the corner.

"I told you I don't speak wolf unless I'm in wolf form."

"Hamy?" Thomas asked, walking around the corner.

Hamilton scrambled to his feet and stepped out from behind a pile of boxes.

"Damn!" Hamilton grabbed Thomas' outstretched hand and shook it. "Where the hell have you guys been?"

Philtzer popped around the corner and sagged with relief. "Man! I wasn't sure you'd make it here."

Hamilton shook his head. "We almost didn't. That's a long freaking walk!"

"Sorry about that." Philtzer winced. Alma was quite a few miles from the mine. "Sophia?"

As Philtzer looked around for her, she crept out from behind the boxes and sat beside Hamilton. She was still on the leash and didn't look happy. Her ears were back and her lips were curled in a silent growl.

"Sorry, honey. You wanna go home?"

She stood and shook her entire body.

He gave her a sympathetic smile and gestured to the truck. "Come on. Let's get the hell out of Dodge."

PUT A PIN IN IT

Madraeus sat behind his desk, staring across the room. The chess set had been packed away, and the midnight blue walls were visible through the empty bookshelves. Upstairs, a small renovation was happening to hide the nature of the detention cells. Soon, the movers would come for the two very comfortable leather armchairs and Madraeus' desk. Sadness washed over him. He had liked it here. It had started to feel like home, but it didn't matter now.

"You look terrible," Rami said as he entered the study. "Nearly as bad as 1871."

Madraeus stiffened. He was aware that his time in the mine had left him rough, but he didn't think it was as bad as when they had been under siege in Paris.

"Have you called Whitney?"

Madraeus stood and paced to the far end of the study.

Rami leaned on the desk and watched his friend. "You will have to talk to her at some point."

"I have other concerns."

"You are being a coward."

Madraeus spun around and glared at Rami. His eyes were black, and his fangs extended. Waves of menace radiated out from him.

Rami slowly stood.

Madraeus shook, trying to control his raging emotions. Finally, he retracted his fangs, and his eyes faded back to chocolate brown.

"My apologies, Rami," he said hoarsely. "I am not..." He gestured vaguely.

"The last few weeks have been a strain on you. I am sorry, my friend. I should not have pushed you."

Madraeus sighed and rubbed his face. He felt old.

"Come see what I have found." Rami's deep voice echoed in the emptiness of the room.

Madraeus stood and followed the giant to his office.

"As you know, Whitney's Dreaded Filing Project has revealed a disturbing trend in shipments."

"Yes," Madraeus nodded, "you thought you could track Cecelia's movements through the discrepancies."

"Indeed." Rami gestured to the world map he had tacked up on his office wall. It was covered in clusters of red and blue pins. "The red pins are the locations that have received high concentrations of blood shipments and travel activity through our brokers. I may not have them all. This is just what Whitney had found so far."

"That is a lot of pins." Madraeus crossed his arms and leaned against the desk. "And very spread out. What is she doing?" he muttered.

Rami held up the little metal disk with the rabbits on it that they had found in the mine.

"The Hares..." Madraeus stared at the disk. The pieces snapped together. "She's camping out where the Old Sources are trapped?"

"It is the most likely scenario." Rami gestured to the map. "I picked some of the sites at random." He pointed at the pile of ancient tomes on his desk. "There is a correlation between where shipments are concentrated and stories of creatures or demons."

Madraeus looked back at the map. His eyes moved from one cluster of pins to another. "How did I not see...?"

"Do not beat yourself up over it." Rami stared at the map. "This is a pattern that could only have been seen from a great height, and we live in the trenches."

Madraeus snorted. "Nice thought, but we are still responsible for finding and stopping her."

"We can rule out where she has been," Rami said. "I have Marcus cross-checking the shipment locations with reports of crime scenes similar to the mine and any increase in missing persons."

"Like the ones that Unkhabami mentioned?"

"Yes—" Rami's phone rang. It was Marcus. He put it on speaker and set it on the desk.

"These are in order of the shipment dates and the dates on the police reports," Marcus said. He began to rattle off the names of towns across China, India, Africa, North America, and southern Europe. "The last ones showed Germany and Colorado."

While Marcus spoke, Rami added pins to the map and drew a line showing the trail of death left behind by Cecelia.

Madraeus shook his head. "Too many dead bodies. We're getting noticed. It's only a matter of time before the authorities discover the Races."

"I think they are pretty close to figuring it out already," Marcus snorted.

"How much do you think they know?" Madraeus asked. As a private investigator, Marcus kept an unofficial ear to every official line of information he could find.

Marcus sighed. "There are too many incidents for them not to connect the dots."

"See what you can do about *disconnecting* the dots."

"Sure, corrupt a file here and there, easy enough." They could hear Marcus grinning through the phone. "The difficulty comes if they start working together. Then we are talking about multiple copies of files in multiple government systems."

"I have every faith in you," Madraeus said.

"Who wouldn't?" Marcus laughed and hung up.

"This was so much easier when global communication wasn't a thing," Madraeus grumbled.

"I fear that is not the end of our troubles," Rami said, studying the map.

"Why?" Madraeus gestured to the clusters of pins. "Most coincide with Marcus' findings. It may be that we just haven't found invoices connecting the others."

Rami turned to the boxes of files stacked against the wall. "It is possible, but..."

"But?" Madraeus looked at the map. "The blue pins?"

Rami nodded. "I looked into who authorized the shipments."

"When I was captured," Madraeus rubbed his forehead, "I was surprised at the size of her army. She has a lot of supporters. More than I thought possible."

Rami turned back and handed a stack of papers to Madraeus. "That is the list of traitors who have signed those invoices."

Madraeus read through the report. He looked up. "Is this true?"

Rami's grim expression told him all he needed to know. This went beyond anything that Cecelia had tried before. "Cecelia's tried to take over a town here or there. But this?" He held up the papers. "This is a full-scale coup."

Rami sighed. "I do not understand why they would join her."

In his mind, Madraeus heard the hissing voice. *Join ussss.*

He shook his head to clear it. Madraeus looked at the list again and then at the map. His gaze flitted across the map, counting blue pins. "The blue pins are traitors. The red: her army. What are all these single pins?"

He pointed to a red pin in England. "Lady Douglas, maybe?" He indicated one in Northern Canada. "Lefour?" Then to one in Chicago. "Marcus?" Madraeus tapped a pin in India. "Bodhendra? None of them would betray the Races."

"And this one is Unkhabami's village," Rami said.

Madraeus stood with his hands on his hips, staring at the map. "Why would Cecelia go anywhere near the Priestess?"

Rami stared at the map for a long time. His eyes shifted to the pin showing the mine's location and then to the individual pins Madraeus had pointed out. Fear filled Rami's face as he looked back at the pin in Unkhabami's village.

Madraeus watched Rami's gaze travel across the map. "What are you thinking?"

"Unkhabami is there, Lady Douglas, Furaha" he pointed out the pins, "and we are here. All powerful obstacles to whatever Cecelia is planning."

"You think some of these pins are targets?" Madraeus' gaze swiveled back to the map.

Rami nodded. "Cecelia wiping out the competition?"

For a moment, the hissing voice filled Madraeus' head. *You cannot ssstop usss!*

Madraeus shook his head. "We are so far behind in this mess."

"It is time we caught up then!" Rami rumbled. "We must weed out her agents, and then we can find a way of stopping her."

"I'll make some calls. Then we'll speak to the council."

WELCOME BACK

"We should go to Myers' place," Thomas said.

Sophia, squished in between Philtzer and Cody in the front seat, whined and cocked her head.

"I don't know." Philtzer half turned in the seat to look back at Thomas. "I'm thinking that we should head back to the office."

Sophia growled.

"But all the stuff we found in the mine is still at Myers' with Vivian. She was going to keep looking for clues."

"But it's been a couple of days. They may have hauled it all back to InfiniCorp."

"Doubt it. We're moving the whole office. Why take more stuff there?" Thomas tried to hang over the seat, but Sophia growled at him again. "Will you stop that? I'm not even touching you!"

Sophia shook her head, making her ears flap. She scooted around, turning so she could watch Thomas.

"Honey?" Cody coughed discreetly. "You're sitting on me."

Sophia whined and moved again this time almost sitting on Philtzer. He tried not to smile and didn't say anything. She was having a hard enough time and he didn't want to make it worse. She was stuck in wolf form due to her lack of clothing, and she was not happy that she had no say about where they went.

"I don't see that we need to hurry back, the vamps aren't going to be awake for hours anyway." Hamilton put in. "It's not like we can do a lot until they are up."

Philtzer nodded. Multiple trips up and down the mountain rescuing people had taken nearly all day.

"We can help Vivian and talk to Myers. Maybe they know something we don't." Thomas glanced out the back window again, looking for pursuit. "We've been on the mountain since the battle. I haven't heard from anyone in days."

"Alright, Myers' it is." Philtzer nodded then reached over and tried to scratch Sophia's ears. She flinched and growled at him. "You'll like Myers. She's old but nice."

Sophia eyed him silently.

"Who is she, you ask?" He smiled. "She is a gazillion-year-old oracle who runs a temp agency and is always fussing about something. Kinda like a favorite grandma."

Sophia snorted.

"Eww! Doggie snot!" Philtzer scrubbed at the wet spot on his arm.

"Whitney's probably still there too." Hamilton leaned forward to hang over the seat. "And that Sandra woman."

"Whitney." Philtzer smiled a sad, crooked smile. "I'm surprised she's still in one piece."

"She almost wasn't," Thomas said quietly.

"What do you mean?" Philtzer swiveled around to stare at him.

"I forgot," Thomas shook his head, "you were gone by then. Whitney was attacked in the tunnel by an enemy vamp. Nearly killed her. They took her to Myers' and Kirkland gave her a transfusion."

"Damn." Philtzer breathed out slowly. "You sure she's still alive?"

Thomas shrugged. "Whitney was still unconscious when we left."

"When was that?"

"After Rami and Madraeus went back to the mine, we unloaded all the weapons from the raid and the boxes of papers Cecelia had left. Hamy, Cody, and I were gonna head back up to the mine to see if we'd missed anything. But when we were coming up the road that turns toward the mine, a bunch of police cars passed us and turned. So, we took the long route and saw them crawling all over the yard outside the shaft house. We took up surveillance 'til you called."

"So, you have no idea whether or not she survived?"

Sophia glanced at Philtzer. She laid her ears back flat against her head when she saw his serious expression and nudged him with her nose.

"The boss will go nuts if she dies." Philtzer looked at her sadly, then explained. "I think he's in love with her. Even though he won't admit it."

They rode in silence for a while. None of them wanted to see what Madraeus would do if Whitney died. They had heard stories about his past, just rumors, but enough to be more than a little afraid of him if he lost control.

Sophia whined at the tension she could feel coming in waves from the men surrounding her. Philtzer looked at her and shrugged. His smile didn't reach his eyes.

"Don't worry, Whitney is tough. She'll make it," he said, trying to ruffle the fur behind her ears. She ducked his hand.

"Yeah," Thomas murmured from the back seat as if trying to convince himself. "She's tough."

"She'll make it." Hamilton agreed quietly.

They drove the rest of the trip in silence. When they arrived at Mrs. Myers' sprawling estate, Myers opened the door and waited for them at the top of the stairs.

"Philtzer!" She gave him a genuine smile. "Am I glad to see you!"

"Hey, Mrs. M!"

Sophia stayed by his leg as he trotted up the steps.

"Boys!" She smiled warmly as Thomas, Hamilton, and Cody came up behind Philtzer. "And who is this?" She turned and smiled down at Sophia, but her eyes seemed to see more than she let on.

"Meet Sophia Sinclair." Philtzer made an over-dramatic bowing gesture.

Sophia bared her teeth at him.

"As in Regina Sinclair?" Mrs. Myers raised her eyebrows and stared at Philtzer.

Sophia growled.

"Stop getting mad at me about that!" He frowned down at her in mock annoyance. Then he turned to Mrs. Myers and whispered, but not quietly, "She's grumpy because we all know her mother and she doesn't."

"Oh, you poor dear!" Mrs. Myers' motherly instinct kicked in as she sank down in front of Sophia. "Don't you worry, we'll soon have that remedied. And don't let them give you a hard time. They're just a bunch of overgrown children."

"Am not!" Thomas protested.

"Oh, hush!" She glared at him and then looked back at Sophia. "I take it since they are men and you are still wolf, you need some clothes?"

Sophia dipped her head and wagged her tail.

"Come with me," she said to Sophia, then turned and walked back into her house. The men followed her without an invitation. "We have a lot to talk about."

"How's Whitney?" Philtzer asked.

"Whitney's fine," said a voice from the living room door-way as they passed.

"Whit!" Philtzer exclaimed and ran over to her.

"Hey, Philtzer." She smiled at his puppy-like exuberance as he squeezed her in a painful hug. "Ahhooww!"

"Oh! Sorry, sorry!" He gentled his embrace but didn't let go. "They said you were..." he trailed off as he pulled back to look at her. She looked like death was near. She was pale and way too thin. Her skin was molted from bruises that were in various stages of healing. "Man, you look like crap again!"

"Thanks?" She laughed for the first time in days. "It's nice to see you too."

Thomas grinned. "Welcome back to the land of the living!"

Whitney smiled back at him. Then she looked down at the little brown wolf that had stepped closer to her and was staring at her with wide dark eyes. "Hi."

"This is Sophia," Philtzer explained. "She's the one who let you guys out of your cell."

Whitney glanced at him and then back at the wolf. "Thank you."

"We having a party in the hall?" Sandra asked as she came out of the living room behind Whitney. She stopped short when she saw Sophia. An expression of fear and revulsion crossed her face.

"This is Sandra," Whitney introduced her. "She was my cell-mate for a while."

Sophia whined.

"Children?" Mrs. Myers cleared her throat and gestured toward Sophia. "Wouldn't this conversation be better when we are *all* able to participate?"

"Right." Whitney smiled at the werewolf. "Sorry."

Mrs. Myers led Sophia up the stairs to find some clothes.

Philtzer hung an arm around Whitney's shoulders and steered her toward the kitchen. "Let's eat."

A COUNCIL DIVIDED

"I don't care what you think!" Madraeus glared at each of the council members on the conference room screen. "You can deny it all you want, but this is the truth. Cecelia has gathered an army."

As the council members argued about the implications of his announcement, Madraeus leaned back against the conference table and looked down at the carpet. The witches had done a good job cleaning the room after using it for a conjuring space. He cringed at the memory of the herb-laced smoke that had filled the room and the pile of dirt Unkhabami and the coven had used while casting their spell to find Whitney.

"I still think you are jumping to conclusions!" Councilwoman Furaha's dismissive voice brought his attention back to the meeting.

"I saw the evidence with my own eyes," Madraeus countered.

"He says he witnessed this army, but where are they now?" Li Wan gestured vaguely.

"They fled," Rami rumbled.

"Then they are no longer a concern," Furaha concluded.

"Wrong!" Madraeus shoved away from the table. "If they are allowed to regroup, they could cause no end of damage. Look at the mess they left at the mine."

"You have disposed of those left behind?" Lady Douglas asked.

"My people took care of the bodies of the Races, Lady Douglas." Madraeus' tone was clipped. "We burned the human bodies, but unfortunately the police arrived before the evidence could be removed."

"I want to know why it was allowed to get this far in the first place?" Dr. Paris Stanley banged his fist on his desk.

"We had no knowledge of her intentions," Rami said.

"Why not?" Stanley jumped on his admission. "You are the head of this council, Madraeus. You are supposed to prevent this kind of incident. But you were running around chasing this mortal woman and have put us all in jeopardy."

"I was not chasing a mortal woman!" Madraeus' lip curled. He could feel his fangs elongating. "I was trying to catch a rogue vampire."

"While putting us all in the public eye!" Stanley jeered. "You are not worthy of your position if you can't catch one vampire!"

"If that is how you feel, then I will be happy to step aside," Madraeus hissed.

Lady Douglas sat forward. "I don't believe—"

"Yes!" Stanley eagerly leaned closer. "Perhaps a change of leadership is just what this council needs!"

"I'm sure you have someone in mind, Stanley," Madraeus snarled. "Cecelia perhaps?"

"That is highly inappropriate!" Furaha snapped. "Why would you suggest such a thing?"

"It is my firm belief that there are those on this council working with Cecelia," Madraeus looked at each of the faces on the screen, "and I will not work with traitors!"

There was a collective gasp followed by angry protests.

Madraeus glanced at Rami and nodded. Rami sent the 'go ahead' text to the teams stationed outside the traitors' houses.

Lady Douglas rapped her knuckles on the desk in front of her. "Ladies and Gentlemen! Please!"

Madraeus shouted above the din. "I have evidence gathered from our invoices that point to sympathizers on this council who have been shipping goods to Cecelia. Accounting records show they are also supplying her with operating capital."

Silence descended.

"Whom do you accuse?" Lady Douglas asked.

There was a quiet moment as Madraeus slowly made eye contact with the culprits. "Paris Stanley. Bentaresh. Li Wan."

The accused cried out, their voices overlapping.

Paris Stanley was the loudest. "How dare you! I'll get you for this!"

Rami raised his voice. "Those with ties to Cecelia will be detained and questioned."

Chaos erupted on the screens showing Stanley, Bentaresh, and Li Wan. The other council members watched as Madraeus' people raided the traitors' locations. The sounds of shouting and fighting blasted out from the conference room speakers. Suddenly the noise cut off as three screens went dark.

Those left on the call sat silently.

"I think that proves my point," Madraeus said.

Lady Douglas was the first to speak. "This is a deeply disturbing turn of events."

Bodhendra, a small Indian gentleman, leaned closer to his camera. "This is a serious time for us. This council has stood for centuries. It is a hard pill to swallow that so many have turned against the tenets of our society."

"Unfortunately, that is not the only issue. There is a high probability that each of you could be targeted," Madraeus warned. "May I suggest increasing your security."

"She wouldn't dare attack the council directly!" Bodhendra gasped.

"Cecelia is moving on a grander scale than ever before," Lady Douglas said. "She already has an army and if she is successful in gathering the Old Sources, then it is a small step to wipe out the council."

"It is," Madraeus sighed.

Lady Douglas sat up straighter and sighed. "Madraeus, I believe that I speak for what remains of the Council. You have our full confidence."

"Then may I suggest that we start to rally our own supporters? Cecelia has plans in motion and we have no idea what her end goal is. We must be ready for anything."

"We are late to this race," Furaha agreed. "We must recruit as many to our side as possible."

"I only hope that it will be enough." Madraeus shook his head.

"Do whatever you have to do," Lady Douglas said.

"I will," Madraeus said, "but you need to understand that things will get worse before they get better."

Lady Douglas nodded. "They always do."

DINNER AND A THOUGHT

It didn't take the four men long to cover the kitchen in dishes. They raided the refrigerator and the cupboards, pulling out everything that sounded good.

Whitney wandered into the kitchen but soon scampered back to the door to avoid the chaos created by hungry werewolves cooking. Sandra stayed by the door with her arms folded and her jaw hanging slack.

Elizabeth Martindale tapped her cane on the floor behind the girls. "What is happening in here?"

"Men cooking," Sandra said at the same time as Whitney said, "Werewolves cooking."

Thomas juggled spices while Cody made something sizzle and pop in a frying pan on the stove. Philtzer sang all the instrumental parts to his own theme song while he chopped peppers, and Hamilton opened and closed every cupboard door as he looked for ingredients.

"Oh my," Elizabeth said.

Philtzer grinned at the trio of ladies watching them. "If you're gonna watch the show, you may wanna tip."

"Maybe we should set the table?" Mrs. Myers asked.

The girls turned to see her standing behind them. A now-dressed Sophia stood a few feet behind Myers as if afraid she wouldn't be welcome.

"Come along." Myers turned and walked down the hall. "You too, Sophia," she said over her shoulder as she led them to the dining room and directed them to the China cabinet.

"Don't worry," Elizabeth said to Sophia as they pulled plates out of the cupboard and handed them to Sandra and Whitney, "you'll get used to being herded like a sheep. It happens all the time around here."

"Are you...?" Sophia stuttered to a stop.

"One of them?" Elizabeth snorted. "No. I'm just here by association. You see, Whitney is my granddaughter and she works for Mrs. Myers, which got her neck deep in this mess." She jerked her head toward the kitchen.

Behind her, Whitney sighed. "Grammy, it's not that bad!"

"Not that bad?" Elizabeth rounded on her granddaughter. "You've almost been killed, what? Three times now? Four?"

"I'm fine, Grammy. I'm still here." Whitney said without much conviction. She followed Sandra around the table, carrying the plates while Sandra set them out. "Besides, there's nothing I can do about it now."

"I know this is hard to accept, Elizabeth, but we are not the enemy," Mrs. Myers said as she counted out forks.

Elizabeth thumped her cane against the hardwood floor. Whitney flinched.

"You're not going to convince me that what he did was right," Elizabeth snapped, glaring at Myers.

Myers glared back. "I shouldn't have to."

Sandra banged one of the plates down a little too hard, gaining the attention of the older ladies.

"Sorry," Sandra said with zero apology in her tone.

Whitney kept her eyes on the plates in her arms.

"Great!" Sophia muttered. "Another dysfunctional family."

They all stared at her. A flush spread across Sophia's face as she realized she had said that out loud.

"I'm sorry," she stuttered.

"It's alright," Mrs. Myers smiled as she placed the cutlery on the table. "I imagine you are confused and a little overwhelmed. Let's see if we can help with that."

Sandra snorted. "Where'd you wanna start?"

"Why don't you tell us who you are?" Mrs. Myers pulled out a chair and gestured for Sophia to sit.

"It's a long story," Sophia warned as she sat down.

Mrs. Myers sat next to her. "They always are, dear."

Sophia managed to speak about her attack without stuttering as badly as she had when she'd told Philtzer. She told them about her dealings with Spark.

Whitney watched her as she spoke. Something about her story sounded familiar, like she had heard it before. Whitney pushed the thought aside because the women were invaded by men carrying steaming dishes and platters.

"Make way!" Philtzer called, swooping in and depositing a platter of steaks and a bowl of sautéed mushrooms on the table. "Grub's up!"

"What'd we miss?" Thomas set down a platter of fried chicken.

Cody and Hamilton followed them in with dishes of vegetables and sauces. The werewolves took the empty spots at the table and started to dig in.

"Boys!" At Mrs. Myers' exclamation, they slowed down and ate with better manners. "Thank you, that's better."

Whitney smirked and elbowed Philtzer. He grinned at her around a mouthful of chicken.

"So, what'd we miss?" Thomas asked again.

"We were just doing a rendition of 'the story so far'," Sandra said, reaching for the chicken.

"Oh, nice!" Philtzer swallowed and sat back. "Did you make it to the part where a devastatingly handsome wolf swoops in and rescues the beautiful but misguided lady wolf?"

"You didn't rescue me!" Sophia blurted, choking on her food.

"Uh-oh," Thomas taunted. "You're in trouble now!"

"And I am not misguided! I just didn't get the whole story."

Sophia started to talk about Spark finding her at the hospital. Hamilton sat back and frowned at Sophia.

"Sparks the white wolf, right?" Hamilton asked. "And she found you the day after you were attacked?"

"Yeah." Sophia frowned back at him. "Why are you looking at me like that?"

"Detective Sanders!" Whitney blurted, cutting off whatever Hamilton had started to say.

"What?" Sandra glanced at Whitney.

"Detective Sanders," Whitney repeated.

"Who's he again?" Cody asked.

"That detective pestering Whitney." Philtzer looked at Whitney. "What about him?"

"On the day of the funeral," Whitney glanced at Hamilton and Philtzer, "remember? Sanders came to the office and started asking me about Justin again. He said that there had been another attack." She switched her gaze to Sophia. "He said there were four guys who had their throats torn out."

Sophia shuddered at the memory. She took a drink of water but stopped when she realized they were all looking at her.

"When were you attacked?" Whitney asked.

"April 17th."

"Same day," Whitney murmured.

"That's weird." Cody reached for the chicken again without noticing the tension that swept across the table.

Whitney and Hamilton were staring at Sophia.

Philtzer's gaze switched from Whitney to Hamilton. "What are you two on to?"

"I was just thinking that this Spark character found Sophia awfully fast," Hamilton mused. "Almost as if she knew where to look."

"You think she knew about Sophia's attack?" Thomas stopped eating.

"How long does it usually take for you to find a new werewolf?" Whitney asked, her gaze bouncing from Hamilton to Philtzer.

"Sometimes years." Hamilton shrugged. "Even if it's an attack like Sophia's, we don't always find them right away."

"So, if Spark was there the next day saying, 'Hey there, let me show you how to be a wolf,' then she had to be watching pretty close." Whitney looked at Hamilton.

Thomas joined the conspiracy. "There have been an awful lot of new wolves around lately."

"What better way to gather an army quickly?" Cody set his chicken down.

"That explains why so many have joined Cecelia." Thomas exchanged a look with Philtzer. "If you want an army that's loyal, make them and then tell them whatever truth you want."

"Wait, what are you saying?" Sophia paled. "You think I was attacked on purpose?"

The color drained from Philtzer's face. "We need to talk to the boss ASAP."

CRAPSHOOT

"Where are we going again?" Cody asked, splitting his attention between driving and looking at the numbers on buildings.

"The Dead Beat Lounge, number 1440," Hamilton said, looking at the paper in his hand.

"How do we even know this ain't just a crapshoot?"

"Rami got this guy's name from the list they confiscated."

"Yeah, but how do we know that list is legit?"

"Paris Stanley is a geneticist and historian. If he compiled a list of potential werewolves based on their genetics, it's probably pretty accurate."

Cody shrugged. "I'm just saying that Stanley may not be trustworthy. I mean, he was working for Cecelia. When Madraeus outed him in front of the rest of the council, he would've been livid. Why not leave a red herring to mess with us? He could have planted a fake list before he high-tailed it."

"Wow. That's supervillain-level thinking," Hamilton chuckled. "But best to check anyway."

"I guess." Cody squinted at a building on his left with a huge crowd out front. "Hey, that's it."

Cody continued past the club and pulled his pickup into a parking lot a block away. He winced when he saw how sketchy the lot looked.

"Somebody's gonna steal my pickup if I leave it here."

"Nobody'll steal it."

"Even drug dealers wouldn't be caught dead here!"

Hamilton glanced around and then laughed. "Then I guess no one will be around to steal your precious pickup."

"Very comforting." Cody grimaced. "So, who are we looking for?"

Hamilton looked down and read. "A guy named Jeff Munroe."

"Any other bits to go on?" Cody looked over Hamilton's shoulder at the paper. "What's this guy look like?"

"Just says his name and that he's a bartender," Hamilton shook his head, "but it does say 'unknown factor P'."

"What's that mean?"

"I have no idea." Hamilton folded the paper and shoved it in the glove box. "Let's go find out."

"Should we do a sweep on four feet first?"

"Normally, I'd say yes, but did you see that crowd?" Hamilton said, getting out. "This has to be the busiest nightclub in Denver."

"Weird for such a dangerous part of town," Cody said, resettling his cowboy hat.

They could hear the bass thumping as they walked down the sidewalk. Hamilton watched the crowd as they approached the front door. It wasn't really a waiting line per se, but more of a continuation of the party that spilled out onto the street.

Hamilton stepped into the crowd, snaking his way closer to the door. He held his breath as he passed through clouds of smoke and vapor. Cody stayed on his heels until a woman tripped backward into his arms.

"Whoa there," Cody said, catching her before she hit the ground. "Ma'am?" He froze, supporting her with his forearms under her armpits, blushing a little as he noticed that she had lost most of her clothes.

She stared up at him through glassy eyes. "We should get a room."

"Um," Cody stuttered. "I..."

Hamilton appeared at his elbow and leaned down to look the woman in the eye. "He'd like to stay and play, but he's working."

Cody snapped out of his embarrassment and lifted the woman to her feet. He let go, wiped his hands off on his shirt, nodded to the woman, and looked at Hamilton. "Thanks."

"Come on." Hamilton turned and walked up the stairs to the entrance.

They stepped through the door and moved past several couples who were making out in the hallway. The door to the main club was just a PVC-strip curtain, blurring the flashing lights and movement beyond it. Reaching out, he moved the plastic strips aside and stepped through.

Strobe lights pulsed with the beat, and green neon tubes snaked in every direction, giving the room a sickly glow. As the music changed, the neon tubes turned pink.

They stepped out onto a wide balcony that ran around the upper half of the room, giving them a good view of the packed dance floor. Bracing their elbows on the balcony rail, Hamilton and Cody leaned over and looked down. Directly under the balcony, a line of booths ringed the dance floor. They were all full. The dance floor itself was so crowded, it looked like a mosh pit. A bar ran the full length of the far wall where patrons waved money and jostled for space.

"Holy shit!" Cody took his hat off and scratched his head.

"You notice something weird about this place?" Hamilton shouted, stepping back from the railing.

Cody leaned down to hear him over the music. "You mean other than it's busier than a one-armed monkey with two bananas?"

"What?" Hamilton stared at Cody, trying to process his comment. He gave up and shook his head. "Never mind. I meant there are no bouncers. No one is making trouble."

"That ain't right." Cody looked around. "Ain't a proper bar without a fight, but people are definitely enjoying themselves." Cody pointed at a group of women who seemed intent on losing all their clothes as quickly as possible.

"Their dates are gonna go nuts."

"Don't think so, look." Cody pointed again.

The men dancing with the women didn't seem to be bothered at all. Quite the opposite. They joined their impromptu strip tease and were all laughing together. Hamilton watched a big man, who could have been a tank, saunter up to the group. He was obviously a stranger to them, but he picked a girl out and started to dance with her. The man she was with didn't get jealous or upset. He just joined them instead.

Hamilton asked, "You think it's drugs?"

"Must be." Cody shook his head. "I'da kicked his ass."

Hamilton turned his attention to the bartenders. He had no idea which one was Jeff Munroe. Watching the busy bar, he realized they would need a bulldozer to get through that crowd. One of the disco lights glinted off a mirrored door near the bar, drawing Hamilton's attention.

A man stepped out and surveyed the room, then walked behind the bar. He was tall and lean. Dressed in a white shirt and black vest, he looked like a Las Vegas dealer. Something about him made him stand out from everyone around him like he was shiny and everyone else was dull.

"Come on," Hamilton said, tugging on Cody's jacket.

They worked their way through the crowded balcony until they found the stairs. Hamilton heard Cody shout something about needing Moses, but he didn't want to stop their momentum to find out what he'd said. By the time Hamilton and Cody had crossed the dance floor, the man was gone.

Hamilton glanced at the people surrounding the bar. Most of them were already so drunk they couldn't stand up, but the staff still served them drinks. *There is no way this place is adhering to liquor laws.*

A waitress came out from behind the bar with a full tray of drinks. She walked to the mirrored door and stepped through. Just for an instant, Hamilton caught a glimpse of the room beyond.

Hamilton elbowed Cody and pointed to the door. Cody nodded.

Expecting resistance, Hamilton opened the door slowly, but no one stopped him. Instead of the gaudy neon of the bar, this room displayed elegant red and gold wallpaper. Scattered throughout the room were black-lacquered gaming tables, and every seat was taken.

He let the door shut behind them, and the blaring sounds of the bar became muffled. From farther back in the room, Hamilton heard the clicking of the Roulette wheels and the rattle of dice at the Craps tables. The nearest tables were surrounded by patrons playing Blackjack. He'd had no idea there was an underground casino in Denver, and if the piles of chips were anything to go by, it was a very lucrative establishment.

As Hamilton scanned the room looking for the man he'd seen earlier, his eyes kept blurring slightly. He shook his head, trying to clear his vision. He squinted at the nearest table, but instead of his eyes blurring, he glimpsed what looked like glitter hanging in the air above the cards. He stepped closer, watching the game. The players were making ridiculous bets on slim chances as if they had no control over their impulses.

He stepped back and whispered to Cody, "There is something seriously wrong here."

REGINA AND THE WOLF

Philtzer handed the binoculars to Sophia. "This is definitely the place."

They had come to Moran, WY to find one of the names on the list that Madraeus had confiscated from Cecelia's sympathizer. Sophia had been expecting an actual town, but it wasn't really a town. It was an unincorporated community that existed to collect fees for the Grand Teton National Park.

The only buildings in 'town' were the post office, the ranger station, and a gas station. Philtzer wasted no time charming the rumor monger working at the post office into spilling all the local gossip. Unfortunately, it was all about strange animal sounds in the night and the tragic loss of their very own Ranger John Ellis, who had been mauled by a bear, leaving behind his teenage son.

Philtzer expressed the proper amount of horror and sorrow, found out the general direction of the weird sounds, compared it to the address that Rami had given them, and happily bounded off into the woods.

The Ellis cabin stood in a little clearing. A pole carport stood empty on the south side, and an old, sky-blue pickup sat off to the west side of the house. The tires were all flat.

Sophia looked through the binoculars at the cabin. Deep gouges crisscrossed the wood, a testament that something had tried to get in. Her eyes followed the trail of scratches across the door and along the wall to where they became concentrated again at the broken window. Someone had tried very hard to get into this cabin.

"I don't think a bear did that."

"Nope." Philtzer took the binoculars back and studied the cabin again. "I'd say several werewolves, maybe a few vamps."

"Think this Kyle Ellis is still alive?"

"Only one way to find out." Philtzer eyed the trees and then stepped out into the clearing.

Closer to the cabin, they found several scorch marks. Philtzer glanced at them but didn't comment. Sophia lingered, wondering if her imagination was playing tricks, but the burn mark looked like a person.

Philtzer walked up and knocked on the massive oak door. "Kyle Ellis?"

"What'd ya want!" a woman's voice snarled. The menace in her tone wasn't hard to miss despite being muffled by the layers of wood.

Philtzer froze. He cocked his head and called out, "Regina? That you?"

Sophia glanced sharply at Philtzer.

"Who wants to know?"

"Oh, get off it, you old bitch! You know who I am!" Philtzer grinned at Sophia's shocked expression.

"Philtzer?"

There was a lot of banging from the other side of the door, and a loud scraping sound came as something heavy was moved.

Sophia wasn't sure which was scarier: that they had barricaded themselves in like that or that she was about to meet her mom.

"It's stuck! Hold on!" Something banged on the wood a few times, vibrating the door, then it swung open.

"Reggie!" Philtzer grinned, but the grin died as soon as he saw her.

Regina Sinclair looked like she had barely survived a war. Bandages covered her left eye and most of her neck and shoulder. Her flannel shirt was encrusted with blood, and the leg of her jeans gaped open to reveal another bandage.

Philtzer gaped. "What happened?"

Regina didn't even look at him; she was scanning the woods behind them.

"Get inside!" Regina snarled. Stepping to one side, she motioned them in with the shotgun she held. When they didn't move, she reached out and grabbed Sophia's arm without looking at her and shoved her through the open door.

Philtzer quickly followed her in. They had to dodge the wardrobe that sat at a right angle just inside the door. A skinny teenage boy with dark brown hair stood behind it, watching them.

Sophia looked around. They stood in the main room, and at the back were two doors. One looked like it led to the bedrooms and one to a kitchen. The cabin wasn't huge, but it was comfortable. At least, it had been once.

Now, all the furniture was shoved up against the windows and doors. Boards had been nailed over every opening that the furniture wasn't blocking. Once-loved family portraits hung askew on the walls, and trinkets of a life well-lived lay scattered amongst the broken glass that littered the floor.

Regina slammed the door shut and secured the locks, then she slung the strap of the shotgun over her shoulder. Turning, she grabbed one side of the wardrobe while the young boy pushed on the other side. Together they maneuvered the heavy piece of furniture back in front of the door.

Finally, Regina turned to face Philtzer. "Hey, Phil."

Sophia stared at the woman. She could have been looking in a mirror.

Regina winced and resettled the shotgun on her shoulder.

"What happened?" Philtzer asked, pointing at her eye.

"This? Oh, nothing. Just got some mascara in my eye."

"You're never gonna let me live that down, are you?"

"Nope." Her grin widened as she glanced at Sophia. "I—" She froze. "Who are you?"

Philtzer did a little spokesmodel impersonation. "Reggie, meet your daughter."

"Sophia?" Regina breathed in disbelief. The two women stared at each other for a long time. Regina lunged forward and hugged Sophia. "I never thought to see you again!"

Philtzer stared at his mentor like he'd never seen her. *Regina doesn't hug. Regina doesn't cry.*

"I don't understand," Sophia muttered as she slowly brought her hands up to awkwardly return the hug.

"I'm so sorry!" Regina cried. "I never wanted to leave, but your father—"

"Wait!" Sophia disentangled herself from her mother's embrace. "What about my father?"

Regina took a step back and looked her daughter over as if she couldn't believe she was real. "He didn't think I would be good for you."

"What?"

"Dennis didn't think I would be a good mother after he found out what I was. He asked me to go." She looked down. "He didn't want me to accidentally turn you into a monster."

"Dad said that?" Sophia stumbled backward. "Dad always told me that you left because you didn't want to be tied down with kids."

Regina shook her head. "It's true that I never wanted kids, but once I had you—"

"No." Sophia backed farther away from her mother. "I don't believe you." She turned and fled through the door that led to the kitchen.

"Sophia!" Regina started to follow, but a hand on her arm stopped her.

"Let it be for a while, Reggie," Philtzer said gently. "She's had a lot dumped on her recently. She just found out she was a wolf, but not in a good way, and then found out about you. So, let her adjust."

Regina nodded reluctantly, watching the door that her daughter had disappeared through.

Philtzer looked at the boy who was still standing near the door. "You Kyle Ellis?"

The boy nodded but said nothing.

Regina looked at the skinny teen and then back at Philtzer. "How do you know his name?"

"We came to find you, but it looks like we're too late."

"Too late for what?" Regina narrowed her eyes. "What's going on, Phil?"

"Cecelia," he said with a shrug.

"Explain," Regina said.

"Later." Philtzer gestured to the damaged room. "First, I wanna know why you are locked up in here instead of running."

MEANWHILE, BACK IN THE CONGO

UNKHABAMI PACED SLOWLY THROUGH the underbrush. The mist had receded leaving a damp layer of moisture on the leaves that dripped onto her back as she passed. Her spotted coat twitched with each drop of water. The trip home from the United States had been exhausting. She hated flying. She was a were-cat. Cats did not belong in the sky.

Tourists and airports, she thought.

She should never have left her jungle. Weeks ago, she had awoken in the middle of the night with a burning need. Prophecy was like that. It waited for no one. Sweating and panting, she had answered the call. She had entered the trance that would allow her to peek into the Universe and see what was coming.

Her visions had almost killed her.

The rage and violence that burned and seethed in the not-so-distant future had terrified her. War was coming. Not just a war of men, but one of demons.

Her pelt shivered and twitched as she remembered the curling serpent from her dream. It had consumed the world, devouring it in darkness. Except for one thing. Her visions had shown one fragile moment of hope that could stop the disastrous future.

The entire reason that she had left her sanctuary in the Congo was to see for herself the girl who would decide their future: Whitney Martindale. Whitney was the point on which so much turned.

Unkhabami sniffed and laid her ears back. *Much good that did!*

Her warning to Madraeus had gone unheeded. And now, her prediction that Whitney would be the spark that sent them all to disaster had come to pass. The descent into darkness was starting. There was no way to stop the coming war.

Blood and violence. The future would be nothing but blood and violence.

The memory of her vision filled her mind. A slight chance remained. Whitney Martindale was the key. But a terrifying choice awaited her, a fickle possibility that could save them all. Or destroy them.

Unkhabami shivered.

She could see the edge of the forest just ahead. She had only been gone for a couple of weeks, but it seemed like a lifetime.

Despite the danger hanging over the future, she was glad to be home. A contented purr rumbled from her throat as she stepped from the shadows.

She froze with one paw in mid-air. Awareness shivered down her spine. Her pupils dilated. Something was wrong. She ran her eyes over the tiny group of buildings that formed her village. The waning light of the sunset made the small clearing glow in a golden light.

The village was dead quiet. There was no sound of children playing. No sound of men and women talking or laughing. No chickens or pigs scampered between the huts. Not a single thing moved.

Cautiously, Unkhabami stepped forward. She crossed the open space between the trees and the huts, quickly finding cover against the closest building. She froze and listened again. Her eyes scanned every shadow. She stalked forward on silent paws, following the rough mud wall. When she came to the entrance, she quickly ducked past the blanket hanging across the door.

The home was empty. The sparse furnishings had been shattered. Her nostrils flared. It smelled of death.

Unkhabami's heart thumped faster. She dashed from hut to hut trying to find any of her villagers. Every house told the same story: destruction and death.

She had been their Priestess for nearly one hundred years. She knew every piece and part of every life. She had protected them, laughed with them, cried with them, and attended their births and deaths. And now they were gone.

The warm light from the sun was fading. The temperature dropped. But it was more than just the sun stealing the warmth, something loomed. Tendrils of the coming evil brushed against her pelt, making it twitch.

Time was short. Terror and desperation pushed her to run faster through the village. Frantic to find anyone still alive, she almost missed the tiny whimper coming from her own hut. She darted toward it. She dashed through the door, changing as she entered.

As soon as she had become human, a small body slammed into her. She staggered back a step as her arms wrapped around the child clinging to her hips.

"Child! What has happened?"

"Demon!" The child shook in terror.

"Demon?" Unkhabami tried to see her face. "Where is your mother? Your father?"

The child only sobbed and held on to her tighter.

Unkhabami looked around the hut. Two or three other faces peeked out at her from the shadows. It would make sense that they would hide in her hut. To keep the village safe from the forces she dealt with, she had placed warding spells on her hut; the protection would have repelled evil as well.

Outside something screeched: piercing and chilling, like claws raking a blackboard. Goosebumps raced across Unkhabami's skin. No animal that lived in the jungle could make that sound.

The child froze, staring at the flimsy blanket hanging across the door. Her eyes bulged white with terror.

Unkhabami physically walked the child backward across the room. She had to pry the girl's arms loose from around her hips. She pushed her down beside another little girl who was hiding behind a pile of books. Immediately they clung to one another. Unkhabami put a finger to her lips and mimed for them to be quiet and stay where they were. The last of the sunlight leaking around the blanketed doorway winked out.

Outside, the thing screeched again. It was closer. She could hear its thumping footsteps mingling with a scraping sound as if it were dragging its feet between steps.

Thump. Drag. Thump. Thump. Drag. Thump.

What was it? She cast about, her eyes searching for something she could use against a demon, if that's what it was. Without details, she didn't know the right weapon. She had to find out what she was dealing with.

Unkhabami shifted to leopard and stalked cautiously toward the door. She tried to gather information without giving away her presence. She listened and sniffed. The stench of evil and decay burned her nose. Fear followed the scent into her mind.

Ghoul!

She shook her head trying to clear it. She backed away from the doorway, shifting back into a woman.

Thump. Drag. Thump.

If there was one ghoul, there would be more. A bite from a ghoul would fester and kill its victim. The dead would then rise again as a second ghoul. She swiveled her head to stare at the children hiding behind her.

The missing villagers? They are the ghouls? Unkhabami started to tremble.

Thump. Drag. Thump.

The sounds were coming from all around the hut.

We are trapped!

The night echoed with the screeching of ghouls. The children covered their ears. Unkhabami reached out to them and whispered, "If we stay hidden until dawn, the sun will drive the ghouls away."

The children nodded, placing their trust in the priestess. However, Unkhabami's attempt at reassurance was cut short as the ghouls converged on her hut.

Unkhabami jumped as the walls reverberated with pounding and scratching as the monsters tried to get in. The children ducked their heads and cowered against the ground.

Unkhabami eyed the mud walls. She closed her eyes, thinking, *We will never make it until dawn.*

A Wolf in the Woods

"We've been fighting off the undead and a bunch of werewolves."

"But the coast is clear now. We walked right in here." Philtzer gestured to the door. "Why haven't you left? You taught me never to get pinned down."

"Don't try to turn my lessons back on me, boyo." Regina glared at him. "We have tried to leave." She pointed to her eye. "This is what I got."

"All right then." Philtzer crossed his arms. "What happened?"

"I heard some rumors that something dark was coming. Everyone's been really edgy," she shrugged with the shoulder that wasn't bandaged. "I was headed back to Denver to talk to Madraeus and stopped for gas."

Out of the corner of his eye, Philtzer saw Sophia edge back into the room. Regina hadn't seen her yet. "You really should get a phone. Denver's been compromised."

"Great," Regina snorted, reaching up to rub her shoulder.

"Doesn't matter." Philtzer waved his hand. "How did you come across Kyle?'

"I had just filled up when an SUV full of 'tourists' stopped for gas and started to beat the crap out of him." Regina nodded her head toward Kyle. "It triggered his wolf genes."

Philtzer looked at the kid.

He stared at the floor in front of him, looking mutinous.

"Anyway, we got away." Regina shrugged. "Came here to get his stuff and split, but they followed. Turns out they weren't just tourists. They were wolves and vamps."

"We held off the wolves for a while, but then night came, and the vamps joined them. We took a couple out, but they blocked us from getting to the truck. We had to retreat."

Philtzer moved to the window and peered out.

"It got quiet out there, so we tried again." Kyle came to stand beside Philtzer. "But they'd slashed the tires on the truck."

"We made a run for the trees, but they caught us. We barely made it back here." Regina sighed, patting the shotgun. "And we only have one shell left."

"How many are there?" Philtzer looked back at her.

"I think seven, but don't quote me."

Kyle turned to Regina, "With their help, can we make it out?"

"I don't know." She held his gaze. "I'm not going to sugar-coat it. I ain't exactly in peak fighting condition, and you ain't trained." She looked at Philtzer. "That leaves you."

"Can you fight seven wolves?" Kyle asked.

"Not alone." Philtzer shook his head. "Why did they let us waltz in here?"

"Three birds with one stone," Sophia muttered.

"What?" Her mother turned, just realizing that she'd come back.

"I was just thinking," Sophia shifted uncomfortably, "if they could get in here, they'd get Kyle. Letting us walk in would let them kill you *and* us. That's less they have to fight later."

"That's a happy thought." Philtzer tried to laugh.

"Just sayin'." Sophia shrugged. "I've been with them. It's how they think."

"Them who?" Kyle asked.

"Crazy vamp named Cecelia," Philtzer explained. "She's building an army, wants to destroy the mortal world. You know, psycho ex-girlfriend stuff."

Regina glared at Sophia. "What do you mean you've been with them?"

"Well, Mom," Sophia snapped, "they were there for me when I became a monster. Unlike you."

"But you're not with them now," Regina said quietly.

Sophia snorted. "Yeah, lucky me."

"We could all be lucky if we go now instead of standing here talking." Philtzer peered out a crack between the window frame and a curio cabinet that had seen better days. "Let's make a run for it. Our car is just through those trees."

"Phil," Regina sighed, "my leg ain't up to running."

He looked back at her and thought, *She'd never admit to weakness. She must be in worse shape than she's saying.*

"All right. How about I go get the car and come back? You all jump in and we beat it?"

Kyle nodded. "Sounds reasonable."

Regina nodded, and Philtzer started to strip.

Sophia blushed and turned away. Over her shoulder, she asked, "How you gonna carry the keys?"

Philtzer stopped and looked around.

"Wait." Kyle ran off into the bedroom and came back with a school lanyard. "Here."

"Cool." Philtzer clipped the keys onto the lanyard and slipped it over his neck. He looked at Regina. "If I come running back in a hurry, open the door this time."

"Yeah, yeah." Regina gave him a shove toward the door.

Kyle and Sophia shouldered the wardrobe back from the door. Sophia unlocked it and looked at Philtzer. She looked as though she wanted to say something but stopped.

He winked. "Be back soon." He slipped out, shifting into a wolf as soon as he was through the door.

Philtzer stood on the porch for a moment, smelling the air. He couldn't detect anything, but that didn't mean there wasn't anything there. He dashed down the stairs and across the lawn past the scorch marks on the drive. The air became cooler as he passed into the trees. The keys jingled softly as he ran. It was only about a mile to reach the car. If he was lucky, he would be there and back in no time.

Off to his right, he heard a crashing sound. Philtzer skidded to a stop and listened. Something was coming through the trees at high speed. He crouched down into a large clump of ferns.

Seconds later, two wolves came crashing through the grove. One stopped to sniff the ground, but the second one ran on.

Philtzer eyed the wolf. He bunched his muscles, ready to pounce. He waited until the wolf glanced the other way before bursting out of the greenery. On impact, they rolled, and Philtzer came up biting. He took a couple of nips from his enemy before he managed to take a chunk out of the other wolf's shoulder. The wolf yowled in pain.

Before Philtzer could take another bite, the second wolf tackled him. They rolled, each struggling to get a hold on the other. He felt his ear tear. Then the other wolf rejoined the scuffle.

Philtzer twisted and rolled, stifling a howl as teeth sank into his neck. He started to panic. He was losing. He had to get free and run! Ripping his hide from the wolf's jaws, he launched himself sideways and then took off at a run. He sprinted through the trees, bursting out into the clearing. Out of the corner of his eye, he saw two more wolves coming at him from off to the left. He ran straight for the cabin, hoping the door would open.

As he neared the porch, he heard scraping sounds. He took the stairs in a flying leap and slammed against the closed door.

He spun around, teeth bared. Four wolves dashed across the lawn, coming straight at him. Philtzer growled. He wasn't going down without a fight.

Behind him, he could hear scrapes and thumps. The door opened.

"Get in!" Sophia screamed.

Philtzer spun and dodged through to safety just as the wolves reached the porch. Without pausing, he shifted back to human and helped to shove the wardrobe back against the door.

Philtzer sank to the floor, panting. "Well," Philtzer winced, "that didn't work."

"You're bleeding!" Sophia dropped to her knees beside him and pressed her fingers against the wound on his neck.

From outside, they could hear scratching and pounding as the wolves tried to get in.

Regina glanced at Kyle. "Bandages."

"Right." Kyle disappeared into the kitchen and came back holding the first aid kit. "There's not much left in it."

Regina knelt next to Philtzer and started to treat his wounds. She stopped and glanced down at Philtzer's chest. With one finger, she lifted the lanyard and held it up in front of his eyes.

"Where'd the keys go?"

Philtzer stared at the empty lanyard. "Oops."

DEAD BEAT

Hamilton and Cody wandered through the casino, watching patrons winning and losing incredibly large amounts of cash. The winners jumped up and down, giggling and screaming, but the losers merely doubled down to try again.

"Why isn't anyone getting upset? They're losing and they don't care." Hamilton rubbed his eyes. The blurring sensation was getting worse.

"Is that him?" Cody pointed to a Blackjack table at the back.

Hamilton shook his head to clear his vision and squinted. The man he had seen earlier was behind the table dealing. "Yeah, that's him."

As they approached the table, the man glanced up.

"You Jeff Munroe?" Cody asked.

"Depends on who's asking."

"We want to talk to you."

"Pay to play, boys," he said while divvying out a new hand.

Cody glanced at Hamilton. "You got any cash?"

Hamilton frowned but pulled out his wallet.

"New player," Jeff said as Cody sat down.

Hamilton watched Cody play through two hands, winning them both. He noticed Jeff watching Cody. Hamilton thought he could see just a hint of something in the dealer's eyes. Glitter sparkled just above the table and then Cody started to lose every hand.

Under the pretense of watching the roulette wheel on the next table, Hamilton took a few steps to the left. He turned slightly to see Cody's face but still kept an eye on the dealer.

Hamilton's eyes widened.

The normally calm and patient expression on Cody's face had been replaced by an angry, predatory glare. Cody watched the dealer's hand as if he would bite it at any moment.

Hamilton's gaze switched to the other players. The winners looked entranced, almost euphoric. The losers shared almost the same intense expression as Cody. The only difference was that instead of angry, they looked desperate, almost like addicts searching for a fix.

Hamilton studied Jeff Munroe. He dealt the cards calmly, watching Cody. With every new card, the glittery haze grew thicker and with it Cody's intensity. Hamilton had never seen his friend like this before.

Suddenly it all clicked: the glitter, the addiction vibes, the complacency. This was magic. In that second, Hamilton knew what the 'P factor' was that Stanley mentioned in the report.

"You're a pixie!"

The dealer's gaze shot to Hamilton. He dropped the cards and spun around to run.

"Wait!" Hamilton shouted just as Cody lunged forward to clamp a hand around Jeff's forearm, knocking chips and cards all over the floor.

Jeff froze and stared at the scattered cards. He looked at Cody. "You need to leave here. Now!"

"Not gonna happen!" Cody snarled.

"If you don't leave now, you're going to get your asses kicked."

"Don't threaten me!" Cody growled.

"Dammit!" Jeff tried to pull free, but Cody wouldn't let go. "I'm not threatening you! I'm *warning* you!"

"Wait," Hamilton stepped closer, "what do you mean?"

Cody snarled and started to shimmer. The pixie's magic had robbed him of control and left him feral.

"No! No! No!" Hamilton knew he had to diffuse the situation before Cody shifted into a werewolf in front of the whole casino. He grabbed Cody's hand and tried to pry it loose. "Look, we came here to warn you. People are coming. Bad people."

"I know!" Jeff shouted, trying to pull free. "I saw it in the cards. You need to leave!"

"Saw it in the cards?" Hamilton stopped fighting with Cody's hand and stared at Jeff. "You see the future?"

Jeff twisted his arm, trying to break loose. "Not exactly. I just know you need to be somewhere else. Now!"

"You're a pixie and a Weaver?" Hamilton gaped. "And a werewolf?"

"A what and a what?"

Before Hamilton could answer, Cody snarled and shuddered. Hamilton doubled his effort to pry Cody's hand open. "Calm down, man! You can't shift in here!"

"Is he a werewolf?"

Hamilton looked back at Jeff. "Yes, and your pixie magic is messing with his control!"

"I didn't know!"

"Dial it back or we're gonna be in a helluva lot of trouble!"

Jeff stared past him at the door to the bar. "You're too late."

The sound of gunfire shattered the night. Jeff jerked backward, freeing his arm. Cody reacted badly, snarling and shifting as he spun toward the door.

Terrified patrons screamed and jumped to their feet. Tables crashed to the floor scattering cards, chips, and dice everywhere. Not knowing which way to run, they pushed and shoved in every direction. Some ran for the door leading to the bar but were pushed back as panicked customers poured in to escape the shooters on the dance floor. Others ran for the back of the room in search of an exit. Screams and gunfire merged with the blasting music to create a cacophony of confusion and terror.

Hamilton searched the panicked crowd. He'd lost both Cody and Jeff. He flinched as a woman screamed near his ear. Just then he caught a glimpse of a furry tail dashing through the door to the bar.

"Not toward the guns, dammit!" Hamilton muttered as he pushed through the crowd, trying to reach the door.

He shoved his way through. Stumbling sideways, he fell behind the bar. He poked his head up for a second, surveyed the situation, and groaned. Five men with automatic weapons were spread out across the club. Two were still on the balcony, firing out across the crowd; and the other three were on the dance floor, converging on the bar. They punched or shot anyone that got within range. Hamilton didn't see Cody anywhere.

Ducking back down, Hamilton looked around for some kind of weapon. He glanced to his left and was surprised to see Jeff. He had expected the man to have run since he was the target, but he was crouched down behind the bar loading a handgun instead.

Hamilton grinned. "Bold choice."

"Ain't my first rodeo."

Hamilton shouted over the sound of screaming and pounding music. "Are you really a Weaver and a pixie?"

"I don't know what the Hell I am." Jeff dug through a box on the shelf behind his head, looking for more ammo.

Gunfire peppered the back wall of the bar, making both men duck and cover their heads. Bottles shattered, spraying alcohol and glass everywhere.

"If we get out of this, we need to talk," Hamilton said as he shook glass shards out of his hair.

"If." Jeff leaned forward, grabbed a bottle of whiskey from under the cabinet, and took a swig.

Hamilton reached into his pocket and pulled out a card. He handed it to Jeff.

"If we get out of this and we get separated, call this number and we'll talk."

"You the good guys or something?" Jeff asked, tucking the card into his shirt pocket.

"Something like that."

More shots hit the racks of booze above them. They ducked.

"And them?" Jeff jerked his thumb toward the invaders.

"They work for a vampire named Cecelia. She's trying to start a war. You're a potential recruit. You have werewolf genes. They're trying to turn you."

"Great." Jeff took another swig.

"I take it your magic isn't gonna help much here."

"Why do you think I have this?" He held up the gun.

Hamilton cocked his head, listening. Something had changed. Instead of the panicked screams of bar patrons, the air was filled with shouting and snarling, followed by more gunfire.

Hamilton poked his head up in a fair imitation of a ground-hog to see the invaders had gone on the defensive. Cody, his clothes hanging off in tatters, darted out and tackled one of the men. His teeth snapped at the man's throat as they wrestled.

"If you're gonna fight, now's the time," Hamilton shouted to Jeff as he sprang over the bar, shifting in mid-air.

He pounced on the nearest man, knocking the gun from his hand. The man didn't hesitate to fight back. Hamilton took a few hard jabs in the ribs, knocking him to the side. His enemy shifted into wolf form and lunged at Hamilton, but a blast from Jeff's gun dropped him.

One of the men on the balcony opened fire on the dance floor. The few people left inside screamed and rushed for the stairs, creating a bottleneck. Several people fell and were trampled by the crowd behind them.

Jeff aimed and fired, dropping the man near the top of the stairs.

The other man on the balcony fired blindly.

Jeff ducked back behind the bar.

Bullets ricocheted off the wall, hitting the DJ booth. The music cut off abruptly. Sparks shot outward from the sound equipment, igniting the spilled alcohol. Bright-colored flames raced across pools of liquor to engulf the stage area. Smoke billowed and the screeching fire alarm drowned out the sounds of screaming.

Hamilton flinched, whining. He shifted back into human form to protect his sensitive ears. He staggered to his feet and looked around. The few intact strobe lights created a stop-motion effect. Through the smoke, he could see Jeff running across the dance floor to the screaming crowd on the stairs.

A burst of glitter filled the air around the stairs. The crowd stopped screaming and settled down enough to make it up the stairs. If they were lucky, they would all make it out in time.

Hamilton looked to the quickly spreading flames and then back across the room. Cody, in human form, lay sprawled on the dance floor. Hamilton staggered forward, holding his ribs. He glanced at the balcony for the invaders. They were gone.

Dropping to his knees beside his friend, Hamilton reached out to Cody. He felt something warm and sticky. He checked for a pulse. Hamilton sighed in relief when he found one.

Jeff appeared at his elbow. "We need to get out of here."

"Help me lift him."

Hamilton grabbed one of Cody's arms and Jeff grabbed the other. They staggered toward the stairs with Cody between them. The fire blazed at their backs. It was a slow climb.

Smoke billowed out around them as they reached the main door. Together they carried Cody away from the building through the crowd of confused and crying patrons. Sirens screamed in the distance as the authorities came to the rescue.

"They're gonna come for you again." Hamilton puffed as they made their way back to Cody's pickup.

"Let them," Jeff grunted as they lowered Cody to the ground.

Cody groaned as the fresh air revived him. Hamilton glanced down at his friend. When he turned back, Jeff had disappeared.

"What happened?" Cody coughed and lifted his head. "I'm beat."

"We got our asses kicked."

"What? How?" Cody struggled into a sitting position and winced. He looked at his blood-smeared forearm and then looked toward the inferno that used to be the nightclub. "Oh."

"Yeah. Oh, is right." Hamilton leaned down, offering Cody his hand. "Come on we need to split."

UNKHABAMI'S WAR

Unkhabami knew they could not wait until dawn. If she and the children were to survive, they had to make a run for it. For a moment, her courage failed her.

I cannot fight the men and women that I love! Unkhabami trembled as images of her village, friends, and family invaded her mind. Grief washed over her. *No! They are gone. All that is left are monsters!*

Resigned to her fate, she tried to think. She couldn't fight them in leopard form. Teeth and claws were her only weapons, but biting a ghoul would only infect her. She would have to fight as a woman. She needed a weapon.

Unkhabami whipped around and dashed to the worktable, grabbing a robe from a peg on the wall and pulling it on. It wouldn't be much protection, but little was better than nothing.

She lit the small torch affixed to the wall above the table. Moving quickly and quietly, she mixed herbs into a small bowl and added liquids from several vials. She flinched as another screech pierced the night. Her hands shook. She closed her eyes and took a calming breath. Raising her face to the Heavens, she held the bowl aloft, muttering an invocation. She lowered the bowl.

Turning, she edged closer to where a bow and quiver of arrows stood next to the door. Alika had left them with her to be blessed. She had meant to return them to him before her trip. Tears blurred her vision for a moment. She rubbed at her eyes and then reached for them, keeping an eye on the door as she moved. A flurry of scratching at the walls made her jump back without retrieving the weapon.

Unkhabami glanced at the children. She had to stop the ghouls before they could break through. The spells protecting her home were holding, but the night would last longer than the spells.

Once again, she crept forward toward the bow. This time, she snatched it. Retreating a few steps, she set the quiver down and pulled the arrows free. There were only eleven. She prayed that would be enough. She was a good shot, but there would be no second chances if she missed.

With trembling hands, she dipped each arrow in the paste she had made. Then reached over and pulled a long knife from the table and smeared the paste across the blade.

The scratching and screeching from outside rose in volume. The ghouls sounded frustrated.

Unkhabami quickly sheathed the arrows again and swung the quiver onto her back. She hung the knife from her wrist with a leather cord and then grabbed the torch. The flames danced shadows across the room as she moved. She turned and looked over her shoulder at the frightened children. The whites of their eyes shone in the darkness.

"Stay hidden," she commanded, then turned toward the door. Taking a deep breath, she dashed forward and ripped the blanket aside.

A ghoul stood just outside the threshold. She didn't recognize it as anyone from the village. It must be the original monster that had come to destroy them.

All muscle and sinew, it stood about six feet tall. Its arms and legs were too long for its torso. Scraggly tufts of hair stood out from its head in all directions. Its fingers, misshapen and too long for a normal hand, ended in sharp, pointed claws. It saw her and screeched, baring its multiple rows of needle-thin teeth.

She thrust the torch into its face. It shrank back and howled in pain. Unkhabami ran past it into the darkness away from the hut. The scratching and scrabbling from behind her stopped as the pack followed her. When she was about halfway to the forest edge, she threw the torch to the ground and turned so the fire was behind her. It would be all the protection her back would have.

The nearest ghoul rushed forward with its claws reaching toward her. It was Bina; she had lived next to Unkhabami for nearly twenty-nine years. Her transformation into a ghoul had made her beautiful face hideous and deformed.

"You are no longer Bina!" Unkhabami cried as she pulled an arrow free, nocked it, drew back, and let it fly.

It struck the chest of the monster, but the ghoul didn't even slow down. Behind it, others closed in. The priestess drew and shot three more times. Each arrow hit what was once a villager. A cry of despair escaped from the Priestess as she raised her arms above her in a V shape and shouted, "Kuleta jua!"

Power crackled through the blackness of the surrounding jungle and converged on the village. As her words pulled magic in to combine with the herbal paste she had smeared on the barbs, the full power of the sun burst forth from the heads of the arrows. The ultraviolet fire burned the wounded ghouls from the inside out. They flailed around screaming and burning.

She should have beheaded them, but there was no time. More were coming.

Unkhabami fired arrow after arrow.

Time after time, she called for the Sun. "Kuleta jua!"

Five more ghouls burned, but more monsters emerged from the forest beyond.

"No!" Unkhabami hissed as she recognized her friends and neighbors: Alika, Kwau, Pasua. Every missing member of the village came hobbling and stumbling toward her with sharp needle teeth bared.

Rage and grief twisted her gut as she readied her last two arrows, letting them fly one after the other. They found their targets. Tears streamed down her face as Unkhabami called for the Sun once again.

One of the burning ghouls stumbled and fell against a kindling pile. The dry wood caught fire instantly and spread. Within moments, the nearest hut was ablaze. From there, the hungry fire jumped from building to building.

The children!

Unkhabami rushed forward, dodging flailing monsters, but she wasn't nimble enough. A ghoul's burning claws made contact, ripping her chest and shoulder. She screamed as pain spread across her left side. She staggered, barely avoiding the raging fire. Pain hit her again as a second ghoul, thrashing against the flames consuming it, knocked her to the side, but not before slashing her back and singeing her skin. Unkhabami scrambled away from it and dove into her hut. She stumbled forward and seized the nearest child.

"Come!" She gritted her teeth against the pain and grabbed the others, pulling them together in the middle of the room.

Smoke seeped in around the blanket on the door. Crackling sounded above them. The fire had reached her hut.

"We have to run for the forest!"

"No!" One of them screamed and tried to pull away. "I won't go out there!"

"The hut is burning!" The Priestess grasped the child again and dragged her to the door. "I will protect you. Just stay together. Hold hands and don't let go!"

She waited just long enough for them to obey and then hauled them out the door.

The village glowed as bright as day. The fires had combined to become a raging storm. Crackling timbers and screaming ghouls deafened the tiny group. Unkhabami looked around desperately for an escape. Finally, she saw an opening in the chaos. She ran, pulling the children along behind her.

Crossing the clearing seemed to take hours, but finally, they reached the trees. The sudden darkness blinded her, but she kept running. Branches and leaves slapped against her as she crashed through the jungle, making too much noise to hear if anything was chasing them.

They kept running.

Her legs ached. Her lungs burned. Her seared skin throbbed. The deep gouges on her back oozed blood, but she couldn't stop. Her shoulder was cramped from the odd angle it was bent at to keep the children with her. She could feel a thousand cuts on her face, arms, and legs from the brush she barged through.

Still, they ran. After an eternity, the sounds of screaming faded behind them. She slowed enough at one point to pick up the youngest child who had lagged behind.

They ran again.

Finally, the light of dawn reached the forest. Unkhabami slowed to a walk and eventually staggered to a stop. The children collapsed to the forest floor. Breathing in gasps, they lay shaking from fear and exhaustion.

The priestess turned and looked back the way they'd come. All was quiet. Unkhabami shifted into a leopard. Pain flared in her wounds as the skin stretched to accommodate her new form. She sniffed the air. She couldn't smell the ghouls, only forest and smoke. She hoped that the fire would kill them all. She shuddered. She couldn't face going back to see if they were destroyed.

A hand touched her shoulder. She looked back to see the children staring at her. Turning, she led them into the foliage to a hollow made by two trees. Unkhabami nudged the oldest girl toward it. All four children climbed into the hollow and crouched together. She scanned the forest one more time and then curled into the opening of the depression, guarding them with her body. She felt them snuggling up against her, clinging to her until they fell asleep.

She purred, but her thoughts were troubled. She licked her wounds, hoping they would close, hoping they weren't infected. It looked like she would have to travel back to the United States again, but first, she would have to find somewhere safe for the children to hide. They were the last of her people. Sadness washed over her, followed by a raging anger.

She had not intended to become involved in this war, but the enemy had sent ghouls to destroy her home. That was a mistake. Now, she would fight until her last breath.

SPEED BUMP RALLY

PHILTZER TOYED WITH THE empty lanyard as Regina bandaged his neck and ear.

"It's fine." Philtzer winced. "There's a hide-a-key in the wheel well with a spare key."

"That's all fine and dandy, but how are we gonna get to it?"

Something hit the door, hard, making them all jump.

"They're gonna get through." Sophia stared at the door. "There has to be something we can try!"

Philtzer pulled on his pants. His expression was thoughtful but turned mischievous.

"You have an idea?" Regina asked.

"Maybe." He looked at her. "Your truck still work?"

"Yeah," Regina shook her head, "but the tires are slashed, remember?"

"Doesn't matter. It's an old truck. It has metal rims. It'll last long enough."

They all flinched as the glass broke in the side window.

"Long enough to do what?" Kyle asked, running over to push the cabinet tighter against the window.

"Wipe them out."

"That's nice, but how?"

"Well..." Philtzer paused for dramatic effect and pulled on his shirt.

"For crying out loud, Philtzer!" Sophia snarled. "Just tell us!"

"Spoilsport!" He gave her a quelling look. "I'm gonna run them over."

Silence stretched, broken only by the scratching and banging coming from outside.

"Come on, give it up. I'm awesome." He motioned for them to start clapping. When nothing happened and they continued to stare at him, he whined, "Oh, come on!"

"You're nuts." Sophia crossed her arms. "How are you going to even get into the truck? There's a lot of teeth out there, and you didn't do so well last time."

Philtzer thought for a minute. "You got any meat?"

"This is no time to think about your stomach, Phil," Regina huffed.

"That's not why I want it!" He frowned at her but suddenly grinned. "Although a nice steak dinner wouldn't be turned down."

Ignoring his cute puppy routine, Regina sighed, "What's your plan?"

"If you have fresh meat, there'll be a strong smell of blood. We toss it out on the opposite side of the cabin. The smell will draw them. They won't be able to resist. They'll be all 'oh yummy, yummy!' and while they are distracted, I pop out the window nearest the truck and vroom, vroom!" Philtzer mimed driving. "I'll run over as many as I can, and you can all run out and kill the rest."

"We're gonna be outnumbered," Sophia protested.

Something banged against the back wall of the cabin. They all jumped again.

"Yeah, but it wouldn't be the first time." Philtzer shrugged confidently, although his eyes said that he didn't think it would be that easy.

Finally, Regina nodded. "I hate to admit it, but that's not a bad plan."

"I'm in." Kyle rubbed his hands together.

"You seem to have taken to this life pretty fast," Sophia accused Kyle.

He shrugged. "Kill or be killed."

Regina walked over and rested a hand on her daughter's arm. "I know this has been hard for you. And I am sorry that this happened. I left because it was supposed to avoid this. I did what was best for you."

"You think so?" Sophia challenged. "It didn't stop me from becoming a monster."

"You're not a monster. There was no way I could have known that Cecelia would start hunting down wolf descendants. Most have normal lives and grow old never knowing there's magic in their veins."

"Magic?" Sophia blanched. "I turn into a wolf and kill people! How is that magic?"

"That isn't all a werewolf is! There is so much more! When this is finished, I'll show you," Regina promised.

"It can be awesome, Soph." Philtzer added, "Don't you remember running on the mountain? How free it was?"

"I remember running for my life with a strange wolf chasing me," Sophia grumbled.

"Oh, come on, you liked it." He nudged her with his elbow.

The sound of glass shattering came from the direction of the bedrooms.

"Hello?" Kyle waved his hands impatiently to get their attention. "Can we get back to the 'things trying to kill us' problem?"

"Right," Regina said.

Philtzer headed for the kitchen. "Is the meat in here?"

Kyle followed him.

"Is this really gonna work?" Sophia asked her mother.

"What choice do we have?"

"He's gonna get himself killed," Sophia protested.

"You haven't known him that long, have you?"

"No."

"Don't let his happy-go-lucky routine fool you." Regina smiled. "His hare-brained plans usually work."

"Usually?"

Regina didn't have the chance to answer because Philtzer and Kyle sprinted back into the room.

"New plan! New plan!"

Regina whipped around and stared at the kitchen. "Is that smoke?"

Sophia's eyes grew huge. "They set the cabin on fire?"

"Time to go!" Philtzer shouted. "Which window is closest to the truck?"

"Bedroom!" Kyle pointed.

Smoke rolled out of the kitchen, creeping along the ceiling. The flames crackled and snapped as the fire spread.

Philtzer started to shove the wardrobe away from the front door. "I'll draw them off. You get in the truck!"

The back wall of the cabin was already engulfed in flames.

"Kyle!" Regina grabbed his arm and pulled him toward the bedroom.

"Come on, come on, come on!" Philtzer mumbled, pushing against the wardrobe.

Sophia rushed to help him move it.

"Get going!" He growled at her.

"I'm not leaving you!"

Philtzer grabbed the door handle and looked at her. "Let's make it fun then!"

He threw open the door, and they rushed out onto the porch.

Regina had been right. There were seven of them. They were standing back from the porch, ready to catch their quarry as they fled the fire.

Philtzer grinned and bounced slightly on his toes. He put his hands to the sides of his head and wiggled his fingers while shouting in a sing-song voice, "Nah, nah, nah, nah, nah, nah!"

The wolves looked up at him and lunged.

He grabbed Sophia's hand, jumped off the side of the porch, and took off toward the woods. The wolves were in hot pursuit.

"What are you? Twelve?" Sophia shrieked as she ran.

"It worked didn't it?"

Behind them, the truck rumbled to life.

The enemy wolves skidded to a halt and turned. Figuring out they had been played, they ran back toward the cabin.

Regina's old blue pickup emerged from the far side of the burning building. She gunned it and rammed into the nearest wolf, mowing him down like old grass. The others dove to the sides. She swerved to hit them. Spinning the wheel and ramming the accelerator to the floor, the back end of the truck slid around. The split rubber on the tires flapped as it peeled off the rims.

One after another, the wolves fell under the careening truck. Once she passed the last one, Regina did a one-eighty and ran over them all again.

The injured wolves struggled and flailed as they tried to get to their feet.

Philtzer knew they had to move fast to finish this fight. Shifting in mid-stride, Philtzer lunged for the throat of the closest wolf. He bit and ripped.

One down, six to go, he thought.

Regina slammed on the brakes, sliding to a stop. Reaching behind the seat, she pulled out a samurai sword. She threw open the door and jumped out, weapon in hand.

Kyle sat wide-eyed in the passenger seat, watching as Regina beheaded the closest wolf.

Two down.

A shot rang out from the door of the pickup as Kyle tried to help.

Three down.

Philtzer lunged for another neck, but the wolf was ready for him. He rolled and bit and spun and clawed. Philtzer snarled in anger. He curled into a ball, twisting as he went. Jaws closed around his neck. He felt his wound reopen and fought harder.

Suddenly, the wolf lost his hold as the impact of another body knocked them all sideways. Philtzer came up snarling and saw Sophia ripping the muscle off their opponent's leg. While the wolf howled in pain, Philtzer went in for the kill. *Four down.*

He turned to find his next fight and saw Regina standing over the headless bodies of two wolves.

One left. Philtzer spun around and found Sophia standing over the broken body of the last wolf. She had ripped his jugular, and he was bleeding out.

"I can't believe that worked," Kyle whispered.

Philtzer surveyed the damage that they had done to the enemy. He couldn't believe it either. He thought, *Honestly, there is no way that should have worked.*

Regina grabbed the nearest body and started to haul it toward the cabin, yelling over her shoulder, "No evidence."

Kyle followed Regina's lead and hauled the bodies to the fire. Philtzer shifted back into a man and looked back at Sophia. She hadn't moved.

"You okay?" He called to her. She turned her head toward him and laid her ears back flat against her head. He walked over to her.

"Thank you," he said, squatting down in front of her. "I know you didn't want to do this, but they would have killed me if you hadn't helped."

She whined, and he reached out to stroke the fur of her neck. For once, she didn't shy away. "It won't always be like this, you know." He smiled. "There are a lot of perks that you haven't gotten to yet."

She whined again and looked at the wolf she had killed.

Philtzer looked down at the wolf's body. "I know. I had a hard time getting over my first kills too. Honestly, I hate it." He laughed bitterly. "I just wanna run free and have fun, but I don't want people like Kyle to suffer because I didn't fight." He looked back at her, "You know what I mean?"

Her answer was a non-committal growl.

"Come on, let's finish disposing of these guys and split." He stood and motioned her to the cabin.

GOOD NEWS OR BAD NEWS

HAMILTON STOOD FACING THE door of the Orchard Employment Agency. He shouldn't be so nervous, but the idea of coming here terrified him. He didn't like playing the messenger, especially when his news was both good and bad. He wondered again if he was making the right choice. He had tried to call Madraeus and Philtzer, but neither had answered.

He took a deep breath, blew it out slowly, and entered the office.

"I'd like to see Mrs. Myers, please."

"Mrs. Myers is not seeing anyone this afternoon."

"She'll want to see me."

The receptionist eyed him with a mixture of judgment and speculation. He smiled awkwardly at her.

She leaned forward to speak into the intercom, "Mrs. Myers, someone is insisting they see you."

"Kaylee. I said I wasn't to be disturbed."

"Tell her it's Hamilton."

"He says his name is Hamilton."

There was a pause. Hamilton shifted nervously.

"Send him in."

With an 'it's your funeral' expression, Kaylee gestured toward Mrs. Myers' office door.

As Hamilton reached for the knob, he realized his hand was shaking. He tried to remember that Mrs. Myers had always been a motherly type to all the Races for more than two millennia. He had spent a lot of time with her and at her house for social and business reasons. This time was no different, but a small voice in his mind said, *It is*.

He entered the office and was surprised to see Mrs. Myers had her back to the door. She was watching the news on a small TV.

"Hamilton," Mrs. Myers said without turning around.

He shut the door quietly and stepped closer. He glanced at the TV and cringed. The reporter stood in front of the burned-out remains of the Dead Beat Lounge.

"...authorities are still looking for leads on the mass shooting and resultant fire that happened Tuesday night. Witnesses say that multiple shooters were involved. Authorities are looking for a bartender who allegedly fired back at the shooters. However, there have been no developments in that search. We have obtained footage of the shooting from an eyewitness. Please be aware that this video is graphic and may disturb some viewers."

The camera flipped to a video that had been recorded on someone's phone. It showed the club in all its pulsing neon glory with the crowd dancing and having a good time. Then it all changed as patrons started screaming. The camera view swiftly changed to show the floor and someone's leg as the owner of the phone ducked, but the sound of gunshots could still be heard. The image twisted and bounced. Despite the chaotic filming, the shooters could be seen firing into the crowd.

Hamilton winced. His chagrin quickly turned to anxiety when he saw a wolf streak across the screen and tackle one of the shooters. It was Cody.

"Barbara, was that a dog we just saw?" the news commentator asked. "And was it wearing clothes?"

"Yes, in an odd turn, several witnesses reported that a dog attacked the shooters and then disappeared."

The commentator in the studio gave a little fake laugh, before saying, "Only in Denver—"

Mrs. Myers switched off the TV. She turned in her chair and pinned him to the spot with an icy glare. "Is there something you want to tell me, Hamilton?"

Hamilton swallowed. "Actually, there's more."

"Oh dear," Mrs. Myers sighed and gestured toward the chair facing her desk, "you better sit."

Hamilton settled himself into the chair.

"Was that Cody?"

He nodded.

"Hmm." Mrs. Myers sounded concerned and disappointed at the same time.

Hamilton cringed. "We went to find one of the names on Paris Stanley's list. Things didn't go as planned."

"That is an understatement." Mrs. Myers frowned. "A fire. A mass shooting. Caught on camera."

"It wasn't all us!"

She shook her head, "You'll be lucky if the council doesn't ask for your head."

"We showed up to talk to the guy, and the shooters burst in afterward. We just tried to stop them from killing anyone. The fire was accidental." He couldn't bring himself to tell her that Cody was caught on camera because he was out of his mind on pixie dust.

"And the man you went to find? Did you at least bring him back?"

"Not exactly."

"What does that mean?"

"He was the bartender they mentioned. He pulled out a gun and went after Cecelia's men."

"So, he is hiding from the police?" Mrs. Myers shrugged. "All the more reason to bring him to us."

"I don't think that'll happen."

"Don't tell me that Cecelia's men got him!"

"No, no. They were dead or gone."

"Then, what is the problem?"

"Umm..." Hamilton squirmed. "He disappeared as soon as we made it outside. I don't think we'll be able to find him unless he wants to be found."

"Marcus should be able to find him. He can find anyone."

"Jeff Munroe isn't just anyone." Hamilton took a breath and plunged forward. "He's not just a potential werewolf. He's a pixie."

"Oh." Mrs. Myers sat back as she pondered the implications of a werewolf pixie.

"And a Weaver."

"What?" Mrs. Myers shot to her feet, making Hamilton flinch. "How do you know this?"

"Before we could warn him about the men. He said 'he saw it' and tried to get us to leave, but it was too late."

"A pixie, a werewolf, *and* a Weaver?" Mrs. Myers sank to her seat. "He can't be a Weaver."

"But he knew what was going to happen before it happened." Hamilton sat forward. "That's a Weaver's ability."

"You don't understand." Mrs. Myers shook her head. "There are seven Weavers. There can only be seven Weavers. Seven continents, seven seas, seven sciences of the universe, seven cosmic rays, seven sisters, seven planets, seven sages. Only seven!"

Hamilton stared at her. He had never even heard of half the things she was raging about. He had never seen her this upset before.

"There cannot be an eighth!" She stood and started packing her briefcase. She slammed the lid shut and picked up her coat and purse.

"Why not?" Hamilton stood.

Completely ignoring his question, she marched to the door and yanked it open. She headed straight for the main door, barely stopping to say, "Kaylee, I'll be out for the rest of the day."

Hamilton snapped out of his surprise and dashed after her. He caught up with her on the sidewalk.

She muttered, "Eight!"

"Myers?"

She glanced at him but didn't stop. "Do you realize the mess that he could cause? Pixies can't help but be mischievous. It's in their blood. And werewolves? Ach! A pixie werewolf that can affect the futures of everyone around them?"

"He didn't seem deliberately malicious," Hamilton offered.

"Even well-intentioned meddling in the fabric of fate can be a disaster!" Mrs. Myers stopped and turned to Hamilton. "You are going to find Mr. Jeff Munroe and bring him to me!"

LEFT BEHIND

"I STILL THINK THIS is a bad idea," Whitney's grandmother grumbled as she pulled into a parking space.

"It'll be fine," Sandra reassured her. She glanced at Whitney, who looked like she wanted to run screaming or maybe throw up.

"Nothing good can come from continued association with these... people." Elizabeth pursed her lips.

"Good or not," Whitney sighed. "I have to at least talk to them. I need to know what I'm supposed to do."

"I don't see why you couldn't just ask Myers," Elizabeth said as they got out of the car.

"I tried." Whitney shrugged. "She was busy."

Sandra looked around as they entered the main lobby and crossed to the elevator. Elizabeth hobbled after them.

"You know what you're gonna say yet?" Sandra glanced at Whitney out of the corner of her eye as they rode up to the 27th floor.

"No."

"Cool."

The doors opened, and they stepped out into the mini-lobby that led to her apartment and InfiniCorp. Whitney stopped for a moment and looked around. It hadn't changed: deep carpets, lush plants, and silence. She didn't know why she thought it would be different. Maybe she just expected it to have changed since she had.

She turned toward her apartment door and unlocked it but didn't open it.

"Whitney?" Elizabeth asked, placing a hand on her granddaughter's arm. "You all right?"

"Yeah." Whitney tried to smile. "I just haven't been in here since..." she shuddered at the memory, "since Justin tore the place apart trying to kill me."

"That's all over. He's gone now." Elizabeth wrapped her in a warm hug. "We don't have to do this now. It can wait."

"No, I need to." Whitney took a breath, blowing it out slowly. She opened the door and stepped inside.

Nothing happened.

"That was anticlimactic," Sandra said, following her into the apartment.

"Good." Elizabeth glared at Sandra.

"This is nice," Sandra said, poking her head into each room.

Whitney wandered around for a few minutes just looking. It wasn't as bad as she'd thought. It didn't really seem like the same place. The redecorating job they had done to clean up after

Justin's attack had wiped away the destruction as well as the memories.

"Guess we should head over to the office." Whitney opened the front door and stopped. Across the hall, a sign was tacked to the InfiniCorp office door. It said 'Closed due to illness'.

"Better use the back door." She did a one-eighty and led them through the kitchen.

The hallway was so quiet. She checked the front office, where her desk was, but it was empty. She glanced into Rami's office. It was empty too. A sliver of doubt worked its way into her mind when she noticed his little glass paperweight was gone.

"Where is everyone?" Elizabeth asked, tapping her cane on the floor absently.

"I don't know." Whitney shook her head. "Maybe they're in the apartments."

She retreated down the hallway and opened the door that led to Madraeus' study. The bookshelves were barren. The chairs and desk were gone. Whitney quickly moved to the other door. She yanked it open and charged into Madraeus' apartment.

The silence was deafening.

Whitney dashed to Madraeus' bedroom, hoping that he would be there to yell at her for disturbing him, but it was vacant. She looked around in despair. Her eyes lingered on the bed. In her mind, she could see him sitting there, glaring at her, as she told him about her crazy plan for trapping Justin.

"Did they move out?" Sandra asked from behind her.

Whitney glanced at Sandra and then pushed past her and ran for the kitchen.

Elizabeth watched her granddaughter's frantic searching. Closing her eyes and shaking her head sadly, she turned and hobbled back to Whitney's apartment.

Whitney took the spiral stairs two at a time. Sandra followed her. Whitney ran from room to room looking for someone, anyone. But every room was empty.

Finally, she turned to the hall that contained the cells. She remembered searching them for Justin. She had anxiously wanted to remain undiscovered then, but this time, she was desperate to run across someone.

The cells were gone. They were all small offices now, as if the cells had never been there.

Her world started to collapse. She had been so scared to see Madraeus, but now, she wanted nothing more than to see him. She didn't want to be left behind: discarded like an old broken toy. Pain and betrayal hit her like a baseball bat to the belly. She doubled over and wrapped her arms around her stomach. She'd never felt so abandoned.

Sandra knelt beside her and tried to comfort her, but she didn't know what to say.

At that moment, the sound of the secondary elevator echoed through the silence. Whitney's head shot up. She looked at Sandra and scrambled to her feet. She rushed out of the room and ran straight for the back elevator. She stopped short of running into the doors and waited, bouncing on her toes.

Finally, the door opened and she came face to face with the occupant.

"Thomas?" Whitney exclaimed.

"Whit!" He cracked a smile and then frowned. "What are you doing here?"

"I thought I was coming to work!" She barely held her tears back.

"Oh..." Thomas squirmed, "umm, this is awkward. I guess we shoulda called."

"Where is everyone?"

"Well... some are here. Some are there."

"Thomas..." Whitney warned.

"Wow!" Thomas grinned. "You kinda sound like the boss."

Whitney rolled her eyes. "Just tell me what is going on."

"I don't know, Whit, Madraeus might not want you involved anymore," he hinted.

Whitney glared at him.

"Don't look at me like that. I just think he wants you safe, that's all."

"I'm never gonna be safe until Cecelia's taken care of, you know that."

He looked down at his toes and shrugged. "I know that, and you know that, and Madraeus definitely knows that. It's probably why he doesn't want you involved."

"Thomas!"

"All right, but you didn't hear it from me." He held up his hands. "That theory of yours and Hamy's matched the stuff that Rami found in the filing and in some info that the council confiscated from a couple of traitors. Rami had this big ol' map with all these pins in it. It was awesome, kinda like a spy movie." He grinned. "Anyway, they think they can track Cecelia and stop her from getting her hands on more recruits or at least clean up where she has been, so the cops get off our trail."

"So, where is this map?"

"That's why I'm here, we kinda forgot it."

"Show me!"

ARRESTED DEVELOPMENT

"Where did all the rest of the stuff from the office go?" Whitney asked as she followed Thomas to Rami's office.

"New home," he said as he trotted down the stairs.

"Where?"

"Don't know yet. Rami had it moved and will let us know."

"They didn't even tell you?" Sandra asked.

"Safer that way."

"How?" She challenged as they moved through the study.

"Look, if our secret is compromised, we leave. We have safe houses, but sometimes the exposure is too great, and we have to do a full-scale disappearing act. This is one of those times. The less each of us knows, the better. That way, if any of us are captured, we can't betray the others. We all follow our plans, and after the crisis is over, we'll be contacted. They'll let us know where we're starting over at."

"So, you don't know where everyone went?" Disappointment clouded Whitney's face as they entered Rami's office.

"Come on, Whitney," Thomas tried to ease the pain he saw on her face, "it's gonna be all right. I know where a few of them are." He gestured to the wall where the map was hanging. "Some are looking for potential wolves that Cecelia might attack and some are tracking down this whole rabbit thing."

"What rabbit thing?" Sandra asked, coming into the room. She looked at the map, then took out her phone and took a picture of it.

"You know that disk they found with the three rabbits on it." He saw the look of confusion on their faces and cringed. "Oh. You didn't know about that, did you?"

"No, but you're gonna tell me."

He turned away. "I don't think I'm supposed to."

"Come on, Thomas." Whitney grabbed his shirt front and pulled him back around. "You know, if you don't tell me, then I'm just going to go looking on my own and probably have something horrible happen to me in the process. So, save me the trouble and tell me now."

"Fine," he groaned, looking between Whitney and Sandra. "Cecelia kept mentioning that we were chasing the wrong rabbit."

"Right. I remember her saying that in the mine."

"Well, turns out that there is a rabbit theme to all this. It wasn't just random. They found this metal disk with three rabbits chasing each other around in a circle," he drew a picture in the air, "and their ears make a triangle in the center. Madraeus said it was—"

He stopped talking and looked toward the door that led to Whitney's office. His nostrils flared.

"What is it?" Whitney whispered.

He didn't have to answer because a loud banging came from the door.

"POLICE! OPEN UP!"

"Oh shit!" Thomas lunged forward and grabbed the map, ripping it from the wall. Pins scattered across the floor, making little tinkling sounds. He spun around, stopping with his face inches from Whitney's. "You haven't seen me or heard from anyone else. Understand?"

Whitney stared at him dumbly. His eyes were dark, and his whole body radiated menace.

She nodded.

He pecked a quick kiss on her forehead and then sprinted for the back elevator.

Sandra grabbed Whitney's hand, pulling her through the door and down the hall.

"Where are we going? Whitney hissed.

"It would be better if you were in your apartment than in a deserted office when the police get to you."

"Couldn't we just run like Thomas?" They dashed into her kitchen and stopped.

Sandra shook her head and pointed. Elizabeth stood at the open door, talking to the police.

"Whitney is here, but why do you need to see her?" Grammy sounded so innocent. Sandra and Whitney stared at each other, holding their breath.

"We would really like to speak to *her* about that, Mrs. Martindale."

"It's Detective Sanders," Whitney mouthed. "He's not gonna go away."

"So go talk to him."

"Ah, crap!" Whitney cursed as she walked out of the kitchen to the front door. "Detective Sanders? Is everything all right?"

"Ah, Ms. Martindale." He smiled smugly as he looked her over.

Whitney became overly conscious of her pale complexion. She hoped her bruises weren't showing. She pulled her sleeves a little farther down over her wrists.

"I was just trying to find someone to talk to at your company." He gestured to the sign on the door behind him. "Who's ill?"

"Umm, that would be me, actually." Whitney shrugged, trying to sound embarrassed.

"Uh-huh." Detective Sanders looked her over again, giving her the impression that he thought she was lying even though she looked like death. "Would your boss be around?"

"Not that I know of." She shrugged, inwardly regretting that she was once again trying *not* to lie to the police. "He left on business."

"Any idea when he'll be back?"

Whitney shook her head. She could feel her grandmother watching her. She didn't think she could lie in front of Grammy. At least so far, she had been able to tell the truth.

"Well, maybe you can help me."

"I'll try," she said, trying not to squirm.

"Do you know a man named Thomas Sun-Dancer who works for your boss?"

"I know a Thomas, but I don't know his last name." It suddenly occurred to her how little she knew about any of the people she worked with. *Thomas is right,* she thought, *knowing less will keep me from accidentally betraying anyone.*

"Do you happen to know his whereabouts?" Sanders watched her intently.

"No, I don't." *Truly,* she thought, *he could have gone anywhere after he ran off.*

"Have you seen him recently?"

"No." It was her first actual lie.

The elevator door opened. An officer dashed out and ran up to Detective Sanders. "His Jeep just busted out of the garage past our men. They are in pursuit now."

Detective Sanders looked back at Whitney.

"You wanna revise that last answer?"

Whitney stared at him blankly.

He shook his head. "All right, Ms. Martindale, have it your way." He reached a hand toward Whitney. "I'm gonna need you to come with me."

"I don't see a reason for that!" Elizabeth stepped up and put her hand on the Detective's arm. "Whitney hasn't done anything."

"Mrs. Martindale, please," he reached down and removed her hand, "your granddaughter has been hip-deep in quite a few messes lately, and I'm sick of getting the runaround. She can either come with me and answer my questions willingly, or I'll arrest her and charge her with obstruction."

Elizabeth thumped her cane against the floor. "What exactly has she been involved in?"

"Well, let's see. There're the deaths at The Loop," he ticked them off on his fingers, "the disappearance of Justin Palmer, and now she's lying to me about Thomas Sun-Dancer!"

"Wait just a minute!" Elizabeth cried. "How can you accuse my granddaughter of all these things? I know my Whitney! She's a good girl!"

"Yeah? Well, your 'good girl' hasn't been telling you everything. There's something funny going on, and she knows what it is." He reached out and clamped a hand on Whitney's arm.

Whitney gasped as he hit her bruises. Sanders frowned and looked at her arm. Glancing up, he saw the panic in her eyes. In an unexpectedly swift movement, he yanked her sleeve up, revealing the network of bites and bruises. He stared at her wounds and then looked at her face, taking in her appearance with new eyes.

"What the hell have you gotten into?" he breathed. "I think you have a lot of explaining to do. Come on." He tugged her toward the elevator.

"No!" Elizabeth rapped her cane against the floor. "You can't do this!"

Whitney tried to put on the brakes, but she didn't see a way out of this. Even if she broke loose from Sander's grip, she didn't have the strength or the energy to run very far. They would catch her, and she would have to explain why she ran. Better to go with him and try to act dumb again. She glanced over her shoulder at Sandra, who stood just inside the door of her apartment, trying to remain unnoticed.

'Call Myers,' Whitney mouthed and was relieved to see her friend nod in understanding.

RESEARCH AND RABBITS

SANDRA LISTENED TO ELIZABETH defend her granddaughter as the police escorted Whitney out the door and into the elevator. The sound of arguing faded as the elevator doors closed.

Sandra waited to be sure they were all gone before stepping out of the kitchen. She took out her flip phone and hesitated. She didn't know Myers' number, nor could she look it up. When that vampire, Vivian, had given Sandra the phone, she had made it clear that it was so they could keep track of her, not because they were being nice. So, calls and text only, no internet.

Scanning the room, she moved over to the desk and pulled open drawer after drawer, looking for a phone book. Finally, she found it and flopped it open. Flipping through the yellow pages, she found the number for the temp agency that Whitney worked for.

She pulled out her phone and dialed.

"Orchard Employment Agency."

"May I speak to Mrs. Myers, please?" While she waited on hold, she walked back toward the door, cracked it open, and glanced out into the mini-lobby to make sure no one could hear her.

"This is Mrs. Myers."

"This is Sandra. We have a problem."

"What is it?" Myers' voice lost its pleasantness.

Sandra closed the door and took a few steps into the room. "Whitney's just been arrested."

"What?"

"We're at the office, and this detective showed up looking for Thomas. He had just left, but Whitney told the cop she hadn't seen him. Then this other cop came and said they were chasing him. So, the detective got mad and said Whitney was hiding things. He saw her bites and bruises, and now he's really mad. They just left for the police station."

Silence greeted her diatribe. "Mrs. Myers? Are you still there?"

"Yes."

"So, what do I do?"

"Nothing."

"Nothing? I can't just sit here! Someone has to do something! I thought you guys were all about keeping things secret!"

"We are. And this will be taken care of." Mrs. Myers' voice was stern but not angry. "Whitney has been through this before. She knows what's at stake and what to do."

Sandra felt slightly mollified. "But you're going to help her, right?"

"Of course! As I said, this will be handled, but I don't want you doing anything that will make things worse. Where is Whitney's grandmother?"

"She followed them down in the elevator. I imagine she's going to the Police Department. She was pretty upset."

"Are you still at InfiniCorp?"

"Yes."

"All right. Go back to my house. Whatever you do, don't get involved with the police," Mrs. Myers warned before hanging up.

"Don't get involved?" Sandra muttered as she paced across Whitney's apartment. "I'm supposedly dead. The dead can't talk to anyone."

She stood in the middle of the room with her hands braced on her hips. Her eyes snapped to the computer sitting on the desk. She looked at her phone. Absently, she tapped her fingers against the back of the case.

"Not that I don't trust you, Myers," she mused as she moved over and opened the laptop, "but it's time for a little 'handling' of my own."

While she waited for the computer to finish booting, she opened the picture she had taken of the map with her phone. She studied the pins in the photo as if they would suddenly make sense. When the computer was ready, she jumped on the internet.

"Three rabbits," she mumbled as she typed.

Her search only found really bad rabbit jokes.

"Rabbits, rabbits." She sat back, staring at the list the search had provided. Nothing helpful stood out. She looked up multiple variations of the words rabbit, bunnies, and hares.

Greatly discouraged, she typed in 'ancient rabbit symbol'.

"WHOA!" She sat back. The first thing that popped up was a picture just like the one that Thomas had described: three rabbits chasing in a circle. There were thousands of pictures: some were in stone or stained glass, others were wood carvings or metal disks like the one Thamas had described. There was a map showing all the locations where historians had found the symbol so far. Sandra looked at her picture of Thomas' map and then at the screen.

"What?" she murmured skeptically. Most of the pins matched the symbol locations. "That is way too coincidental."

She scrolled down the pictures for a while. A fascinated smile took over her face. Then she went back and started clicking on links to information.

"This is freaky! China, England, Germany, Switzerland." The Three Hares had been found in countries across Europe and Asia dating back to the 6th and 7th centuries, spanning all religions. "These little buggers are everywhere."

She clicked on a few more sites. The same information was repeated over and over. The symbol was found in churches and temples, in caves, and on buildings, but no one knew what they meant. The only thing anyone agreed on was that the hare represented magic or spiritual forces. She changed tactics and looked up the mythology of hares and rabbits. She read story after story about hares and immortality intermingled with myths of Gods and Goddesses.

"Unity, a continuous cycle, the moon, rebirth, immortality..." Sandra skimmed the pages, muttering to herself. "Yeah, that doesn't sound like the Races at all."

She found the link again to the map of where the symbol had been discovered. A large number of them had been found in England: 17 churches in Devon alone.

She looked at the map on her phone again. There was a huge concentration of red pins in the UK.

"Man, now I see how conspiracy theorists get to be crazy." She shut down the computer and began to pace the room. She needed to tell someone about this, but she wasn't sure they'd listen to her.

A knock at the door made her jump. She froze, scared that it was the police again. The knock repeated.

"Ms. Conners?" called an unfamiliar, English-accented voice. Sandra didn't know anyone with an accent. "Ms. Conners, we know you are there. I think we can be of some help to each other."

Cautiously, Sandra stepped closer.

"Ms. Conners, could you please open the door?"

"Who are you?"

"My name is John Danos."

"Doesn't ring a bell."

"I represent The Three Hares."

Sandra froze. "That was unexpected," she murmured. "How do you know about me?"

"We know a lot about the situation you find yourself in. If you would like to open the door, we can discuss it."

"How do I know you aren't going to do something nasty to me?"

"As I said earlier, I think we can help each other."

"You're gonna have to be a little more specific, bud."

Through the door, she heard him sigh and say something that she couldn't make out.

"You alone?" Sandra called.

"No, I have a colleague with me."

"Once again, not really helping your case."

"Her name is Barbie Calvin."

Sandra snickered, "A bunny named Barbie?"

"Please, Ms. Conners? We really need to speak with you," the woman said. She sounded Welsh.

"You guys sound kinda far from home!"

"We've come a long way. Could you open the door?" he asked.

"You want to stop the woman who locked you in a mine? We can help with that," the woman added.

Sandra stepped back and stared at the door in surprise. She moved to open it but stopped. She looked around for something to protect herself with, but nothing was handy. She trotted out to the kitchen and searched the drawers until she found a butcher's knife.

"All right," she called as she returned. "I'm gonna open the door, but don't try anything funky."

"You have my word," he said immediately.

THE THREE HARES

Sandra opened the door.

A short, rotund man with black-framed glasses stood in the doorway with his arms crossed. The woman standing behind him was taller and blonde. Both were young and looked like they spent too much time in their mothers' basements.

"May we come in?" he asked.

Sandra stepped back and allowed them to enter the apartment.

The man nodded a thank you. Looking around, he took a seat on the couch. The woman followed him in and sat down beside him. He gave Sandra an assessing once-over and then smiled at her expectantly. Sandra stayed near the door, standing as far from them as she could.

"I see that you are cautious. That's good." He nodded. "If you are going to survive your dealings with these monsters, you will need that instinct."

He waited for Sandra to respond, but she just continued watching them.

"All right," he resumed, unfazed by her reaction. "We represent a group of concerned citizens, if you will. We try to help those victimized by the monsters."

"Concerned citizen?" Sandra interrupted. "You're going to have to do better than that. You see, I've seen a lot of weird stuff lately, and just being a 'concerned citizen' ain't gonna fly with me."

He ran his eyes over her, reassessing. "Very well."

"Usually, we try to be more circumspect," Barbie said. "Most people find us a little eccentric."

"You mean most people think you're nuts," Sandra corrected.

"Ahem." John cleared his throat. "Since you've already had dealings with the monsters, it's the truth for you. We are the Ancient Society of The Three Hares."

"Ancient Society, huh?" Sandra looked the pair over. "You don't look like much."

John bristled. "I hardly think our looks come into it!"

"Really?" Sandra asked, "And what does your secret society do?"

"It is our duty to hunt, trap, and if necessary, destroy the monsters of this world."

"Oh," Sandra nodded, "that's nice."

"Please," Barbie held up her hand, "I know it sounds strange, but—"

"Honey, I've been locked in a mine so I could be used to feed vampires." Sandra crossed her arms, leaving the knife pointing up past her shoulder. "We're a bit past strange."

Barbie's eyes grew large at the appearance of the knife, but John smiled again. "We believe we can help you."

"You're about three months too late on that one, pal." Sandra glared back at him. "Quit acting like a politician and tell me what you want."

"That woman who locked you in the mine? She's planning something bad," Barbie blurted. "Really bad."

"So?" Sandra shrugged. "I know that already."

"But do you know what she is planning?" John leaned forward.

Sandra thought he had the look of a cat that had not only eaten the canary but a few expensive parrots as well. She didn't like that.

Leaning back against the door, Sandra thought out loud. "The Three Hares symbol is all over the place. Cecelia is building an army. You hunt, trap, and destroy." She fell silent at the look of surprise on John's face.

He quickly tried to hide it.

Sandra stood up straight. "She's springing your traps! That's what the Three Hares symbols are! They're markers to the traps!"

Barbie and John exchanged a look of alarm.

"Sorry, did I spoil the big reveal?" Sandra cocked her head in mock sincerity. Her expression changed quickly to anger. "Now that that's out of the way, tell me what you want from me."

"That's complicated," John hesitated.

"I'm all ears."

"What do you know about Egyptian Mythology?" Barbie asked.

Sandra frowned at the change in subject. "The usual stuff, I guess."

"Do you know about Apep?" John looked up at her.

"Never heard of him."

"Apep is the snake demon, the World Eater. Sometimes known as Apophis? For thousands upon thousands of years, he has tried to consume the world in darkness," Barbie said. "He was the night as Ra was the Sun."

John took over explaining. "Legends say that he resides just below the surface of light. He can't come into the light, so he tries to bring darkness to the world. He tries to stop the sun from rising every night by battling Ra in the Underworld."

"Sounds like a real jerk," Sandra interrupted.

"I wish you would take this seriously!" John snapped. "We are talking about the fate of the world!"

Sandra glared at him. "So far, all you've done is tell me some vague, old story."

"What we've told you is Cecelia's goal." Barbie stared at her intently. "She is freeing all the monsters the Society has trapped over the centuries. The army she is building is for Apep."

"That sounds bad."

John shot to his feet. "It's horrendous!"

At his shout, Sandra jumped, uncrossing her arms to hold the knife in front of her.

John didn't seem to notice her defensive move as he continued to rage. "If she frees Apep again and pairs him with an army, an apocalypse will be upon us!"

Silence followed his outburst.

John's eyes dropped to the knife. He looked up at Sandra. After a moment, he sat down and took a calming breath.

Sandra lowered the knife a little. "You said 'free Apep again'. What does that mean?"

"Apep has been defeated and banished to the underworld repeatedly throughout history. He always rises again." Barbie's voice quivered.

"But you said 'free him *again*'. Doesn't that mean that he is locked up already?"

"For now," John hedged.

"All right," Sandra said when it was apparent that he wasn't going to say more. "I'm still not getting why you want me. You have Mr. Evil Snake Guy locked up, and you know Cecelia is trying to let out all your monsters. You've marked all the traps or whatever, so you don't need me to find them. I am not trained in supernatural warfare, so I'm not equipped to fight. I have no power or influence on any of this. So, once again, what do you want?"

John pressed his lips together, refusing to answer.

"Really? You came to find me, go through all this bullshit, and now won't say why?" Sandra marched to the door and yanked it open. "You can go."

"We need help!" Barbie jumped to her feet. John grabbed her arm, trying to hush her, but she shook him off. "No. You can be the mysterious conspirator if you want to, but I'm not playing this game anymore, John. I'm scared." She looked at Sandra and pleaded, "We need help. Please?"

Sandra slowly closed the door and turned back to the couch. "Why?"

Barbie took a few steps toward her and away from John. "We are being hunted."

"Hunted?"

"Our Society has been around for centuries. I can't remember why it was started," Barbie began.

"It was started because the gift of immortality was being abused!" John interrupted.

"It doesn't matter right now." She waved away John's words. "We have tried to protect mankind. There are creatures out there that are way more of a danger to humans than nuclear weapons. Our ancestors managed to trap or destroy innumerable enemies, but the most dangerous is Apep. In the beginning, he just tried to stop the sun from rising by simply standing against Ra every night, but then he kinda branched out."

"Branched out?" Sandra resettled the knife. Her palm was sweaty.

"He started to interfere in the civilizations of humans. He sought out individuals who were of a like mind and taught them terrible magic. He took every opportunity to bring chaos and destruction into the world."

"Then, somehow, he discovered that if he infected humans with his venom," John snarled, "it created demonic monsters!"

"Vampires," Barbie clarified. "Those he infected were powerful, and like their master, they were creatures of the night. Daylight was their destruction."

"Like Cecelia?" Sandra guessed.

"Yes," Barbie nodded.

"They must all be destroyed!" John said with a gleam in his eye. "They are a plague, infecting others, just like Apep. Their bite creates more vampires."

"We studied those second-generation vamps. They were never as powerful as the ones originally infected by Apep. Unlike their tamer offspring, the originals often lost their humanity and were prone to Apep's evil tendencies. He also seemed to retain a hold on them, like he could influence their actions. After we had imprisoned him, Apep's hold wasn't as strong as before. The spells we used to confine and bind him dampened his power, but he could still affect his first-generation offspring to an extent."

"So, you think Cecelia is listening to the All Psycho Snake Radio in her head, building an army to free her..." Sandra looked from John to Barbie, "Boss? Father? Creator?"

Barbie blew out a whoosh of air and nodded. "Essentially, yes."

"The Three Hares have hunted down these monsters for hundreds of years. We destroyed or trapped every one we could. There were some, though, that we couldn't stop. We tried and failed again and again to destroy them, but they always evaded us."

"Like Cecelia?"

John nodded. "Yes, and the CEO of InfiniCorp, Madraeus Ravilla."

"Madraeus?" Sandra gaped. "You tried to kill Madraeus?"

"He's a monster!" John spat.

"He saved my life!"

"He's murdered thousands!"

"Please!" Barbie was on her feet again. She looked from Sandra to John. "We are not here to argue. Regardless of what he is or what he's done, we need him!"

John sat back and crossed his arms, staring straight ahead at nothing.

Sandra resettled the knife and looked at Barbie. "Need him for what?"

GOOD COP, BAD COP

IN AN INTERROGATION ROOM at the Denver Police Department, Whitney sat, tapping her fingers on the metal table. Detective Sanders had escorted her into this room and then disappeared again. She tapped out a random rhythm and looked around. It wasn't the same room that she had been in after Justin had attacked her at The Loop. That one had been nicer. This one had paint chipping off the walls and a crack in the two-way mirror. She had the feeling that she was no longer being considered a victim.

Whitney tried to plan out what to say, but nothing sounded good. Hoping that she would suddenly become a competent liar didn't seem like a viable solution either. She could deny some of the charges that Sanders had mentioned to her grandmother, but not all. The last time she was here, she had managed to avoid most of the questions he had asked by being vague and only telling half-truths. But she had the feeling that it wouldn't be enough this time.

Detective Sanders seemed to think he was onto something. He didn't seem like the kind to let anything go. Whitney thought he was more of a 'dog with a bone' kind of guy.

"I'm never getting out of here," she sighed and then glanced warily at the two-way mirror, wondering if there was anyone in there watching her.

I better not talk to myself too much, she thought. *Knowing my luck, I'll talk myself right into prison.*

The door opened, making her jump.

"Ms. Martindale?" Detective Sanders came in, followed by a younger man in a cheap black suit carrying a small stack of files. "This is Agent Milner of the FBI."

Ah, that explains the cheap suit, Whitney chuckled to herself as she tried to control her face. He was taller than the detective and a lot better looking, but he had a harsher expression than Sanders.

"Ms. Martindale." Agent Milner stepped forward and extended his hand. Whitney hesitated for a moment and then shook it. "We'd like to ask you some questions."

Whitney tried to smile. "I figured I wasn't here for a pedicure."

"Right," he said dryly as he moved around the table to sit in one of the two chairs across from her.

Detective Sanders took the second seat. Milner set the file stack on the table and noisily scooted his chair up to the table.

Sanders just sat down and looked at Whitney with an un-readable expression.

Whitney moved both of her hands off the table and folded them in her lap. She looked from Sanders to Milner to Sanders again, saying nothing. At the moment, she felt very uncooperative and had no intention of making this easy.

"I understand that you were the victim of an attack at The Loop by one Justin Palmer?" Milner sat back and crossed his arms.

"Yes." Whitney was taken aback by his direct stare. She had expected him to be more like Detective Sanders, fussing with paperwork and spending all of his time writing notes and checking files. His icy blue eyes never left her face. It made her nervous. It was too much like her grandmother when she knew Whitney was up to something.

"Why did he attack you?"

"I don't know," Whitney stammered. This was really not going like she had hoped. Milner was too intense.

"How did you manage to escape without injury that night? Everyone else who went into that bathroom came out injured or dead. Except you. Can you explain that to me?" His voice was calm and almost gentle.

"I can't." Whitney shrugged. "I grabbed the trash can and started swinging. I didn't want to let him near me."

"Detective Sanders tells me that you were later chased by a giant dog. I believe it was after the funeral?" He glanced away, but only long enough to get a confirming nod from Sanders. "Kinda weird. But interesting timing, don't you think?"

"I hadn't really thought about it."

"May I see your arms?" Milner sat forward and extended his hand across the table.

"Why?" Whitney self-consciously pulled her sleeves down.

"Please, Ms. Martindale." He waited, staring straight into her eyes.

"I don't see why you need to look at my arms." Her heart pounded harder. "What is this all about?" She nodded her head at Sanders. "He comes to my apartment, telling my grandmother all kinds of crazy things and scaring her, then drags me down here. Why are you treating me like some criminal?"

"We're not treating you like a criminal, Ms. Martindale." Sanders slowly shook his head. "You aren't in handcuffs, yet."

"Then what do you want?"

Milner leaned his elbows on the table and rested his mouth against his folded hands. He stared at her for a long time, holding her gaze. With effort, Whitney looked away and glanced at Sanders. The older cop hadn't moved.

"Were you in the Sherman Mine?" Milner asked.

Whitney jumped at the sudden sound and looked at him. "The what now?"

"The Sherman Mine," he explained, "you know, the one that has been on the news lately?"

"Oh," Whitney stalled, trying to come up with a good answer, but nothing popped into her head. "I guess I didn't know its name. I really don't pay attention to the news much."

"Just answer the question," Sanders said.

She looked from Milner to Sanders. "Why?"

"Look, Ms. Martindale. We know you were there." Milner sighed. "It would be a lot easier for all of us if you just told us the truth."

Whitney blinked, swallowed, then blinked again. She couldn't bring herself to speak. There was no way she was going to tell them anything. Madraeus may have betrayed her trust by killing all those prisoners in the mine, but she wasn't about to betray the Races. She felt obligated to keep their secret despite her personal feelings about Madraeus.

"We found your fingerprints on the bars of a cell in the mine." Sanders finally sat forward and leaned on the table. "Your arms are evidence enough that you were not treated well. So, why don't you just tell us what happened?"

Whitney's heartbeat increased to panic speed.

"We know there is something else going on here, Ms. Martindale." Milner turned on the icy stare again. "I've been investigating similar events all over the country. I know that something unnatural is happening." He pointed to her arms. "Whoever they are, whatever they are..." Out of the corner of her eye, Whitney saw Sanders frown at Milner. "They are hurting people. I want to stop it. I can help you if you let me."

"I'm sorry. I can't tell you anything," Whitney whispered.

"Oh no, Missy, you tried that with me before." Sanders sat forward and tapped the table with his finger. "You can't just keep avoiding the questions. I know you are mixed up in something. You may feel some misguided loyalty to whoever is doing this, but it's time you stopped trying to protect these people. There are sixty-six people dead in that mine." Whitney winced at his harsh words. "Your friend and all those people at The Loop. Dead!" Tears threatened as he continued. "Those four men in that alley. Dead."

The ones that attacked Sophia, Whitney thought, trying to distract herself so she wouldn't cry.

"None of those people deserved to die," Sanders finished. "Please, just help us stop these killers."

Milner started opening files and pulling out selected pieces.

"I'm sorry," Whitney started, but she was cut off by Milner tossing several photos in front of her.

The crime scene photos showed piles of bodies in dark places. Their gaunt faces and vacant eyes stared up at her. Whitney swallowed the bile rising in her throat. Milner tossed a couple more photos in front of her. These showed bodies with bite marks and torn flesh. Whitney shuddered. Two more photos landed on the pile. They were of men lying in awkward positions. The bodies were barely recognizable, as if they had been savaged by animals.

Her hands shot out from under the table and covered the photos. "Please!" Whitney closed her eyes. Her tears finally managed to escape down her cheeks.

"You can help us stop this from happening again," Milner pressed.

"Just tell us the truth," Sanders added.

"I can't!" Whitney said without opening her eyes.

Silence filled the room. It was more than a pause in the conversation. All the noise from the building had stopped. She couldn't even hear a breath in the stillness.

Slowly, she opened her eyes.

ENEMY OF MY ENEMY

Sandra stared at the Hares in silence. She couldn't believe what she was hearing.

"Madraeus Ravilla is powerful enough to stand against Cecelia. They are both first-generation offspring created by Apep. For years, we have tried to find a way to…" Barbie hesitated as if she didn't want to finish.

"Kill them?" Sandra supplied.

"Yes." John sat forward eagerly. "They must be killed. This world would be better off without their kind."

Barbie rolled her eyes at John and then looked back at Sandra. "What I'm trying to say is that over the centuries—"

"Over the centuries, you've tried to kill him," Sandra shook her head, "and now you want his help?"

"Yes, without our help, he will be too late."

"But," Sandra looked from Barbie to John in confusion, "you just said that you needed *his* help."

"Yes." Barbie nodded. "Cecelia is hunting down every Warren and exterminating every Hare."

"Wait," Sandra held up a hand. "I'm confused. What's a Warren?"

"Warrens are what we call the small groups of our Society. There is one posted at every prison or trap we've created. We don't leave the monsters unguarded."

"And she's been—"

"Murdering all of them!" John hissed. "And then she lets the monster they guarded out to roam free."

Sandra shivered at the hatred in his tone. She reached up and ran her fingers through her hair as if it would brush off the ominous feeling.

"There are only a handful of us left," Barbie said. "We've pulled most of our people back to guard Apep, but there aren't enough of us to stop her when she comes."

"So, you've come to get help from the only vampire stronger or at least as strong as her?" Sandra asked.

Barbie nodded. "Exactly."

"I don't understand why you came to me."

"We came here hoping you could help us convince Mr. Ravilla to help us."

Sandra blinked a few times.

"You know him," Barbie offered.

"Yeah," Sandra laughed at their unbelievable suggestion, "I talked to him for ten seconds, and he didn't kill me! That doesn't mean I can go around asking him to help people who've tried to murder him!"

"Our information says that Whitney Martindale does, though," John hinted, "and you are her friend."

"I barely know her either! We were just stuck in the mine together!"

"You aren't giving yourself enough credit."

"I think you two are expecting too much." Sandra snorted. "Just because that saying says 'the enemy of my enemy is my friend' doesn't mean everyone is going to get along and help each other. Besides, Whitney's just been arrested. So, she ain't helpin' anyone."

"What?" John jumped to his feet.

"Why are you surprised?" Sandra gave a humorless laugh. "I thought you," she mimicked his tone from earlier, "knew all about our situation."

"We didn't know that!" Barbie shifted in her seat. "When did this happen?"

"Maybe an hour ago," Sandra shrugged.

"Why are the police after her?" John asked.

"There's this detective that thinks he knows something. He's sure that Whitney is the key. So, he took her in for," Sandra made little quotation marks in the air with her fingers, "questioning."

"What does he think he knows?" John stalked toward Sandra.

"I don't know!" Sandra snapped, holding the knife out toward him.

John stopped short, eying the blade. "We have to do something!"

"It's being handled," Sandra said.

John narrowed his eyes. "By whom?"

"Whitney told me to call Mrs. Myers. I did, and she said it would be taken care of."

"Mrs. Myers?" Barbie said thoughtfully.

"Yeah." Sandra watched them suspiciously. "What about her?"

John turned back to Barbie.

"If we want Whitney, we need to get to Mrs. Myers," John said.

"Can you take us to her?" Barbie asked.

"I don't think that is such a good idea. I'm barely on their 'okay' list. I don't think they're gonna like me bringing you there."

Barbie nodded. "We're aware of the dangers."

John planted his feet and crossed his arms as if reciting some superhero oath. "We are prepared to take the risks."

"Yeah? Well, I'm not." Sandra shook her head. "There are more than just vampires running around, you know? When we left, there were a couple of witches and several werewolves at her place. I'm not getting into the middle of a war."

"We will try our best to avoid conflict," Barbie promised.

"I'm more worried about them ripping your heads off when they find out who you are."

"They can try," John said, looking a little too eager for the chance to defend himself.

"I have no desire to get into a fight." Barbie gave him a warning glare and then looked at Sandra. "Perhaps you should call and warn them?"

Just as Sandra opened her mouth to answer, the sound of loud voices came from outside the apartment's front door. Barbie and John spun to face the door. Sandra crept to the door and pressed her ear against it.

An authoritative voice said, "Go ahead and open it." There was a crash. "Search everything."

Sandra turned back to the Hares and whispered, "I think it's the police!"

"They can't find us here!" John glanced around.

"Is there a back door?" Barbie asked, looking around as well.

Sandra pointed with the knife. "There's a way out through the kitchen, but it leads into a hall that's attached to the offices."

"Can we use it to get past them?" Barbie took a couple of steps toward the kitchen.

"I don't know." Sandra shrugged. "There's a second elevator at the back."

"You think we can make it?" Barbie's voice shook.

"I don't want the police looking for me," Sandra warned. She looked at the door and then at the kitchen, then back at the door. "What if we just go out the door all calm and nice, pretending we aren't being hoodlums, and go down the elevator?"

"Really? You want to waltz out of here?" John threw his hands up. "Just like that?"

"Yeah, just like that." Sandra pointed the knife at him. "You never heard of 'fake it 'til you make it' or 'hiding in plain sight'?"

"Of course," he snarled back at her, eying the knife, "I just don't think it's going to work."

"I'm willing to try." Barbie stepped closer to the door and pressed her ear against it like Sandra had. "I can't hear anything."

Sandra crept into the kitchen and listened at that door. It was louder. She quickly moved back into the living room. "I think they've made it into the hall."

She stepped up beside Barbie and listened at the door. When she didn't hear anything, Sandra reached down and clasped the doorknob. Slowly, she turned it, trying not to make any noise. The bolt released, and she cracked the door open a sliver. Pressing her face against the crack, she peered into the mini-lobby.

The main door of InfiniCorp was standing open. She couldn't see anyone in the office, but she could hear the sound of drawers opening and closing and snippets of conversation. Sandra turned her gaze to the elevator. There wasn't anyone standing in front of it. She jumped at the sound of a knock at the kitchen door and the knob jiggling.

Sandra felt Barbie's hand on her shoulder. "We have to go now!"

Sandra nodded and opened the door further. She glanced around once more, seeing no one. She yanked the door open the rest of the way and walked quickly to the elevator. Barbie and John were right on her heels. She pressed the button and waited. Every few seconds, she looked over her shoulder at the office door. Discovery was only a breath away.

Her heart pulsed so loudly in her ears that she didn't hear the ding heralding the elevator's arrival. The doors opened, and John shoved her into the waiting car. Barbie hit the 'Door Close' button. Sandra held her breath until the doors closed again.

As the elevator descended, she realized she was still holding the butcher's knife from Whitney's kitchen. She held it up, staring at it dumbly. She looked around the elevator and then down at her outfit. There really wasn't any place to put it, but she couldn't be seen walking around downtown with a huge knife.

"Here," Barbie said, noticing her predicament. She didn't try to take it away. She just adjusted how Sandra held the knife so that the blade ran along the back of her forearm. "Your arm hides it then."

"Oh," Sandra moved her arm experimentally, "thanks."

"No problem."

"I'm surprised you aren't trying to make me get rid of it," Sandra murmured, watching the floor number display.

"Nah." Barbie shrugged, also watching the floor numbers. "I think you're gonna need it."

TRICKY PIXIE

Whitney gaped. Both Milner and Sanders were frozen. She stared at them, waiting for them to say something or at least blink.

Seconds ticked by.

She leaned to one side, then the other. Their eyes didn't follow her movement. She sat forward, leaning closer and closer. Whitney's eyes grew huge as neither of them moved. Slowly, she reached out one finger and poked Agent Milner's hand. There was no reaction at all.

"Holy crap!"

She sat there almost as frozen as they were, not knowing what to do. Whitney glanced at the two-way mirror and then at the door. She looked at the two men in front of her again.

The door handle moved a fraction, then it moved all the way. Whitney turned as the door opened, revealing a very tall, very beautiful, very blonde woman dressed head to toe in bright pink. She looked vaguely familiar.

"You Whitney Martindale?" the woman asked in a bored voice.

"Uh… yeah?" Whitney wasn't sure if this development was good or bad.

The woman in pink sighed like a teenager on a family vacation. "Come with me then."

"Who are you?"

"I'm Cherry," she said as if everyone should have known that. "You coming or not?"

Whitney hesitated; she couldn't trust anyone anymore. "Sorry, but why are you here?"

"Seriously? I come all the way down here, and all you want to do is ask questions?" Cherry flicked her hair over her shoulder and rolled her eyes. "Whatev'!" She turned and walked away down the hall.

Whitney looked back at the frozen policemen, terrified that they would snap out of it any second.

Better a pink bitchy chick than these two, Whitney thought, and dashed into the hall after her.

"Wait! Wait!"

Cherry turned and struck up a model pose with one hand on her hip and her head cocked slightly in challenge. Whitney skidded to a stop about a foot away from her and stared up at her. She was a lot taller than Whitney.

"I didn't mean to insult you, I was confused!" Whitney stammered. "I just didn't know who sent you."

"Myers sent me to clean up the mess." Cherry sighed, flicking her hair over her shoulder. She turned and walked off again. Whitney kept pace with her as they snaked down the maze of halls. In every room they passed, Whitney could see people frozen, just like Sanders and Milner.

"Did you do this?" Whitney asked in awe.

Cherry rolled her eyes. "Duh, I'm a pixie."

"I don't know anything about pixies," Whitney told her as they passed a man frozen in mid-struggle against several police officers. Arms and legs were going everywhere. "But remind me never to piss one off."

"Good plan," Cherry said with sing-song sarcasm.

"What happens when they wake up or unfreeze or whatever?" Whitney asked, trotting to keep up with Cherry's long strides.

The pixie shrugged. "They'll be a little confused with some short-term memory loss, but they'll recover."

"What about those files and the FBI? Aren't they gonna be looking for me? Won't I be in more trouble for disappearing?"

Whitney looked back over her shoulder to see if things were unfreezing yet and slammed into Cherry. She hadn't realized that the pixie had stopped. Cherry glared down at Whitney and then rolled her eyes.

"Oh, fine!" Cherry sighed and strode back the way they'd come. They backtracked through the police department's unending hallways until they were back in the interrogation room.

Sanders and Milner were still staring at the spot where Whitney had been sitting.

"This is just creepy," Whitney whispered.

"It's not creepy," Cherry said as she moved over to the table. "It's a survival skill. Pixies are always being chased by stupid people who think we're like Tinker Bell: all cute and sweet."

"Aren't you?" Whitney hedged. She was afraid to upset her just in case she decided to leave her behind.

Cherry glared at her. "Do I look three inches tall?"

"I meant the cute and sweet part."

Smiling at the pseudo-compliment, Cherry winked at Whitney suggestively, making her blush. "Well, maybe just a little."

Cherry looked at the files on the table. She slid the pictures into a pile and slipped them into one of the folders in front of Milner. Cherry picked up the whole stack and thrust it at Whitney. She started for the door again, but Whitney stopped her.

"Aren't they gonna know we took these? Won't they wonder why they're sitting in here with no one to interrogate and no files?"

Cherry scowled at Whitney. "You're kind of a pain. Has anyone told you that?"

"More times than you can count, actually!" Whitney snorted. "But you know I'm right."

"Fine!" Cherry huffed another of her put-upon teenage sighs and looked back at the two men. "You know, pixies normally just freeze people and then disappear. We don't worry about the details." She pursed her lips as she thought. "Ah, I know."

She snapped her fingers and, with a little poof of pink sparkly dust, a porn magazine popped into existence in her hand. She opened it and flipped through the pages for a moment. Her eyes lit up, and she smiled wickedly. Cherry leaned forward and placed the magazine in front of Milner. She leaned back, frowned, and then bent back down to unzip Sanders' fly. She stepped back once more, surveying her work. Still not satisfied, she moved Sanders' hand over to Milner's leg.

"There. That should distract them." Cherry looked at her and winked again before walking out the door.

Whitney's jaw hung open in shock. Realizing Cherry was leaving her behind, she snapped her jaw shut and raced after the pixie.

"I can't believe you just did that!"

"You're the one who wanted them to be distracted." Cherry shrugged and glanced at Whitney with her lashes lowered. "Besides, that was fun. Nothing a pixie likes more than a little mischief."

Whitney giggled despite her shock. "Cherry, I think I like you!"

"What's not to like?" Cherry primped her hair a little, smiling. The pixie led her through the halls to the front door of the building.

"My car is just outside. They better not have given me a ticket." Cherry reached out to pull the glass door open.

"I don't think they would've had time." Whitney started to reassure her, but just as the door swung inward, she shouted, "Stop!" Whitney grabbed Cherry's arm, almost dropping the files in her haste.

"What now?" Cherry snapped.

Whitney pointed. "Wolf!"

Just outside the door was a snow-white werewolf. She was sitting back on her haunches; her sky-blue eyes watched the door. Her tongue lolled out as she panted.

"Who the hell is that?" Cherry sounded more annoyed than frightened.

"Spark." Whitney remembered her all too well from the mine. "She works for Cecelia and she's a nasty bitch."

"Nice pun," Cherry giggled.

Whitney frowned but then caught on and gave a little laugh. "What do we do?" Whitney shivered as Spark looked directly at her. "Do we go out the back?"

"Really?" Cherry looked down at her. "You think a little wolf is going to bother me?"

"I don't know." Whitney shrugged.

"Werewolves and vampires don't involve us in their little tiffs for a reason, honey." Cherry opened the door and stepped outside.

Whitney couldn't bring herself to follow.

Cherry bent forward and said slowly and loudly to Spark, "Go away."

Whitney winced. Cherry had pronounced her words in a bad imitation of someone who didn't know how to talk to a person who didn't understand English.

Spark growled at Cherry and slowly came to all four feet. She paced forward, baring her teeth and snarling at the pixie.

"Really?" Cherry was unimpressed.

Whitney shook her head, whispering, "She's gonna kill you!"

About a yard away from Cherry, Spark's body tensed, and then she sprang. Her jaw snapped open, showing all her teeth, ready to rip Cherry apart.

"No!" Whitney burst through the glass door, determined to save the sassy pixie.

"Whatev'!" Cherry snapped her fingers. There was a pop. Pink dust poofed outward in a cloud around the wolf.

Whitney skidded to a halt, her warning dying in her throat.

Spark crashed to the ground at Cherry's feet. The wolf's head was stuffed in a wooden bucket, and her body was tangled in pink yarn. Spark snarled and thrashed, flopping around like a fish out of water as she tried to free herself. The bucket made a hollow thumping sound every time it struck the pavement.

"You coming?" Cherry stepped daintily over the growling mass of pink yarn and white fur. She sashayed over to a bright red Mustang convertible and slid gracefully into the driver's seat.

Whitney took one last look at Spark and hurried to the car.

"Please remind me never to piss off a pixie," Whitney said as she slid in beside Cherry.

The pixie winked and blew Whitney a kiss before giggling and driving off.

PIXIES AND BUNNIES AND FBI, OH MY!

WHITNEY BRACED HER HANDS against the dashboard of Cherry's Mustang.

She had thought Philtzer's driving was bad. She would never forget that ride on the back of his bike. They had flown down alleys and through traffic like a deranged bumblebee, but that was nothing compared to Cherry's driving. Whitney was certain that all of her hair would be gray by the time they reached Mrs. Myers' house, if she didn't throw up first.

It might not have been so bad if she had a normal car, but Cherry owned a convertible, offering zero protection from the world flying by at light speed. All she knew by the time they pulled into Mrs. Myers' gated estate was that she had survived the most terrifying thirty minutes of her life. Whitney sat frozen even after Cherry had gotten out. She clutched Milner's files to her chest and closed her eyes as she savored the thrill of motionlessness.

She opened her eyes when she heard another car pull into Mrs. Myers' driveway. It was an economy rental car. Whitney squinted, trying to see who was in it. They parked next to Cherry's convertible. The back door opened, and Sandra popped out.

"Hey there." She looked the sports car over and then took in Whitney's pale face. "Who brought you home?"

"Cherry, the crazy pink pixie," Whitney answered, watching the two strangers get out of the rental car behind Sandra. "How about you?"

"Two British bunnies." Sandra raised her eyebrows. "Are you going to get out of the car?"

"I think my legs are still frozen in fear." Whitney grimaced and noticed Sandra's bunnies were staring at her.

Sandra glanced back at Barbie and John, then down at Whitney. "We have a lot to talk about."

"Yes, we do," she agreed, handing the stack of files to Sandra so she could get out of the car.

"Whitney!" Her grandmother exclaimed, coming out of the house behind them. She hobbled forward as fast as she could on her cane.

Whitney hurried to meet her.

"Oh, thank God!" She enveloped Whitney in a huge hug. "Are you okay? You're shaking!"

"Hi, Grammy!" Whitney returned the hug fiercely. "Just glad to be alive."

"Come inside." Elizabeth pulled her toward the door.

Sandra nudged the car door shut with her knee. Looking at the two Hares, she jerked her head toward the house in a 'come on' gesture and followed the Martindale women up the steps.

Mrs. Myers met them at the door. "Whitney, I'm glad you're all right."

Whitney smiled at the older woman. "Thanks for sending Cherry to get me."

"I hope she behaved." Mrs. Myers looked over her shoulder to where the pixie had disappeared into the house.

"Depends on your definition of behaving."

"Come inside and tell us what happened." Mrs. Myers stepped to the side so they could pass but caught sight of Sandra and the two strangers. The Weaver straightened to her full height.

Whitney turned to see what had caused her reaction.

Barbie and John were kneeling on the steps in front of Mrs. Myers. Sandra stood behind them with her mouth open, holding the stack of files.

"Great Oracle, we have no sacrifice, but may we enter your presence and learn?" John asked with his head bowed.

"Are you kidding?" Whitney asked, looking from them to her long-time boss. "Mrs. M? What are they doing?"

"They are following a very old custom," she said, glaring down at them.

Whitney couldn't tell from her tone if they were annoying her or pleasing her. "I'm not supposed to do that, am I?"

"No, dear. I no longer accept sacrifices."

Whitney blanched. She was having trouble telling if Myers was joking or not. "You can be kinda creepy sometimes, you know that?"

"It comes with the territory. I have been around a long time."

"Yeah, I guess so." Whitney shivered a little as she remembered the banner at Mrs. Myers' birthday party that had said, Happy 2,325th Birthday.

Mrs. Myers turned her full attention to John and Barbie. In the dimming light of sunset, it looked as though her eyes were glowing. Her voice took on an echoing quality as she said, "Come forth and learn."

John and Barbie bowed lower and then stood.

Whitney glanced at Sandra. She shrugged.

Mrs. Myers called over her shoulder, "Vivian?"

Whitney, who still stood in the doorway, turned to find the young vampire coming up behind her.

Mrs. Myers didn't turn and didn't take her eyes off the two newcomers. "Vivian, please escort our guests to the game room and stay with them until—."

"Very kind of you, Oracle," John interrupted, "but the Hares' mission is of the utmost urgency. We would prefer to speak to you now rather than wait with," John eyed Vivian, "that thing."

Whitney glanced at Vivian. The vampire's nostrils flared as recognition filled her eyes. She hissed and started forward with her fangs out. Whitney scrambled backward. As she tried to get out of the way, she knocked into her grandmother, nearly toppling them both.

"Never forget to whom you speak!" Myers snapped.

Everyone froze. The air crackled with power. No one said a word.

"You have come to me. You do not make demands. Know this: if you disrespect anyone in my house, I will let them gut you where you stand."

Whitney blinked. The world suddenly seemed a lot darker. She had never seen this side of her beloved boss before. Kind and nurturing wasn't supposed to come with teeth and claws.

Without another word, Mrs. Myers turned and entered the house, brushing past Vivian.

Whitney looked from Vivian to the Hares and back again. Although she looked ready to rip the Hares to shreds, Vivian seemed to be in control. The Hares just looked shocked. Elizabeth poked her granddaughter in the back, prodding her forward, but instinct kept Whitney from stepping in between a predator and its prey.

Finally, Vivian turned and walked away. John and Barbie hurried after her.

As Sandra and Whitney stepped into the house, Sandra said, "Damn."

Whitney blew out a long breath. "Yeah." As they passed the living room, Whitney could see Cherry lounging in front of the TV, watching a reality show about fashion.

Whitney shook her head, getting that double vision thing again: scary monsters and normal life. She sighed. *How's a person supposed to live like this?*

They found Mrs. Myers in the dining room. Sandra plopped the stack of files down on the table with a bang and started to leaf through them.

"I'll bring us some coffee," Mrs. Myers said as she walked into the kitchen.

An awkward silence settled over the room until Whitney turned to her grandmother.

"Where did you go when the cops took me to the back?" Her grandmother had tried to follow her into the back halls of the police department, but they wouldn't let her.

"I was about to go home and find a lawyer, but Mrs. Myers called me on my cell phone. She told me to come directly here instead. That she was sending someone to handle the situation," Elizabeth said. Her grandmother poked the floor with her cane. "I'm sorry I wasn't more help."

"Don't feel bad. I always feel like I'm running to catch up around here."

"Myers knew what to do." The bitterness in Elizabeth's voice surprised Whitney.

"Oh, Grammy!" Whitney hugged her. "Believe me, being experienced at this kind of thing is not something you ever want to get."

"I should hope not!"

Sandra looked up from the file she was reading and asked Whitney, "Where did you get these?"

"Police station. An FBI agent named Milner had them."

"FBI!" Elizabeth stared at her granddaughter. "Whitney Elizabeth Martindale! As if getting arrested by the police wasn't bad enough, now you are involved with the FBI?"

"It's not my fault, Grammy!"

"She's right," Sandra stared at the older woman. "These files are from all over the country. They document multiple attacks by, and I quote, 'unnatural predators'. I think this Milner guy might have proof of the Races' existence."

THE LOSING SIDE

HAMILTON STOOD AT THE window, watching the cars file past on the noisy street. It nearly drowned out the sound of Cody's moans. One by one, the streetlights flickered on. Hamilton sighed and turned away from the view.

His second-floor studio apartment was tiny at the best of times, but now it seemed downright claustrophobic. He walked over to the futon and looked down at his friend. Cody shivered in his sleep. Cody was already using every blanket in the apartment. Hamilton looked around and then retrieved his coat from the closet by the door and tucked it around his friend's shoulders.

The bullet wound Cody had received during their adventures in the nightclub wasn't healing right. For nearly a day after that fiasco, Cody had tossed and turned, locked in a fever. None of the normal medical treatments had had any effect on the infection, and Hamilton was starting to worry.

He had left messages for Philtzer and Thomas, but they hadn't called back. As a last resort, he had called Dr. Kirkland. He wasn't particularly fond of Kirkland, but he was a member of the Races, and he couldn't exactly take Cody to a regular doctor. The doc had promised to come by after his shift, so there was nothing to do but wait and think.

The conversation with Myers rolled around in his mind. He had never seen the Weaver lose her composure before. It was a little unnerving. And all that raving about the number seven? What did she expect him to do? He had no idea how to find Jeff Munroe again. They'd barely found him the first time.

Hamilton sighed and wandered over to the little L-shaped section that was supposed to be the kitchen, but was really just a stove, sink, and refrigerator shoved into the corner. He opened the cupboard above the sink and looked at the boxes and cans. He reached for a box of macaroni and cheese but stopped. He tilted his head, listening. The hair on the back of his neck prickled.

Slowly, he stepped back around the corner and tiptoed toward the door. He looked through the peephole. There were several men in the hallway. Hamilton squinted; they had guns. He reared back from the door; it was the men from the club. Quietly and quickly, Hamilton turned and dashed for the futon. He shook Cody awake, covering his friend's mouth to silence his protest.

He whispered, "We have to go! Now!"

Cody blinked, trying to focus.

Hamilton hauled Cody out of the pile of blankets and shoved him toward the windows. He yanked on the cord to pull the blinds up, but only one side worked. He shoved them out of the way and slid the window open.

Through the door, Hamilton heard a gun cock. They were out of time.

Muttering a silent apology, he hoisted an incoherent Cody through the window. At the same moment, gunfire erupted behind him, splintering the front door.

Hamilton jumped out the window, landing on Cody in the bushes below. Above them, the gunfire stopped.

Knowing they only had seconds before their attackers figured out where they'd gone, Hamilton scrambled to his feet, grabbed Cody, and tried to lift him.

"Dammit!" Hamilton snarled. "Why does everybody have to be bigger than me?"

Adrenaline coursed through him as he heard the rattle of window blinds above them. Hamilton dragged Cody out of the bushes and struggled to get him into a fireman's carry. He staggered under the weight but managed to get to Cody's pickup. A bullet whizzed by as he yanked the truck door open.

Hamilton glanced back to see one of the men hanging out the window of his apartment with his gun aimed right at them. Hamilton ducked as the man fired again, but none of the bullets came close. He was either the worst shot ever, or he was just trying to keep them pinned until the others got down to the street.

Not wanting to wait and find out, Hamilton pushed and shoved until Cody was in the passenger seat. He dashed around the front of the truck, nearly getting hit by a passing car as he tried to reach the driver's door.

Hamilton dared a glance toward the apartment as he cranked the ignition. The men were running across the lawn, making a beeline straight for the truck. Hamilton ducked as a bullet shattered the passenger window. More bullets clanged against the side of the truck.

Cody muttered and tried to sit up.

"Stay down!" Hamilton shouted as the truck finally roared to life. He peeled out of the parking spot and sped down the street.

Cody picked at the broken glass in his lap. "What'd you do to my truck?"

Hamilton glanced in the rearview mirror as he drove. "Had air conditioning installed."

When Cody didn't respond, Hamilton glanced over. His friend had passed out again. Hamilton shook his head.

They had to find somewhere safe. He thought for a moment and then drove toward downtown. As he got closer to where Thomas lived, he slowed. Fire trucks and emergency vehicles had blocked off the street. Hamilton pulled over and stopped. The middle of the block glowed orange. Flames and smoke billowed out from Thomas' apartment building.

Hamilton pulled out his phone as he watched the chaos. Thomas didn't answer, so he left a voicemail. "Thomas! Don't go home! Your place is on fire!"

Hamilton hung up and dialed Philtzer. "Come on, Philtzer! Answer!"

"Philtzer's phone," a woman's voice answered.

He breathed a sigh of relief. "Sophia? Where are you?"

"On our way back from Wyoming. You okay? You sound freaked?"

"I am. Tell Philtzer not to go home." Hamilton glanced around. "My place got blasted to bits, and Thomas' place is an inferno."

"Oh, geez!"

Silhouetted against the glare of the fire trucks' flashing lights, Hamilton saw two men walking toward Cody's pickup. One reached into his jacket and pulled out a pistol.

"Tell Philtzer to meet me at that place where Cody punched the bull," Hamilton said in a rush and then dropped the phone onto the seat. Slamming the truck into gear, he sped away.

***

An hour later, Philtzer's rented SUV pulled in next to Cody's pickup in the parking lot of the Saddleback Steakhouse. Hamilton glanced at Cody. He was still sleeping. Hamilton slipped out of the pickup, gently closing the door so he wouldn't disturb his friend.

Sophia got out first and looked around. "Sorry we took so long. He couldn't remember where this place was."

Hamilton nodded. "We were all pretty drunk that night."

Regina and Kyle got out and came around the front of the SUV.

Philtzer grinned and heaved himself out of the car. "Not so drunk that I'd forget Cody punching that thing." He pointed toward the eight-foot-tall fiberglass bull standing under the Saddleback Steakhouse sign.

Kyle eyed the large chunk missing from the bull's nose. "Wow."

Hamilton noticed all the bandages on Philtzer and Regina.

"You all look like Hell," Hamilton said.

"You're pretty too, Hamilton," Regina snorted. "Now, how about you tell us why the cloak and dagger routine?" She looked past him. "And why there're bullet holes in that truck."

Hamilton filled them in. "Cody was nuts on pixie magic. Someone caught it on camera. On top of that, he got shot, and he's not healing."

Sophia looked toward the pick-up where Cody was sleeping. "That's weird."

"There's more." Hamilton told them about the invasion at his apartment and the fire at Thomas' place.

"Somebody likes fire," Regina snorted.

At Hamilton's confused look, Sophia explained. "They tried to burn us out of Kyle's house too." Sophia hooked a thumb toward the sullen teenager leaning against the side of the SUV.

"Yeah, but we managed to get out." Philtzer shrugged, wincing.

"After they had nearly killed us," Sophia snorted.

"We're not the only ones," Hamilton nodded. "While I was waiting for you, I called some of the others. We've lost about fifty percent of the targets from Rami's list. Either they're already gone or dead. I couldn't get a hold of a lot of our people. They could be dead. The ones I managed to talk to said their places had been hit too."

Philtzer rubbed his bandaged neck. "We need to regroup."

"How?" Hamilton gestured vaguely toward the city. "There is nowhere for us to go. Cecilia is trying a full-frontal assault. She's never done that before."

"Do we go back to InfiniCorp?" Sophia asked.

"Nah, it'll be cleared out by now. We'll take Cody to Dr. Kirkland and get our wounds seen to." He looked at Hamilton. "Meanwhile, you go check in with Myers."

"You think Cecelia will attack Myers too?" Sophia asked.

Regina snorted. "I wouldn't put anything past that psycho bitch."

"Seems to me we might be on the losing side," Kyle said.

"Yeah?" Regina yanked open the car door. "Well, I ain't staying on the losing side."

CRUMBLING

"I BELIEVE THAT WE have much to discuss," Mrs. Myers said as she came back into the room with a tray full of steaming mugs.

"Yeah, starting with these files," Sandra said, leafing through another stack of papers.

"Starting with why you decided to bring Hares to my house!" Mrs. Myers snapped.

Sandra flinched and looked at her.

Whitney's stomach went through the floor.

Myers' eyes glowed. "Sandra, you have been allowed your freedom, but that does not include inviting the enemy into my home."

Sandra swallowed hard. "I'm sorry. They said they could help catch Cecelia faster. Isn't that the goal?"

"It is, but I will ask you to remember that you are here by our good graces. Do not presume too much."

"Mrs. Myers," Whitney whispered, "she was just trying to help."

As she turned to Whitney, the glow in her eyes dissipated. "I understand her motives, but neither of you understands the extent of the animosity between the Races and the Hares."

Sandra took a deep breath and said, "History aside, I think you should at least listen to them. They know a lot more than you do about Cecelia's main goal. They told me quite a lot before the police showed up and started searching InfiniCorp's offices."

"They what?" Whitney gaped.

"That's what I was trying to tell you about these files." Sandra held up a folder. "They are onto the Races."

The Weaver didn't look surprised, but she stood and came to look at the files anyway. Long moments passed as Myers leafed through Agent Milner's research.

"This just keeps getting worse." Elizabeth looked at her granddaughter.

"I know." Whitney rubbed her face. "I disappeared out of a police interrogation room. I'm pretty sure they have a warrant out for me by now."

Elizabeth grabbed her granddaughter's hand. "I think you should get away from these people before your life is completely destroyed."

"Grammy, I'm already in this too far." She gestured at Sandra. "We can't go back to a normal life."

"I'm afraid you can't either, Mrs. Martindale," Myers said as she set down the file she was reading.

"What do you mean?"

"The FBI mentions you in the files as a connection to Whitney. If you go home, they will be on your doorstep in a heartbeat."

Elizabeth tapped the floor with her cane. "But that is my home! My whole life is there!"

"I am sorry."

A loud commotion from the hallway, followed by a shout of "Myers!" had everyone on their feet.

"Thomas?" Whitney jumped up and dashed for the hall but skidded to a stop when she reached the doorway.

Thomas had his arm around Unkhabami's waist, supporting her. The Priestess panted as they staggered forward. Her eyes were sunken, and her skin was more gray now than dark brown. Gloria followed them in, carrying a backpack. Quiet and honest, Gloria had always been there to help. She was one of the few witches that Whitney had met since starting at InfiniCorp.

Mrs. Myers pushed past Whitney and rushed to the Priestess' side. "What happened?"

"Ghouls," Unkhabami huffed.

"Ghouls?" Whitney frowned. "What's a ghoul?"

"A creature of darkness. It feeds on corpses," Gloria said as she squeezed past Whitney into the dining room and pulled out a chair for Unkhabami.

"Come on, just a bit more." Thomas practically carried her the last few feet. He carefully set her down in the chair.

"You look awful," Elizabeth said.

"I am healing," Unkhabami said without inflection.

"How did you come across a ghoul?" Myers fussed as she checked Unkhabami's temperature.

The Priestess waved her away. "My village was attacked. Everyone was infected."

"Infected?" Sandra asked.

"A ghoul's bite creates another ghoul," Gloria said as she dug through her backpack and pulled out a dark green bottle. She popped the cork and handed it to Unkhabami.

The Priestess drank slowly. A bit of her normal color returned.

Thomas stood with his hands on his hips. "Cecelia laid a trap in Unkhabami's village. Only a few of the children survived."

"This will not go unpunished!" Unkhabami hissed. "She has taken my home!"

Elizabeth exchanged a loaded look with Sandra, but more noise from the hallway stopped her from speaking.

"Now what?" Myers sighed.

Whitney, who was still standing in the doorway, turned to find Hamilton coming in through the door.

"Sorry to barge in," Hamilton said as he came closer. His face lit up. "Thomas! You're okay! I take it you got my message?"

"Yeah, I didn't get it until about ten minutes ago." Thomas shrugged. "I was dodging the police after they invaded Infini-Corp, but then Gloria called to come help her with Unkhabami at the airport."

"Unkhabami?" Hamilton sobered.

"In there." Whitney hooked a thumb over her shoulder.

They moved past her into the dining room to find Myers and Unkhabami in a heated discussion.

"There cannot be an eighth Weaver!"

"What does it matter?" Unkhabami shook her head.

"I have seen things coming!" Mrs. Myers snapped.

"As have I!" Unkhabami glared at her.

"We must find this man!"

"And do what with him?"

Myers glanced at their curious audience.

"Children, please excuse us. We must speak privately." She waited expectantly, but when no one moved, she began to shoo each of them back out the door.

Sandra wasted no time getting out of her way. She scooped up the files and practically ran for the door. Elizabeth was the last out. As soon as she hobbled through the doorway, the door slammed shut behind her.

"That was weird." Thomas looked at Hamilton. "What's she so freaked out about?"

Hamilton cringed. "Long story."

Sandra edged up to Whitney. "What's the deal? Who is she?"

"Unkhabami is a High Priestess of the Paka Watu. They're were-cats, and she's some sort of medicine woman," Whitney explained. "She tells the future and does actual magic. She's the one who helped Madraeus find us in the mine."

"So, she's not exactly a Weaver like Mrs. Myers then?" Sandra glanced toward the closed door.

Thomas looked up from his quiet conversation with Hamilton. "Nope. More hands on."

"And scarier," Hamilton added.

"Seems to me that everyone around here is," Elizabeth muttered.

"Part of the fun." Thomas winked at her.

"Don't wink at me, boy," Elizabeth harrumphed. "It's rude!"

"I think we have bigger problems," Thomas laughed.

"Speaking of bigger problems..." Sandra pointed to the files.

"What are those?" Hamilton asked, walking over to look at them.

"FBI files that we stole from police interrogation." Whitney crossed her arms.

"Damn, girl!" Thomas poked her in the shoulder. "You been having fun again?"

"This is a problem." Hamilton glanced around the group. "Almost all of us are listed in here."

Whitney hugged herself. "So? What do we do?"

Thomas shrugged. "Stick to plan A: get the hell out of Dodge."

"What about the bunnies?" Sandra murmured to Whitney.

Thomas looked from Sandra to Whitney and back again. "What bunnies?"

"Funny story..." Whitney laughed uncertainly.

"Whitney?" Thomas' voice held all the warning and exasperation that Madraeus' voice usually did when she'd done something stupid. "Start talking."

18TH CENTURY EUGENICS

Thomas stormed down the hall.

"Thomas?" Whitney trotted to keep up with him. "What are you gonna do?"

He didn't answer.

They found Vivian standing with her back to the door of the game room. Her arms were crossed, and she was glaring at the wall.

"Viv? You okay?" Hamilton asked.

She curled her lips and snarled at him.

"So, that's a no." Whitney backed up a little.

Vivian shoved away from the wall. "Those bastards shouldn't even be allowed to live, much less be given safe passage!"

Thomas laid a hand on her arm. "Honestly, once I get some info out of them, I don't give a crap whether you eat them or skin them."

Vivian nodded and turned to open the door, missing the worried look that Sandra sent Whitney.

They found the two Hares pacing around the pool table.

"It's about time!" John snapped. "Where is the Oracle?"

"She's a bit busy at the moment," Thomas said with a pleasant smile. "Now, what's so important that you walked into the wolf's den?"

Whitney glanced at him, wondering what he was up to. He knew exactly why the Hares had come; Sandra had filled them in on everything that John and Barbie had said.

John glanced at Sandra. "We came because we have a common goal: stopping Cecelia from freeing Apep."

"You came because you're scared!" Vivian scoffed.

"I'll admit that," Barbie agreed. "I'm terrified, but scared or not, we have to stop her from getting to Apep."

"Where is Apep now?" Whitney asked.

John and Barbie exchanged a look.

"Where?" Thomas asked again.

Despite John shaking his head, Barbie answered, "Devon. It's in the UK."

"So, how close is Cecelia to getting there?" Whitney asked.

"I'd say pretty damn close." Sandra held her phone out to Whitney. The image showed Rami's map of red pins. "That little cluster is Devon."

Sandra turned to Barbie. "You know where Cecelia is going, and you already have Apep imprisoned. Tell them what you told me. Tell them why you really came."

"We need reinforcements," John admitted grudgingly.

"We need your boss, Madraeus Ravilla," Barbie added vehemently. "He's the only one who can even remotely stand up to Cecelia. There are so few of us left that we can't protect the Key on our own."

"What Key?" Hamilton pounced on that detail.

"Barbie!" John hissed, warning her not to give them too much information, but she ignored him.

"The Key to the trap. It's a girl."

"Wait, what now?" Sandra frowned.

"Barbie!" John grabbed her arm.

"In for a penny, in for a pound, John. I'll tell them anything they ask if it will save lives." Barbie shook his hand off and leaned on the pool table. "It's a spell. It's complicated, and I don't really understand it, but there is a ring around the entrance to the trap. It's made from blood."

Sandra wrinkled her nose. "Eww."

"Wait," Thomas held up his hand, "if we are going to discuss the particulars of a spell, I want someone who understands magic." He left the room.

"Hello, Gloria," Hamilton smiled at the short, red-haired witch as she followed Thomas back into the room. She blushed as she shyly returned his smile, making her freckles more prominent. Gloria glanced around the room, her eyes staying on John for a few seconds longer than anyone else.

Thomas gestured to Barbie. "Please continue."

"I was saying that there is a binding circle around the entrance to Apep's prison. It's made from the blood of the Key."

Gloria nodded her understanding, although she had a repulsed expression on her face.

"You said the Key was a girl!" Whitney accused.

"Yes, but don't worry," Barbie held her hand up to stop Whitney from jumping to the wrong idea, "she's alive."

"At least she was when we left," John mumbled.

Thomas glanced at him.

"Apep can't cross the threshold of the prison as long as the Key is alive," Barbie explained.

"How long has Apep been imprisoned?" Gloria asked, watching them carefully.

"We caught him in 1794," John replied.

"1794!" Whitney gasped.

"Wasn't that when the French Revolution was?" Hamilton asked.

"Yes, like I said, Apep likes to cause chaos." Barbie nodded.

"So, how did you manage to keep him in prison from then until now? If you have to have a Key's blood to lock the entrance, did you just keep finding new Keys?" Thomas asked.

"It wouldn't work like that." Gloria shook her head. "The spell is more complicated than that, isn't it?" She looked at Barbie.

"Yes, only the blood that was in the original binding will hold the spell. If you try to replace it, the trap will open. Unless you can re-bind it faster than Apep can get out," Barbie replied.

"And I don't think that's possible." She shuddered. "I think he hovers at the entrance, waiting."

"Then how have you maintained the lock for over two hundred years?" Whitney asked.

John and Barbie exchanged a look. Barbie answered hesitantly, "The Hares made sure the bloodline continued."

"Huh?" Whitney looked around, seeking help to understand.

"The only way to do that is to carefully breed your Key," Gloria said. Her voice was dangerously quiet.

"You set up a eugenics program!" Thomas blurted.

"Sorry," Whitney shook her head, "still not getting it."

"They pick and choose who they want to breed together so they could get the offspring they wanted. One that had the right amount of genetics from the original Key in order to keep the Key pure enough to hold the trap shut," Gloria explained.

"Oh. Eww." Whitney exclaimed when she finally got it. "You guys suck!"

"How can you do that to someone?" Sandra stared right at John. "How can you take away someone's future like that and force them to follow your little breeding plan?"

"We were trying to protect the world!" John gestured wildly.

"You bastards!" Vivian snarled.

"We are not the monsters here!" John rounded on her. "Your kind has done far worse!"

As they argued, Whitney thought about the mine and Cecelia keeping people as cattle. About Justin burning in the sunlight. About Madraeus wiping out sixty-six terrified prisoners. The Races had done terrible things, but to forcefully breed humans was monstrous too.

Barbie slammed her hands down on the pool table, silencing the room. "The reasons why are not the issue! We must protect her *now*! Apep must not be allowed to enter the world again. That's why we need Ravilla."

"Madraeus is already after Cecelia. Why come to us now?" Hamilton asked.

"Because she is getting close, and we need him now. He is running around trying to find out what she is doing. We can supply a shortcut and take him straight to the source."

"If you want to shortcut, why not just go straight to him? Why come to us?" Gloria asked.

"Because they know that he will kill them before they have a chance to ask," Thomas scoffed.

"Exactly!" John sneered.

Whitney watched him closely. There was something off about him, but she couldn't put her finger on what. Maybe it was just that he was a crazy-conspiracy, secret-society nutball, but she doubted it.

"That's why we need you." Barbie looked at Whitney.

"Me?" Whitney squeaked.

DUTY AND DESTINY

"You're the key," Barbie nodded, "to getting Madraeus to listen."

"Oh, no. I don't think that's a good idea." Whitney shook her head and backed up with her hands out to ward off their crazy ideas. "He's not gonna listen to me."

"We believe he will." John turned his slimy glare on Whitney. "He's never kept a mortal around as long as he has you. He's gone to a lot of trouble for you."

"No, he hasn't!"

"Yes, he has. The Loop, the police, the mine. He's gone through a lot to keep you close and safe." John smiled like he had finally gotten his finger on the pin of a live grenade.

Whitney shuddered. She didn't want to think about Madraeus and how he felt about her. She didn't want to think about how she felt about him either. Not now, not after all those people in the mine. She started to shake. Her breath came in short gasps.

Someone knocked on the door, making her jump. Hamilton turned to open it. Unkhabami came in, supported by Mrs. Myers and Elizabeth.

The Priestess' glance fell on Barbie and John. Her eyes narrowed, and her lip curled. "You defy the sanctity of the Oracle's house."

"Bami, please," Mrs. Myers warned quietly. "I have allowed them entrance."

"Then you are a fool!" Unkhabami turned her feral stare on the older woman.

"We have come for knowledge," John smiled smugly.

Barbie glanced at him and then back at Unkhabami. "We've come for help."

"Help?" Unkhabami bared her fangs. "You do not deserve help!"

"But you are going to help us." John took a step toward Whitney. "One way or another."

"Back off!" Thomas stepped in front of Whitney, shielding her with his body.

"Stay out of this!" John wrinkled his nose. "Stinking werewolf!"

"Not cool!" Whitney shouted.

John stepped forward again, and Thomas growled.

Hamilton grabbed Thomas' arm. "Settle down!" He looked around at everyone. "We are under the gun here, kids."

Barbie jabbed John with her elbow. "He's right. Enough is enough!"

John shot her an annoyed glance. Thomas turned away and leaned against the wall.

While everyone was taking a moment to calm down, Sandra asked, "Exactly what do you think is going to happen if we don't help?"

"War." John smiled smugly as if he wasn't entirely against the idea.

"War?" Elizabeth gasped.

Thomas muttered, "Supernatural World War number who-knows-what."

Elizabeth turned to stare at the werewolf. "There have been more of these wars?"

"Oh yeah," Thomas crossed his arms, "thousands."

"Then why doesn't anyone know about them?"

"Everyone knows," Hamilton chuckled. "Pick any historical conflict, that's probably us."

"I don't understand." Elizabeth frowned at him.

"Myths, legends, all the great battles from history." Hamilton shrugged. "The Races and the Hares were there."

"And therefore, so was Apep, in reality or through his creations. He thrives on chaos," Barbie explained. "There is real truth there under all the details. You'll find Apep or one of his forms in most cultures. The Landon, the serpent in the Garden of Eden, the Midgard Serpent, the Leviathan, Kukulkan. You know, snake mythology is really very prevalent."

"You need a new hobby," Sandra said.

"This isn't a hobby!" John snapped.

"No, your hobby is hunting down innocent people and killing them!" Vivian snarled.

"There's nothing innocent about you monsters!" John shot back.

Barbie grabbed his arm. "John. Please!"

John shook her off and glared at Whitney. "Are you going to help us or not?"

"You are getting a bit too pushy!" Elizabeth rounded on John, and then looked around the room. "She is under no obligation to do anything for you people!"

"She has no choice!" John crossed his arms and glared at Whitney.

"I wasn't talking to you." Elizabeth barely glanced at him.

"Grammy, please!" Whitney rubbed her face really hard. She looked from John to her grandmother and sighed. "I don't know what else to do. If there really is a chance that we can stop Cecelia from freeing Apep, isn't that enough reason to help?"

"Why can't it be Thomas, or Philtzer, or Rami? Why you?" Her grandmother looked close to tears. "You aren't ready for some kind of supernatural war."

"Neither is the world," Barbie said quietly. "I know that it's hard to think of your granddaughter going into such an insane and fantastical situation, but think of what she has already been through. Why not let her see it through to the end?"

"I am thinking of what she's been through already." Elizabeth shook her head. "Madraeus has already put you in danger too many times."

"He isn't the one who put me in danger. He's saved my life again and again."

"You shouldn't go because you feel like you owe him!" Elizabeth punctuated her protest by stabbing the floor with her cane.

"It's not like that." Whitney grabbed her grandmother's hand.

Hamilton leaned forward. "This is about saving the world, Mrs. Martindale."

"But she's just a child!" Elizabeth squeezed Whitney's hand.

"She's not a child," Mrs. Myers said.

"We have seen the destruction that is coming, and Whitney has always been the bright spot of hope," Unkhabami spoke from behind Mrs. Myers. "She has always been the key."

Sandra gave a short laugh. "No pressure."

Whitney looked around the room. Everyone was staring at her.

"I'm sorry, Whitney, but you are the best hope for the world," Barbie said.

"I don't wanna be the best hope for the world," Whitney whined. "I'll mess it up."

"You've done fine so far," Hamilton grinned.

"Are you even in the same whacked-out story as the rest of us?" Whitney gaped at Hamilton, making him laugh.

"Whether you like it or not, you are the best candidate," Barbie reasoned. "He won't listen to a mortal—"

"I'm a mortal!"

"But you're different," Barbie said.

"They're right, Whit, Madraeus... he seems to..." Thomas hesitated, not knowing exactly how to say that they were all pretty sure Madraeus was in love with her.

"Don't say it! I don't want..." Whitney held up her hands, pleading with her eyes. "I can't!"

"It'll be simple." Thomas stepped forward. "You walk up to Madraeus, say 'yo, the bunnies have a shortcut to Cecelia', and then walk away. What he does after that is up to him."

Knowing she was outnumbered, Whitney sank into a chair and said, "Fine. Let's go talk to Madraeus."

"Cool." Thomas clapped his hands together. "I'll make the flight arrangements."

"Wait, flight arrangements?" Whitney's head shot up. "Why?"

"Madraeus left for Europe a couple days ago."

"Ah, crap," Whitney whimpered and let her head fall onto the table with a bang. "Ow."

"Can't you just call him?" Elizabeth asked.

"No!" John said with a gleam in his eye. "We must see him face to face."

Thomas narrowed his eyes, glaring at John suspiciously.

"Saves time." Sandra shrugged. "That's where we have to go anyway. Devon is in the UK, remember?"

John reached out to grab Whitney's arm. "I would feel better if Whitney came with us."

Thomas knocked his hand away. "I don't remember asking how you felt."

"How dare you!" John fumed.

"Look, if you want our help, you're going to have to do it our way." Thomas poked him in the chest. "That's the only way this is going to work. We'll talk to him and then call you."

John opened his mouth to argue, but Barbie cut him off. "He's right, John. The whole point was to get them to bring Madraeus. We can't dictate how that happens."

Whitney watched John. He looked as if he wanted to scream at Barbie, but he swallowed his vitriol.

"Very well," John turned and stalked to the door, "we will await your call."

Thomas looked at Vivian and jerked his chin toward the door. She curled a lip but nodded and followed the Hares to escort them out. Thomas turned to speak to Hamilton.

Sandra watched them leave and whispered to Whitney. "They're intense."

"At least you aren't their trophy prize," Whitney muttered.

Elizabeth came forward to speak to her granddaughter, but before she could, Unkhabami screamed and collapsed onto the floor.

"Unkhabami, what is it?" Mrs. Myers bent over her, trying to help but not finding the cause of the other woman's distress.

"Rami!" The name was dragged from her throat. "Rami..."

"What about Rami?" Thomas was on his knees in front of her, grabbing her elbows and pulling her upright.

Tears streamed down Unkhabami's ashen face. Her eyes were glazed over, fixed on the scene playing out in her mind. "No!"

"Priestess!" Thomas shook her.

Her gaze slowly focused on the young werewolf's face.

"He will fall."

"What?"

"We must go now!" Unkhabami shuddered. "He cannot die!"

FORK IN THE ROAD

While Unkhabami was bombarded with questions, Hamilton's phone rang. He flipped it open, turning pale as he listened. He snapped it shut and looked at Thomas.

"That was Marcus, he's monitoring the police bands. FBI and Denver police are gonna raid us."

"What?" Mrs. Myers shoved to her feet. "My house?"

Sandra shook her head. "Told you Milner was onto you."

Outside, they could hear the sirens approaching.

"Cherry!" Myers dashed out the door and down the hall.

The pink pixie poked her head out of the living room.

"We need time!"

Cherry rolled her eyes and snapped her fingers. Pink glitter shimmered in the air. Whitney stopped and listened: all sound outside the house had stopped. It was just like at the police department.

Thomas shouted. "Clean house!"

Vampires and werewolves dashed through the house, removing all evidence that they had been there.

Myers took Sandra by the elbow. "You and Whitney, go get your things."

Sandra gaped at her. "We don't have that much time!"

Myers glanced at Cherry. "Yes, we do. But don't take too long."

Whitney and Sandra sprinted up the stairs. Cherry stood in the center of the entryway with her eyes closed. A cloud of pink glitter swirled around her.

Minutes later, as Whitney and Sandra thundered down the stairs with their bags, Whitney heard Cherry's shaking whisper, "I can't hold it much longer."

"Time's up!" Whitney shouted.

Mrs. Myers held the door as Thomas carried Unkhabami out, followed by Elizabeth.

"Will you be all right?" Whitney asked.

"Yes, dear." Mrs. Myers gazed back at her calmly. "I've been doing this for over two thousand years. Now, go on, and good luck."

As they dashed to the cars, Whitney marveled at the sparkling pink air. Her inner child wanted to giggle at the existence of pink pixie magic, but the adult in her was terrified that it existed at this magnitude. She said a silent thank you that Cherry was on their side.

Gloria, Unkhabami, and Thomas were already leaving in Gloria's car. There was no sign of Vivian. Whitney jumped into

Hamilton's rental car with Sandra and Elizabeth. As soon as she shut the door, Hamilton sped out of Myers' driveway. Not more than fifty yards from the house, they met a line of police cars frozen in time. The red and blue glare from their light bars illuminated the dust cloud kicked up by their tires.

"There's something you don't see every day," Sandra muttered, looking back at the line of cars.

"Disturbing," Elizabeth muttered.

Whitney sank down in the back seat. She had caught sight of Agent Milner and Detective Sanders in one of the cars as they had passed. Whitney closed her eyes and prayed. If Cherry's magic didn't hold, the police would arrest her and probably cart her friends off to some scary place that only conspiracy theorists knew about. They wouldn't be able to save Rami, Apep would get out, and the world would be destroyed. She wanted to cry. It was all just too much.

Behind them, the night erupted with the sound of sirens. Whitney twisted around in a panic, but then realized that Cherry must have released her hold on time. Whitney sagged in relief as she watched the police continue on toward Myers' house.

Sandra turned and tapped Hamilton on the shoulder. "Where are we going?"

Elizabeth said, "I suggest we go home before anything else can go wrong."

"Easy for you," Sandra snorted, "you're not wanted or dead."

"Dead?" Elizabeth sat forward.

"Yeah," Sandra looked at her, "I'm dead, remember?"

"Well, I'm not. I want to go home." Elizabeth sat back and crossed her arms.

They drove in silence for a while until Hamilton's phone rang.

"Yep. Yep." As he answered, Hamilton glanced at Whitney in the mirror. "Yep."

Whitney leaned forward, wondering what they were saying about her.

"Right." Hamilton hung up and stuffed the phone back into his pocket.

Ahead of them, Gloria's car veered off onto a side street.

"Where are they going?" Whitney asked.

When Hamilton didn't answer, Whitney glanced at Sandra. She shrugged.

"Well?" Elizabeth leaned forward.

"Well, what?" Hamilton asked, watching traffic.

"Don't be cagey, boy. Tell us what is happening."

"I'm taking you to your house." Hamilton glanced at her in the mirror.

"You're taking us home?" Whitney asked. "Didn't we just decide that wasn't going to work?"

"Yes, but I'm taking Mrs. Martindale home."

"What about Whitney?" Elizabeth asked suspiciously.

"Whitney's with us."

"No, she's not. This insanity has gone on long enough!" Elizabeth snapped. "You can drop us both off, and we'll sort this out ourselves!"

Whitney looked up and noticed Hamilton watching her in the rear-view mirror. He didn't say anything, but she knew he was waiting for her decision.

"I don't think I can," Whitney whispered.

"Why? Because of all this nonsense about being the only one who can help? Because Myers and Unkhabami say you should?" Elizabeth snapped. "They are manipulating you!"

"They've been right so far," Whitney muttered.

"That's coincidence!"

"But what if they are right?" Sandra asked, turning to peek over the seat. "What if she really is the key to stopping Apep from starting World War III? Shouldn't she at least try?"

Whitney looked from Sandra to Elizabeth. It was all too real again. She was staring down two roads, one with monsters and one blissfully ignorant of that reality. In that moment, she wanted more than anything to go back down the road where she didn't know about the Races. But it wasn't possible.

"I'm sorry, Grammy." Whitney felt tears running down her cheeks, and she was thankful that the darkness hid her pain. "I have to try."

"You are making a mistake. Your life has been nothing but one crisis after another since you got mixed up with these people."

"It started before that," Whitney said. "Cecilia turned Justin before I worked at InfiniCorp."

"You know what I mean." Elizabeth dismissed Whitney's logic with a wave of her hand. "I almost lost you. What if I never see you again?"

She wanted to tell her grandmother not to worry, that she would be fine. But she knew it wasn't true. She had been nearly killed by vampires twice already; who knew if her luck would hold?

"It'll be all right, Mrs. Martindale. You don't need to worry," Hamilton said, settling his elbow on the windowsill and holding the steering wheel with one finger. "We have a plan."

"I imagine you do," Elizabeth sneered. "But can you promise me that she'll come back in one piece? Healthy and whole?"

Hamilton shook his head. "No one can promise the future."

"But you want us to listen to people who can supposedly see it," Mrs. Martindale snorted.

"That's different," Hamilton said, but his tone lacked conviction.

They drove in silence until they reached Elizabeth's house. Hamilton approached through the alley just in case the police were watching. Whitney walked with her grandmother through the back yard and up to the porch.

When they reached the back door, Elizabeth grabbed Whitney's hand. "I don't want you to go! I have a terrible feeling about all this."

"Grammy, I don't exactly have a good feeling either," Whitney squeezed her hand, "but I don't feel like there's a choice."

"You have a choice." Elizabeth glanced at Hamilton, who was waiting in the car, and then spoke more quietly. "You could go to the police and explain everything. You said that FBI agent knew about the Races. Why not let them handle it?"

Whitney could only imagine how badly the government would react to a supernatural threat. "I doubt they are equipped to handle vampires, werewolves, and snake demons from ancient Egypt."

"Maybe not, but this is too big for us, for you." Elizabeth shook her head. "I have raised you like my own daughter. I have tried not to dictate your life, but enough is enough. It's time to get help."

"I'm sorry, Grammy, but I can't." Whitney hated what she was about to say. "And if they come to talk to you, I need you to keep the Races' secret too."

"You can't ask me that. The evils of this world always have a way of slipping around the rules. What's right is right. If they come asking, I will do what's right."

Whitney stared at her grandmother in the dim light from the neighbor's back porch. There was nothing left to say but goodbye. She hugged her grandmother tightly, causing them both to cry.

"Be safe, baby girl," Elizabeth choked out through her tears.

Whitney nodded. With one last hug, Whitney turned and walked back to the car.

AWAKENING DEMONS

Madraeus paced the hotel room. He hated waiting. The flights had been a nightmare. He hated traveling in a coffin. First of all, it was degrading; second, no one treated coffins with any respect. He had been knocked around and slammed against every hard object from Denver to Germany. Unfortunately, there was no alternative. They didn't have time to wait around and take only night flights.

Madraeus glanced again at the curtains, watching as the bright orange glow of the fading sun dimmed. At any moment, he would be able to leave this room and get on with hunting Cecelia. He had been growing more and more impatient as the hours crept by.

Sssoon.

He spun around. His eyes searched the room. He was sure he had heard a voice. Listening carefully, he could hear the sound of cars passing in the street below and the sound of water from Rami's shower, but nothing else. There was nothing there.

He rubbed his eyes. It was happening again. It had been so long since he had been bothered by that whispering voice.

But now, he remembered.

He remembered how it whispered to him in the night when he was hunting. He remembered how it urged him to indulge in every fantasy that came to mind. Long ago, he had put it down to being infected by Cecelia's demon. Once he had parted ways with her, the voice had dimmed, and finally, about two hundred years ago, when he had taken over as Head of the Council, it had faded away.

Now, after all these years, he was hearing it again. He had heard it in the mine when he had exterminated the threat posed by those sixty-six prisoners Cecelia had left behind. It had been quiet, but it was there. A hissing in his mind. He shuddered. Perhaps it was just being around Cecelia again that had triggered it. Maybe it really *was* her demon infecting him again.

He looked at the curtains. The glow of the streetlamps had replaced the glow of the sun. The door opened behind him.

"I will never get used to the small-mindedness of European architects," Rami rumbled as he tried to duck low enough to get through the door.

"They didn't know anyone your size when they built the building." Madraeus smiled at his friend. "Sun's set."

"Finally," Rami sighed.

"So, where are we going?" Madraeus asked as he picked up a long knife that could have been considered a short sword. He slid it into a sheath built into the back lining of his jacket.

"Across town." Rami pulled a folded map from his pocket and showed Madraeus their route. "I did not want to rent a place anywhere near it in case things go awry."

"As if anything ever goes wrong for us." Madraeus shrugged into his jacket, flipping the collar up. It was black and would help him blend with the shadows.

"Oh, never." Rami grinned at him as he pulled on his dark blue wool coat.

Madraeus moved to the door but missed it by a foot and walked into the wall.

Rami stared at his friend. He had never, ever been clumsy.

"Damn it." Madraeus stepped back and rubbed his eyes with a thumb and forefinger.

"What was that about?" Rami asked.

"Nothing," Madraeus growled. "Let's go."

Rami followed him out the door, closing it behind him quietly. Madraeus scowled as they descended the stairs. First, he was hearing that hissing voice; now he was seeing flashes of Whitney. She had been sitting at a table, looking unhappy. The last thing he needed was to start hallucinating about Whitney. He reached the bottom of the steps and walked outside, taking a deep breath to clear his head. He waited for Rami to join him and point him in the right direction.

As they walked through the beautiful German village, he didn't notice the historical architecture or the quaint shops. He also didn't see the lamp post that loomed directly in front of him. He only saw Whitney careening through traffic in a red convertible.

Rami glanced at him, waiting for him to alter his course. Madraeus just kept walking, staring straight ahead. At the last second, Rami shoved him sideways so he wouldn't walk into the post.

Madraeus stumbled to one side. Regaining his balance, he spun and snarled at the giant with his fangs out.

"Ray!" Rami admonished him, glancing around to see if anyone had seen the fangs.

"Why did you shove me?" Madraeus asked, straightening up and retracting his fangs.

"You were going to walk into that post." Rami pointed behind them.

Madraeus looked at the post and then back at Rami. "Oh, thank you."

"Are you all right, my friend?" Rami regarded him curiously.

"I'm fine." He started walking again.

"You are acting very strange."

"I'm fine," he repeated.

"If we are going into battle, I do not wish to die because you cannot avoid lamp posts." Rami glanced at him sideways.

"I'm not going to get you killed." Madraeus stalked ahead of Rami. He didn't want to admit that he was hallucinating, but

Rami had a point. If he couldn't even avoid a lamp post, how was he going to see an enemy coming? Maybe it would just stop.

He slowed his steps a little so he was walking with Rami again. The giant glanced at him but said nothing. They walked in silence for a few blocks.

Madraeus finally asked. "So, what is this place again?"

"Cistercian abbey built in 1200 something, but now it's a psychiatric hospital."

"Fun." Madraeus rubbed his forehead. "What are they doing in a psych hospital?"

"Maybe Cecelia finally figured out that she needs help," Rami chuckled.

"We're not that lucky." Madraeus' eyes followed the winding path of houses up to an ancient stone building. "That it?"

"Yes."

"You think this is recruiting mental patients or some nasty beast?"

"Could be either."

"You know anything more about it?"

"My research said that monks built the monastery, elaborate and beautiful, but as the years progressed, the monks fell into darker and darker activities. They were accused of being lazy drunkards and Godless men, amongst other things."

"Makes me think that Cecelia's looking for a friend," Madraeus mused. "Maybe there was something in the building that was affecting them."

"It's possible." Rami shrugged. "Are you well enough to fight a demon?"

Madraeus glanced at him sharply, wondering if he knew about the hissing voice. "I've recovered from the mine."

"That is not what I meant, and you know it."

Yesss.

Madraeus stopped and pressed his fingers against his temples.

"What is it?" Rami looked at his friend, but then something caught his eye, and he turned to the monastery. "Look." He pointed up at the bell tower.

A blue glow spread outward from the windows of the steeple.

"What the hell...?" Madraeus trailed off.

A sound, reminiscent of a wooden ball rolling around the rim of a metal bowl, emanated from the abbey. It reverberated off the buildings, vibrating back in on itself. Rami held his ears. Madraeus winced against the pain in his head. The light in the bell tower grew brighter. They were too late.

Rami and Madraeus sprinted up the last bit of road to the abbey.

Even at a distance, they could hear the patients inside the psychiatric hospital wailing and screaming from the pain-inducing sound. Rami took the stairs leading up to the main entrance four at a time. Madraeus took them two at a time. Rami rammed into the double oaken doors, knocking them open. They banged back against the walls. Rami and Madraeus looked around. Beautiful carved stone columns reached up to the arched ceiling, and massive leaded-glass windows lined both sides of the building. Orderlies cowered on the floor, covering their ears against the sound. They looked up in terror at the invading giant.

"Bell Tower?" Rami roared. One of the orderlies pointed down an ornate corridor.

As the two vampires raced across the stone floor toward the bell tower stairs, a sound like a tree cracking apart sliced through the ringing. The creaking changed to a crashing as the ceiling below the bell tower collapsed. Timbers and plaster exploded in every direction as the massive bell plunged down through the floors. The whole building shook from the force of the falling bell. As it crashed at the bottom, Madraeus and Rami were knocked to the floor.

Dust billowed outward, dousing the room in a gritty fog. Except for belated bits of debris bouncing away from the pile of timber and metal, the abbey settled into silence.

LET'S ALP AND SPLIT

Madraeus pushed himself up onto his knees and squinted through the haze at Rami. The giant looked gray from the coating of dirt that covered him. Madraeus scrubbed at his hair, sending a cloud of plaster dust flying. "What the hell just happened?"

Rami sat up and coughed, waving his hand in a futile attempt to clear the dust away from his eyes. He coughed again, spitting dirt into the air. "At least the noise stopped."

They climbed unsteadily to their feet and approached what was left of the tower stairs. The stonework around the door had been obliterated. Bits and pieces of the broken floors from above continued to fall, making donging noises whenever they hit the bell.

Madraeus surveyed the pile of rubble. He reached out and brushed the dust from a raised spot on the crown of the fallen bell. The Three Hares symbol was engraved into the metal.

"Rami, look at this." He pointed to the symbol.

"Those damned rabbits again," the giant grumbled as he tried to swipe the dust off his coat.

Madraeus shoved and pushed until he could get past the bell and into the base of the tower. Waving the dust away, he peered into the dimness above them. A keening sound followed by a flash of movement caught his attention. Looking up, he moved sideways but stumbled as he tried to keep his footing on the pile of rubble.

"Rami, there's something up there," he said quietly.

Rami climbed over the debris to join him. Looking up, he followed Madraeus' gaze to where the stairway's second landing used to be. Something crouched there.

"What is that?" Madraeus whispered.

They watched it until it darted out and across to the opposite side of the tower. There wasn't much for it to sit on, forcing it to dart back again.

Rami shifted a little to get a better view. "Looks like an alp."

"A what?"

"It is a creature out of folklore and legend. It is supposed to be the cause of night terrors. A kind of cousin to vampires. They feed off nightmares."

Madraeus gave a short, humorless laugh. "Guess that's why the monks went all loopy."

"Not a great thing to have in a psychiatric hospital either." Rami glanced down the hall. The orderlies were starting to recover and get organized. "We are going to have company soon."

"You've got to be joking." Madraeus glanced at the hospital staff and sighed. "Right. How do we get rid of it?"

"No idea," Rami rumbled, staring up again.

"Great."

"Looks like it's the old-fashioned way." In a sing-song way, Madraeus said, "Lop off the head, and it stays dead."

Madraeus sighed and started to climb. He sprang from broken beam to broken beam. He grabbed onto part of the busted stair railing and hauled himself upward.

Once or twice, the hand-hold he'd found crumbled away, crashing down to join the rest of the debris. As they neared the top of the bell tower, Madraeus climbed faster. Although he wasn't sure what the alp would do when he caught it, he didn't plan on wasting time.

"Hurry!" Rami warned, watching the orderlies point in their direction.

"I'm trying!" Madraeus grunted. Finally, he drew even with the creature where it huddled just under the steeple's window sill. The alp dodged away from him, trying to escape.

Not more than a couple of feet tall, it was a spindly, hunched shadow with a long, pointed face and tall ears. However, the little hat it was wearing made it look almost silly.

"That's interesting," Madraeus muttered, looking at the hat. Suddenly, the thing shifted into a cat. "You didn't tell me it was a shape-shifter!" he snarled down at Rami.

"Is it?"

It shifted again, this time into a pig. Madraeus climbed a little closer. It changed into a dog and growled at him. Madraeus let his fangs extend and snarled back at the alp. It flinched and shifted back to its normal shape. In one smooth movement, Madraeus reached back, grabbed the handle of his knife, drew it clear of his jacket, and swung. The blade hissed through the air and parted the alp's head from its body.

The head fell. It bounced off a piece of railing that was still clinging to the tower wall, arched through the air, ricocheted off the opposite wall, and then landed beside Rami. A moment later, the body joined it.

Rami stared at the body of the alp as it disintegrated. He looked up to see Madraeus descending, but the climb down was not proving as easy as the climb up. Rami glanced over his shoulder at the group of hospital staff that was approaching and grimaced. Just beyond them, he saw that the police had arrived.

"Stay where you are!"

Madraeus froze and looked down.

The police had surrounded Rami and were rattling off questions in German. He knew he had to stay still or they would see him. Unfortunately, Madraeus could feel the wall starting to crumble under his fingers. He had to move. Looking around, he saw a hole in the wall a few feet to his left. He stretched out his hand and managed to grab the hole, but the small piece of timber that he was standing on gave way, dropping his feet into mid-air.

His feet scrambled against the stone, looking for footing. He could hear shouting below him, but he couldn't spare a glance, or he would drop. The sounds of arguing got louder. Madraeus clung to the hole. His foot searched desperately for somewhere to stand.

Then it all went blank. The tower disappeared. He was in an airport hangar. Thomas held out a bundle of papers. As he reached for them, he noticed his hands weren't his hands.

Realizing that he was experiencing another vision of Whitney's future, Madraeus muttered, "Damn Unkhabami and her stupid spells!" He tried to shake the vision, but it wouldn't go away.

Madraeus blindly scrambled against the wall. Finally, his toe found something sticking out. He struggled to get his foot onto it. When he finally felt stable, he blinked until his vision cleared. Looking down, he couldn't see Rami, only a mob of policemen.

Then, from under the dog pile of police, Rami roared and erupted like a volcano, throwing people in every direction. Once free, the giant ran for the door. Some of the officers who were still standing gave chase.

Unfortunately, one of the officers who had landed on his back on the pile of rubble looked up and saw Madraeus. He started yelling and pointing. Two more officers appeared at the bottom of the tower. They looked up, shouted something in German, and began climbing the pile of debris.

Madraeus glanced around and weighed his options. He couldn't go down, but maybe he could make it to the windows higher up in the tower and escape onto the roof. With no other choice, Madraeus started to climb again. He scrambled back up the way he had come, knocking more of the broken stairwell down as he climbed.

Below him, the police cursed and yelled. Lights from their flashlights dodged and bounced across the walls around him. After a few precarious moments, Madraeus gained the window and pulled himself up into the opening.

The abbey stretched out below him. The buildings formed a square around a garden courtyard. About thirty feet below, he could see the roof of the main wing of the abbey. He swung his legs up and over the windowsill and, without hesitation, dropped to the tiles below. Madraeus landed hard, rolled to his feet, and then dashed along the roof toward the front of the building. When he reached the edge, he peeked over, scanning the street.

Emergency vehicles pulled up and parked in every direction. Firefighters and paramedics ran inside with ladders and medical bags. He could see Rami dodging between them and running down the street with half a dozen officers on his tail. Some of the police cars pulled out again and shot down the street after Rami.

"Can't go that way," Madraeus groaned and sprinted back along the roof toward the steeple. He could hear shouts echoing from inside the tower. He veered away from the steeple, sliding down the tiles until he hit the stone rain gutter at the edge. He scrambled up the steep pitch of the next section of roof.

Grabbing onto the ridgepole, he pulled himself over the top and slid down the other side.

This section of the abbey formed an L shape that blocked the light from the street and cast this side of the building into complete darkness. It was as far from the police as he was going to get. He poked his head over the edge of the roof and looked down at the wall of the abbey. He plotted his route and swung over the edge. He had to hurry. It wouldn't take them long to figure out where he had gone.

Madraeus hung from the edge, clinging to the crenellation. He worked his way to a molded archway and then dropped to a brick column that stuck out from the wall. He shimmied down it the best he could until he was close enough to the ground to let go. He dropped to the ground with a grunt. Madraeus glanced around and then sprinted into the darkness of the nearby trees.

THE GET AWAY

Rami ran for his life.

The police were right behind him. He didn't have time to worry about Madraeus or whether or not the body of the alp had fully disappeared. All he could do was try to get away. If he could lose them, he could go back to the little hotel and wait for Madraeus.

If…

Within a couple of blocks, he had already left behind his pursuers, who were on foot. The police cars, however, were another matter. He was fast, but not faster than a car. Physics didn't allow any predator that much of an advantage. Rami dodged down one street, then another. He slipped through an alley and down a passage between two shops. He glanced back but saw no one.

Rami slowly moved to the edge of the walkway but ducked back as a patrol car crept by. Reversing course, Rami made his way back to the alley, only to be stopped by a second car.

He froze when he heard movement: some intrepid officer was checking the passageway.

For a tiny little town, their police force is on the ball, he thought grimly. He glanced around and sighed, *Nowhere to go but up.*

He looked at the walls, braced his feet and hands, and worked his way upward. He shimmied up as quickly and as quietly as he could. Glancing down, he saw the police officer pass directly under him. Rami froze.

Do not look up! he thought desperately. *Do not look up!*

The man flashed his light around as he moved. He stopped and aimed the light behind him for a moment, and then looked up. He caught sight of Rami and shouted.

Rami snarled and scrambled the rest of the way up. He heaved himself over the lip of the tiles, shot to his feet, and raced across the roof. Jumping to the next building, he ran along it. He could hear shouts below him.

Up was bad, he thought. *I should not have gone up!*

He dashed across the rooftops of the connected buildings. Stopping at the ridgepole, he looked around. Across the street was a clump of trees, a field, and the glass roof of what looked like a greenhouse. He skied down the slate to the edge of the roof and jumped.

Landing hard and rolling, he launched himself at the grove just as the police rounded the corner. They shouted and charged after him into the trees. Ahead, past the greenhouse, lay the open field.

Too open, he thought.

Rami sprinted along the side of the greenhouse. He circled back toward the village. Crouching as low as he could behind a rather large bush, he watched several policemen barge past him in the dark. He waited a moment before running back the way he'd come. Several police cars were parked on the street, so he turned and followed the tree line.

Sliding out of the shadows, he dashed across the road. He thought he had made it, but then he heard a shout. Rami started running and dodging again. The police cars were not far behind.

He had turned in a complete circle and was heading back toward the abbey again. Just over the trees, he glimpsed the flashing lights reflecting off the abbey's steeple. He glanced over his shoulder; the cars were gaining. To his right, he saw a wooded area. Hopping over a small cable fence, he ran straight for it.

Rami disappeared into the shadows of the trees and paused. He could see the lights from an ambulance through the greenery. Closer to the abbey than he had first thought, he turned to watch for his pursuers. They had abandoned their car and were following him into the trees on foot. He heard the crackle of their radios. The light beams from their flashlights cut through the trees behind him. He was surrounded.

"Damn," he snarled, realizing they had called in help from the abbey.

Rami turned and dashed through the trees parallel to the abbey's wall. The ground sloped upward as he neared the edge of the village. He could hear the men behind him. Some were shouting at him, but most were saving their breath for running.

Rami ran harder, nearing the edge of town. The tended trees became a jumble of foliage as he plunged into the forest. Behind him, the police shouted, waving their lights. The ground became more uneven and rocky. The trees thinned.

Rami skidded to a halt, nearly falling into the jagged ravine gaping wide before him. He looked down, but mist hung about seventy feet below the edge, obscuring everything. He could hear water roaring far below. A sharp, cold wind slithered up over the edge, making his eyes sting.

Rami glanced back at the police; they had fanned out into a semi-circle and were closing in on his position. Realization dawned. They'd known about the ravine, and now they had him trapped.

He turned toward the coming line of men and let his fangs elongate. His eyes became black orbs. He balanced on the balls of his feet and readied himself to go down fighting.

A tinkling laugh echoed from the ravine. Rami spun toward the sound. A tall woman stood a few feet away from him with her back to the ravine. Her silver-blond hair hung in braids on either side of her head, swaying slightly in the wind. She had her hands clasped behind her back.

"Cecelia!" Rami snarled.

"Oh, Rami, you always were so polite." She pouted. "Should I leave you to your fate and let the police have you?" She looked past him.

"What do you want?"

"Nothing." She smiled sweetly.

Rami glanced back at the approaching line of police officers, wondering if they had noticed Cecelia. Out of the darkness, several men appeared behind the police.

"Look out!" Rami shouted, but it was too late. Cecelia's men had already dispatched the officers.

Rami turned back to Cecelia only to see her bringing her hand from behind her back, holding a small crossbow.

Rami flung his hand up in defense, but it was too late. She had already fired.

The wooden bolt pierced his chest. He crumpled to the ground, gasping as he tried to pull the bolt free.

"Tsk, tsk." Cecelia shook her head. "None of that."

Her men came forward and grabbed his arms, preventing him from reaching the bolt. They dragged him forward. He struggled, but their grip was like iron. All he could do was stare at the edge of the ravine as they dragged him closer and closer.

He snarled, digging his heels in against the ground, but his strength was failing. His heart shuddered and seized.

"Bye-bye," Cecelia giggled as her minions shoved him over the edge.

He plummeted into the misty darkness.

LOST

THE SUN HAD FINALLY set. Madraeus peeked out the window again. He muttered, "Where are you, Rami?"

After the disaster at the abbey, the police had been out in force all night, combing the streets of the village. It had taken Madraeus until dawn to make it back to the hotel safely. But Rami hadn't shown up yet, and that worried him.

He let the curtain drop back into place and paced the room. Time was running out. He knew it was only a matter of time before the police started searching the buildings. He scrubbed his hands through his hair and flopped backward onto the bed.

"I hate waiting."

He closed his eyes, but they popped open immediately as he felt a weight land on him.

"Well, wait no more," Cecelia purred as she straddled his legs and leaned on his chest with crossed arms.

"Cecelia," Madraeus breathed. He could have thrown her off of him with very little effort, but that wouldn't get him answers, so he stayed still.

"Aren't you happy to see me?"

"Happy isn't the word I would use, no."

"Still angry about the mine?"

"Did you think I would feel otherwise?"

"I was doing you a favor." She traced a finger across his lip. "That Whitney would have only brought you heartache. It's good that she's dead now."

"Whitney's not dead."

Cecelia stiffened in surprise but relaxed again. She shrugged as if it were only a minor detail. "You have more restraint than I do. I wanted to kill her the first time I met her, but then again, you've always been sentimental."

"Unlike you."

"That hurts. You know I'm sentimental about you."

"Why are you here?"

"Can't I just pop by to see an old friend?" She smiled, knowing what his answer would be.

"Cecelia..." Madraeus warned with a growl.

"Oh fine." She pushed against his chest and sat up. "You spoiled my fun."

"I'm glad to hear it."

"Hmm." She traced a circle on his chest. "You made such a mess of the abbey."

"I didn't make that mess. You did."

"Why do you assume it was me?" she asked a little too innocently.

"Oh, let's just say a little bunny told me."

"So, you finally figured out the rabbit clues," she smiled. "Took you long enough."

"This game grows tiresome, Cecelia. Why don't you just give it up?"

"Oh no, we aren't near finished yet." She smiled, showing her fangs. "You could join me."

Yesss...

Madraeus flinched as the voice filled his head.

"You know you want to," Cecelia crooned.

Yesss.

He shook his head, trying to banish the voice.

"Especially after you find out what I know."

"And what is that?"

"Rami is dead."

Madraeus sat up quickly, dumping her on the floor. "What?"

"He's dead!" she snarled, picking herself up off the floor and dusting off her pants.

"Liar."

"Am I?" She stopped and looked him in the eye. "I saw him fall."

"Where?" Madraeus stood.

"Those policemen chased him to the ravine at the edge of town. He wanted to fight, but there were too many of them." Her eyes lit with glee as she spoke. "They kept pushing and pushing him back until he was right at the edge. Then they shot him."

Madraeus glared at her.

She shaped her fingers into the guns that killed him and pretended to shoot. "Pew. Pew! He staggered backward and fell." She leaned forward and whispered, "Smashed to pieces on the rocks below."

Madraeus lunged forward and grabbed her by the neck. He marched her backward until she was pinned against the wall. "You lie!"

"Go look. There's blood all over the rocks at the bottom."

Rami'sss blood, the voice taunted him.

He shook his head. He could feel his rage building.

"It's your own fault," she continued. "You left him to fight all those men on his own."

You left him, the voice accused. *You promisssed not to get him killed.*

"I didn't leave him," Madraeus hissed, squeezing her throat.

Cecelia clawed at his hand.

Your bessst friend issss dead, the voice hissed in his mind. *Kill them. They killed Rami.*

Madraeus breathed faster, and his eyes turned black.

Cecelia tried to pry his fingers loose, but he snarled at her. His long, sharp fangs were mere inches from her face. Cecelia brought her knee up, but she missed, smashing it into his hip instead.

It surprised him enough that he lost his grip on her throat. She swung a right hook at his jaw, knocking him sideways. While he tried to regain his balance, she ran for the door.

Madraeus snarled, plunging after her. He yanked the door open, but she was gone.

He slammed the door shut again and braced his hands against it, trying to get his temper under control. He closed his eyes.

Kill them.

Rami'sss blood.

You left him.

They killed him.

The voice just kept hissing, filling his mind and taking over his thoughts. Madraeus pressed the heels of his hands into his temples. Anger and hatred swept through him.

Kill them.

Rip them to piecesss.

Madraeus snarled as his emotions finally boiled over. He burst out of his room and dashed out of the hotel, following the path across town that Rami had taken. The hissing demon in his head seemed to know the way.

Run. Hurry.

Madraeus found his way through the trees to the precipice.

Rami'sss blood.

Casting about, Madraeus found a way to the bottom of the cliff.

Kill them.

Madraeus roared at the voice in his head. It stopped hissing for a moment as he searched along the river's edge. A jumble of boulders stuck up out of the flowing water. Even in the darkness, the smears of blood were still visible. Madraeus' nostrils flared as he caught the scent.

Rami'sss blood.

The voice hissed with glee, *Kill them!*

The world dissolved into shadows. He didn't remember moving, but suddenly, he was emerging from the trees behind the abbey.

He snapped the neck of the first person he saw without missing a step. Someone shouted at him, but Madraeus barely heard it over the hissing laughter in his head. One after another, the police ran at him. He ripped out one man's throat with his bare hands, another went down from a punch. As he stalked to the abbey, he left a trail of bodies behind him, none of them breathing.

Madraeus came around the corner and found a group of police gathered around a map they had spread out on the hood of one of the police cars.

Kill them.

They killed Rami.

Your bessst friend isss dead.

Madraeus roared in rage. The police turned toward him, but he was already on them. He ripped and punched and bit.

Bodies fell.

Blood splattered.

He turned toward the abbey and stalked forward.

Yesss!

Kill them all!

You are mine! The voice hissed triumphantly as Madraeus took his revenge on everyone he could find.

WHAT DOESN'T KILL YOU...

Whitney had been terrified from the moment that Thomas had handed her a fake passport. Although Thomas assured her that he had taken care of all the paperwork, Whitney was convinced that every security guard in the airport was going to arrest her.

As they landed in Frankfurt, Whitney had joked with Sandra that the hard part was over, but then they saw the news. The local television channels were flooded with images of emergency vehicles and lines of body bags. It was obvious that the authorities of the quiet little village in the middle of Germany had no idea what had killed so many people. But one look at Thomas or Hamilton, and Whitney knew; it was someone from the Races. She was also pretty sure that this massacre was related to Unkhabami's vision.

Despite Unkhabami's prophetic abilities, the priestess could not give any more information about the danger to Rami, only that he would fall. Thomas and Hamilton had agreed that if Rami was in danger, then it was likely that Madraeus was too. The simple trip to recruit Madraeus was quickly turning into a rescue mission.

Thomas found them accommodations in a neighboring town, close enough to investigate but not close enough to draw attention. Leaving Unkhabami in the care of Sandra and Whitney, the wolves left to look for Rami and Madraeus.

Whitney had always wanted to visit Europe, but staying locked in a hotel while waiting for bad news was not what she'd had in mind. On top of that, Unkhabami's frantic impatience had not made the stressful wait any easier.

It was nearly dawn when the wolves returned with Rami's mangled and broken body. Whitney and Sandra scrambled to stay out of the way as Unkhabami and the wolves desperately tried to put Rami back together, but the hotel room was too small to get away from the gore and the blood. When he had a moment to spare, Hamilton gave them the keys to the room he shared with Thomas, and they made a hasty exit.

Now, there was nothing to do but wait. Whitney stared out the hotel window at the trees as they swayed slowly in the early morning glow. She hugged her knees a little tighter, trying to block out what she had seen.

Behind her, Sandra flipped through the TV channels.

The streetlamps went dark as the sun rose. Still, they waited.

Sandra ordered room service. After eating very little, Whitney returned to her chair in the corner and watched the trees.

The sun sank. One by one, the streetlamps flickered back to life. Sandra paced, and Whitney stared. They both jumped when the door finally opened.

"Whitney," Hamilton's face was drawn and gray, "Rami wants to speak to you."

She glanced at Sandra, but Hamilton shook his head. "Just you."

Whitney stood slowly and followed Hamilton.

As soon as she walked through the door, she put her hand over her nose. The smell of blood and antiseptics was overwhelming. Hamilton stepped around her and went to the window, shoving it open. He turned and started picking up discarded bloody towels.

On the bed, Rami lay on his back with his eyes closed. Unkhabami sat in the chair on the far side of the bed. Her eyes were closed, but her lips moved silently.

Thomas, who had been sitting on the side of the bed, got up and came over to Whitney. He said quietly, "His blood was on a rock at the bottom of the ravine. We found him about a mile downriver, caught in a drainage culvert."

Whitney wrapped her arms around her waist in a self-soothing gesture. "Is he going to be okay?"

Thomas nodded. "Yeah, Unkhabami is doing her thing," he wiggled his fingers like a magician, "and we both donated some blood. Might take a few days for him to be back to normal, though."

Whitney shivered.

"What happened?"

"Cecelia shot him. But that isn't the worst of our problems."

She looked up at him. "What do you mean?"

"Madraeus." Thomas rubbed his chin. "He's the one that wiped out the town."

In her mind, she saw all those body bags from the news. *All those people! It's the mine all over again.*

She could only whisper, "Why?"

"I don't know," Thomas sighed, "but he is still out there. We need you to stop him."

The room tilted. Thomas caught her.

"Whitney?" Rami's voice was a rasping shadow.

Thomas helped her closer to the bed.

"I am sorry, Whitney," Rami gazed up at her. His eyes were still mottled red from the broken blood vessels. "I know no other way."

Whitney shuddered. She wasn't sure if she had the courage or the strength to walk into that village and confront the raging monster that Madraeus had become.

"I don't think I can do this." The words clawed their way out of her throat, leaving behind shame and fear.

"I have faith in you." Rami winced as he tried to reach for her hand.

"Don't move too much!" She hurried to stop him. She laid her hand on his shoulder, careful to avoid any bandages.

Whitney looked at Unkhabami. Her eyes were still closed, chanting. She looked terrible.

"How do you know he'll stop if he sees me?"

Rami closed his eyes for a long moment before looking back up at her. "I cannot guarantee anything, Fair Maiden, but I do know that he loves you, and I hope that will be enough to stop him from hurting you."

"Everyone keeps saying that he loves me." Whitney sighed, swiping her hair back from her face. "How can he love anything? He's been killing people right and left."

"He is hurting."

"Yeah," Whitney snorted, "everyone he gets near."

"No, I mean he is hurting inside." Rami tried to shake his head, but pain forced him to stop. "He is trying to protect the Races."

"That may be his excuse for the mine, but what about this poor little village?" Whitney shook her head. "You think he's finally gone nuts?"

"No. I do not know why he is..." Rami tried to articulate his thoughts. "Something is wrong. He is not himself. In the last few days, he has been acting strangely. Distracted."

"Distracted by what?" Thomas asked.

"I do not know." Rami took a shaky breath. "Someone must reach him and bring him back." He looked at Whitney. "You are our best chance."

"I don't wanna do this," she whimpered, burying her face in her hands.

"If I could go, I would."

"I know." She let her hands drop and looked at the gentle giant.

"I wish there was another option," he murmured sadly.

"Me too."

"You can do this," Rami whispered.

"Well, if I can't," Whitney's voice trembled, "it won't matter 'cause I'll be dead."

Rami closed his eyes. "Good luck."

BRAVERY 101

Thomas stayed to have a quick word with Hamilton while Whitney went to say goodbye to Sandra.

"You really think this will work?" Sandra asked as Whitney dug through the suitcases and found her jacket.

"They seem to think so."

"But do you?"

Whitney thought about all the times Madraeus had come to her rescue. He had been her champion against wasps and rude businessmen, against vampires and inquisitive detectives. He had saved her life. She thought about the quiet, intimate times—the kiss in the mine.

Maybe he does care for me. Maybe I stand a chance. She remembered the body bags. *A small chance.*

Thomas opened the door and peered at them. "Are you ready?"

"No," Whitney mumbled. She turned to Sandra. "If I don't come back, take care of Grammy for me."

Sandra nodded. "I will."

Thomas smiled at her reassuringly as he held the door. They walked down the stairs to the hotel's lobby in silence. A thousand scenarios played out in her mind. Whitney tried to plan what she would say, but how could anyone know what would happen when confronting a crazed predator? She wondered if lion tamers felt this way every time they got into the cage.

She shook her head, *Don't think about it. Just one foot in front of the other.* Whitney took a deep breath and stepped out into the twilight.

It took only a few moments to drive to the little village where Madraeus had wreaked such havoc. As they drove into the town, Whitney scanned the deserted streets, alert to everything. It seemed that self-preservation and fear had taken over and driven the surviving villagers indoors. Thomas parked on one of the side streets.

"Do you know where he is?" she whispered as they got out of the car.

Thomas walked beside her, but his eyes were on the shadows that surrounded them.

"Hamilton and I followed his scent. He ranged all over the town. Not sure if he was evading capture or searching for Rami. But the trail got mixed up with the scents of Cecelia's men." He glanced at her. "The ones that attacked Rami."

Whitney nodded.

"That's when we lost his scent. But from the concentration of bodies," Whitney flinched at his words, "we think he went back to the abbey. He's probably still there."

"But you don't know?" Whitney looked around.

"No."

"All right." Whitney shivered and reached out to grab Thomas' hand. He glanced at her in confusion but then noticed her trembling. He squeezed her hand in reassurance.

The abbey loomed ahead of them. Lights aimed at the lower walls of the abbey highlighted the historical architecture to the most dramatic effect possible. High above them, floodlights illuminated the steeple from all sides. As she watched, a shadow moved across the tower. The angle of the lights made the shadow elongated and creepy.

It was Madraeus. She knew it. Whitney jerked Thomas to a stop.

"What's wrong?" Thomas asked.

Whitney pointed at the steeple. Thomas turned and caught sight of the shadow. They watched as it moved along the roof and disappeared below the roof's edge.

She started to back away, pulling on Thomas' hand. When he didn't come with her, she yanked on his arm.

"Come on!" Her voice shook. "I can't do this!"

"No." Thomas pulled her back up to his side and spoke to her without looking at her. His eyes were on the abbey. "You *can* do this, and you *will* do this."

"But I can't!" She tried to pull away from Thomas, but his grip on her hand tightened. "He's *gonna kill me!*"

Thomas finally looked at her. "He's gonna kill everyone unless you try to stop him!"

"Why can't you guys just jump him?" She stared up at the werewolf, shaking.

"Because there's only two of us!" Thomas snapped. "We'd be no match for him. You don't understand how powerful he is! I've never seen anyone who can fight like him."

Whitney remembered Madraeus taking on two vampires and a werewolf by himself when they had ambushed her in her apartment. He'd torn the head off the werewolf and destroyed her living room in the process. It had been a terrifying night.

"The only thing that's gonna stop him is you or the sun."

Whitney felt like she'd been slapped. Her or death by the sun? She stared at Thomas, feeling trapped and hopeless.

"You can do this." Thomas put his hands on her shoulders and turned her toward the abbey. "I'll stay close, but I don't know what he'll do if he sees me." He gave her a shove forward.

Whitney stumbled a few steps toward the abbey. Once she regained her balance, she took a deep breath and took one step, then another. Closer and closer to the ancient building, she walked on unsteady feet. She stared up at the brickwork on the front of the abbey. If she hadn't been so terrified, she might have thought it was pretty cool.

Her eyes darted from shadow to shadow, waiting for one of them to move, hoping that none of them would. Her heart rattled her ribs, making it hard to use her lungs properly. She jumped at every rustle of leaves and whisper of wind.

Thomas and Whitney crept toward the front of the building. No light came from the massive arched window. The double doors stood open, revealing the yawning blackness beyond. The silence from inside felt like death. Whitney shivered. There was no way she was going in there.

Whitney jumped as something rustled on the other side of the ivy-covered wall that shielded the garden from the street. She froze and looked at Thomas.

He nodded and pointed toward the garden entrance.

Whitney shook her head. She knew she had to go in there, but she couldn't move her feet.

Thomas shot her an eloquent look, reminding her of what was at stake.

She blew out a shaky breath. *Come on, Whitney*, she lectured herself. *You can do this.*

She managed to take a step and then another. Her hands clenched into fists at her side, but it didn't stop the shaking.

Another step and then another. She reached the stone archway that marked the entrance to the garden. She peered through the arch. With a last breath, she stepped into the night-shrouded garden.

The high wall behind her blocked the light from the street, but the floodlights shining on the abbey walls glowed above her. As her eyes slowly adjusted to the dimness, she could see flower beds with their occupants eager to bloom. Trees scattered throughout the alcove spread their branches over stone benches and walkways. Whitney wished she could see it by daylight. It would be beautiful and peaceful if the circumstances were different.

From the shadows at the far side of the enclosure, something growled. The hair on the back of her neck stood up and screamed for retreat, but Whitney stood frozen in place.

INTO THE VAMPIRE'S DEN

WHITNEY PEERED INTO THE shadows. She could just make out a figure crouched behind the flower bed in the corner, watching her from the darkness.

Madraeus.

His head was angled slightly downward, but she knew he was staring straight at her. He rose and stalked forward out of the darkness. His face and clothes were covered in dried blood from his killing spree. His body remained tense, ready to burst into the chase if she ran. He held his hands out from his sides, ready to grab.

She wanted to run, but she couldn't break away. Just like the fragile flowers around her, she was rooted to the ground.

Shaking with fear seemed to be the only movement she could manage. She couldn't even bring a sound out of her throat.

Slowly, Madraeus smiled. The light glinted off his ghostly white fangs.

Hatred and death were promised in every step. He didn't seem to know her. He snarled and surged forward, raising his right arm to slash her.

Whitney prayed her instinct to run would kick in, but she just stared at Madraeus as he bore down on her. Her death was coming so fast, and all she managed to do was breathe faster.

When he was about halfway across the garden, everything changed. A look of confusion replaced the hideous snarl. His steps faltered, and he stumbled. His expression quickly morphed into one of anguished recognition. He threw his head back and let out a soul-tearing howl.

Whitney covered her ears.

Madraeus started forward again.

Whitney cried out in terror and dropped to the ground, cowering in a ball with her arms over her head to ward off the blow she knew was coming.

Nothing happened.

She waited.

Still nothing.

She waited another full second before she peeked out. Everything was quiet. Slowly, she lowered her arms. Her boss lay crumpled in a pile a mere foot from her. Panting, he gripped the grass as if it were a lifeline.

Whitney's eyes darted around the garden, looking for an explanation. She tried to slow her breathing. She could already feel her lips tingling from hyperventilation. Slowly, in jerking increments, she raised up onto her knees and stared at Madraeus.

She reached a shaking hand toward him. "Madraeus?"

He raised his head. His eyes were still black orbs, but they held only anguish now. The malice was gone.

"Forgive me!" With a groan, he scrambled forward on all fours, practically tackling her. She swayed backward but managed to remain on her knees. He buried his face in her stomach. His arms held her in a steel grip, shaking almost as much as she had.

Whitney didn't know what else to do, so she wrapped her arms around his head and held him. She didn't hear Thomas come up behind her until she felt his hand on her shoulder.

She looked up at him. "What just happened?"

"I don't know," he said quietly, "but you're not dead, so it's all good. Let's get him out of here."

Thomas ran to the garden's arched exit while Whitney awkwardly tried to untangle herself from Madraeus. She wasn't making much progress. He just kept mumbling in Italian and pleading for her forgiveness.

"I don't think he is completely coherent." She grunted, still trying to get him to let go of her.

"Doesn't matter as long as he's calm," Thomas said absently as he scanned the street and then motioned for her to bring him forward.

"You're gonna have to help me," Whitney hissed at Thomas.

"We don't have time for this!" Thomas walked back over to grab Madraeus. He reached down to pull Madraeus to his feet, but the vampire snarled and took a swipe at him.

"Oh! No! No! No!" Whitney threw herself backward to keep Madraeus away from Thomas just as Thomas jumped back. Her unexpected move unbalanced Madraeus, pulling him over with her.

"Oof!" All the air rushed out of her as Whitney and Madraeus landed hard. She lay still for a moment, trying to get her breath back.

Madraeus curled around her protectively, muttering in Italian.

Thomas backed off and waited.

Whitney tried to pry Madraeus' arms loose from around her so she could get up, but he wouldn't budge. After struggling for a few moments, Whitney finally managed to extricate herself from Madraeus' grip and staggered to her feet. With a frustrated snort, she straightened her clothes.

"This is ridiculous." She reached down and grabbed Madraeus' arm, hauling him to his feet. She pulled his arm over her shoulders and started walking her dazed boss toward the archway.

Thomas moved out of the garden first. They stepped through the archway and made it about three steps before Thomas stopped.

"Ah crap!" He stared down the street at the line of men and vehicles approaching. The town had called in the army.

"Back!" Thomas snarled at Whitney. She looked up and saw the force of arms slowly progressing toward the abbey. They searched each building and alley as they came. After hesitating a fraction of a second, she tried to get Madraeus to turn around. It was like trying to steer a drunk.

"Can't you call Hamilton to come get us or something?" she hissed at Thomas as she steered Madraeus back into the garden.

"I can try, but we'd be the only car in town moving that isn't the army. Might draw a little too much attention."

"What if we can get away from the abbey's section of town? Then can he pick us up?" Whitney swayed as Madraeus moaned and pushed his face into her hair. She absently patted him like a puppy.

"If..." Thomas huffed, watching the progress of the soldiers.

"We're going to have to get out of this town anyway." Whitney glanced toward Thomas. "We have to get to Devon, remember?"

"Philtzer is supposed to be picking up a cargo van. That way, Rami and Unkhabami can keep doing their healing thing," Thomas pointed at Madraeus, "and we can keep the vamps out of the light."

"So where is he?"

"He was flying in this morning just before lunch," Thomas shrugged. "No idea when he'll get here."

"Great," Whitney sighed as Thomas poked his head back out of the archway.

"They're getting closer."

"Is there a back door?" Whitney asked.

As Thomas ran to do a quick search of the garden, Whitney tried to get a look at Madraeus. She moved so she could see his face. His eyes were glazed as if he wasn't really seeing what was happening around him. It was almost as if he were in some sort of trance.

Madraeus rattled off something in Italian and tightened his hold on her. He had never been anything but completely in control since the first time she had met him. But now, he seemed terrified and desperate. It scared her.

Thomas returned, shaking his head. "It's a solid wall all the way around except for a door that leads into the gardener's shed."

"Can we hide?" Whitney looked toward the shed, realizing as she asked that it was too small. "Can we climb the wall?"

"And go where?"

"I don't know! Why don't you come up with something!" Whitney snapped. "You're supposed to be the expert here."

"I'm working on it!" Thomas looked around again. "I honestly didn't think we'd still be alive at this point."

"What?" Whitney gaped. "You let me walk in here—"

"Relax, Whit," Thomas grinned, "it worked out."

"Worked out, my butt!" Whitney snapped, pointing toward the coming army. "They're gonna arrest us!"

"I doubt they'll arrest us." Thomas poked his head out of the garden again to check the army's progress. "They'll probably shoot us on sight."

Whitney made a strangled, snarly, growly sound of frustration. She pointed away from the army. "What if we just go out the doorway and turn that way? If we hug the wall, maybe we can stay out of their view. We head down the first alley we find and get far enough away that Philtzer or Hamilton can come get us."

"Seriously?" Thomas pointed to the vampire clinging to her for dear life. "Dragging him?"

"You wanna stay here?"

"Good point." Thomas glanced back at the soldiers. "How are you at being invisible?"

HIDE AND SEEK

Whitney took a step forward, but Madraeus pulled her back.

"Please," Madraeus muttered into her neck. "Don't leave me."

Whitney looked at him in surprise. It was the first thing he'd said in English since collapsing. "I'm not going to leave you, but you gotta start walking."

Whitney started forward again, pulling her dazed boss with her.

They struggled and stumbled, but they made it to the archway. Thomas looked out again. The army was almost a block away. He motioned for Whitney to go. She pulled and staggered and pushed, trying to get Madraeus pointed in the right direction.

"It's like a three-legged race, but they tied our heads together by mistake," she complained.

"At least he's not trying to kill you," Thomas whispered as he brought up the rear, watching for discovery. "So far, so good."

As she stumbled against the ivy-covered brick, Whitney griped, "How long is this stupid wall?"

Thomas glanced around. "Shouldn't be much farther."

They staggered on for another few yards until the wall ended and a parking area opened up to their right. Whitney stopped. Only a few cars were still in it. Some were sitting with their doors open. Whitney glanced down at Madraeus, wondering if he'd had anything to do with that. Thomas looked around the parking lot.

"Can we steal a car?" Whitney asked.

"Not from this lot." There was only one driveway, and that opened onto the street the soldiers were searching. "Keep going." He pointed to a small alley at the back of the lot. "There."

"Where do you think that goes?" she asked as she started the complicated process of moving again.

"No idea, but it's not towards the army."

It took an eternity for them to make it across the parking lot to the small opening that Thomas had seen. The werewolf ran ahead into the little alley to see where it led. He returned and motioned for her to follow him.

It was too narrow for her and Madraeus to walk side by side. Whitney had to turn sideways and sort of drag him in the right direction. She stumbled and banged her elbow hard into the bricks.

"This is fun," she grumbled. "How do I get into these situations?"

"There's another parking lot up here. It leads off into a street with a bunch of shops." Thomas said over his shoulder.

An eerie silence settled over the town, amplifying the shouts of soldiers as they searched street after street. For hours, Whitney and Thomas snaked their way through the town with the threat of capture constantly looming. Periodically, Thomas would dart ahead, checking to see if the way was clear. More and more often, he would return and report that the way was blocked by soldiers or police. Whitney felt like a fox slowly being driven into a corner.

Near dawn, Whitney huddled against the back wall of a house with Madraeus' head in her lap as she waited for Thomas to return from another scouting mission. She stroked his hair as she watched the sky become lighter and lighter. Soon, it wouldn't matter if the army caught them. Madraeus would be dead, burnt to ash. The thought twisted her gut. She leaned her head back and stared at the sky. *Please don't make me watch him die.*

Thomas came around the corner and sat down with a sigh. "We might have to break into one of these houses."

"Won't the people inside get grumpy about that?" she asked.

"Yeah," Thomas grinned. "Maybe a little."

Whitney looked down at Madraeus. He hadn't moved in a while. She hoped he was going to come out of this psychotic trance soon. He seemed calmer. He had stopped muttering and asking for forgiveness about an hour ago. She counted it as progress.

Suddenly, Thomas sobered and dug in his pocket for his phone. He glanced at the number before answering.

Without even saying hello, Thomas exclaimed, "Philtzer! Tell me you're coming to get us!"

The relief on his face as he listened to the answer told Whitney all she needed to know. She sagged in relief. Rescue was coming. She listened as Thomas rattled off the names of the closest streets.

"Hurry?" she added, although she doubted that Philtzer could hear her.

The sun had almost gained the horizon when Philtzer pulled up with a little box van. He slammed on the brakes and jumped out before the truck stopped rocking. He hurried over to them.

Whitney shook Madraeus' shoulder, trying to wake him. Philtzer reached down to help. Thomas grabbed Philtzer's arm before he could touch Madraeus.

"No!" Thomas and Whitney cried together.

"What! What's wrong?" Philtzer looked at them in alarm.

"He won't let anyone but her touch him," Thomas warned. Philtzer looked down at Whitney.

She shook Madraeus' shoulder again. "Come on, we're going," she said.

Madraeus lifted his head and looked up at her.

"Whitney?" It was the first time he had recognized her.

"Hi."

"Boss?" Philtzer asked. "You okay?"

Madraeus looked up in confusion.

"Philtzer?" He glanced around, trying to reorient himself. He noticed the brightness of the sky. "The sun!" He struggled to stand.

Philtzer and Thomas jumped forward to help him. Madraeus staggered as he stood, but they steadied him.

"Truck's waiting." Philtzer pointed at the van. Madraeus nodded listlessly and let them lead him to the back of the truck.

Now that Madraeus was someone else's responsibility, all the adrenaline that had sustained her through the night suddenly dumped into Whitney's stomach. She rolled over onto her knees and threw up.

"Whit?" Philtzer glanced back.

Whitney climbed stiffly to her feet. She stood on shaking legs and then slowly followed them.

Thomas rolled up the back door of the van. Madraeus moved to climb up into the cargo area but stopped.

"Rami?" Madraeus choked out. He stared into the face of his oldest friend, who was sitting in an open coffin in the back of the truck.

"Yes, my friend." Rami nodded.

Madraeus scrambled awkwardly up into the cargo bay and threw himself down between the two coffins. He grabbed Rami's hand and stared at him disbelievingly.

Thomas grinned at their reunion and climbed into the cargo area, taking a seat on the second coffin. Rami looked much better. He was still not back to normal, but he was healing. Unkhabami sat on a pile of tarps at the head of Rami's coffin. Dark circles rimmed her eyes, and exhaustion etched her face. Her gaze never left Rami.

"Please, my friend, sit." Rami frowned. "You look worse than I feel."

"I thought you were dead!" Madraeus rasped.

"I know." Rami nodded sadly. "I wish you had responded in a less violent way."

"What are you talking about?" Madraeus shook his head in confusion.

"Boss," Thomas sat forward and put a hand on his shoulder, "do you remember the last couple of days?"

Madraeus looked from Rami to Thomas to Unkhabami and then slowly looked down at his blood-soaked shirt. "My God, what have I done?"

Thomas exchanged a look with Rami and sighed. "You better sit down, boss." Thomas slid a hand under Madraeus' limp arm and helped him up off the floor. "We've got something to tell you."

Philtzer looked at Whitney. She was staring into the back of the van, swaying on her feet. Philtzer shook his head and reached up to pull the rolling door shut.

"Come on." He put an arm around Whitney and gently guided her toward the cab.

Whitney crawled up onto the seat and pulled her knees up to her chest.

"Here," Philtzer shrugged out of his coat and handed it to Whitney. She stared at it blankly. "You're shivering."

Whitney glanced down at herself, realizing that it was true. "Thank you." She pulled the coat across her knees and tucked it under her chin.

"You'll be okay," Philtzer said. Stepping back, he gave the door a good shove to get it to shut. "At least, I hope you will," he muttered and ran around to get in the driver's side.

RUN AWAY

Hours later, Philtzer pulled off the road and jumped out. Whitney's head jerked up from where she had been dozing and looked around.

"Where are we?"

He glanced up and down the road. He looked back at Whitney. "Border crossing's coming. Come on."

Whitney felt more confused. "The what?" She climbed out and looked up and down the road. There was nothing but grass and trees in both directions.

Philtzer trotted to the back of the van and banged on the door. "Border."

The van began to rock as everyone inside shifted around. Whitney hugged Philtzer's jacket closed and walked back to join him just as the door rolled up. Thomas looked down at them.

"I've got papers for two coffins and two workmen," Philtzer said, looking into the van where Thomas stood between the two coffins. The lids were closed, hiding Rami and Madraeus from the sun. "That leaves two people without papers."

Thomas looked at Whitney and then at Unkhabami. "How about two per coffin?"

"What!" Whitney backed up a step.

"It's the only place. We have to get across the border, Whit." Philtzer assured her as a couple of cars passed by, buffeting them with a gust of wind. He glanced up and down the road again. "Sooner rather than later, before we make people suspicious."

"Can't I just walk across?"

"No," they said in unison.

Thomas held a hand out to Whitney. She stared up at him, shaking her head. "I can't."

"You didn't think you could face the boss either, but you did. Come on."

"Whit, just do it." Philtzer reached over and hooked a hand under her armpit, propelling her up into the back of the van. Thomas rolled the door shut again to shield them from the sun while they rearranged everyone. Unkhabami was already lifting the lid on Rami's coffin. Thomas turned to open the one Madraeus occupied.

"Thomas, I can't be locked into..." Whitney turned back toward the door. "Not with..."

"Whit, you can do this. It's only for a few minutes while we cross the border, then you can get out again," Thomas said calmly, stepping toward her. She looked down to see Madraeus sitting up in the coffin. She looked from his grave eyes to the blood on his shirt and shook her head.

"I can't." She pulled back. She could feel Rami and Unkhabami watching her.

"Whitney, it is perfectly safe," Rami rumbled.

"Get in, child," Unkhabami added.

Whitney shook her head, struggling against the hold Thomas had on her arms.

"Whit, I love ya to death," Thomas took her by the shoulders and turned her so he could look her straight in the eyes, "but if you don't get in on your own, I'm going to knock you out, and you will have one hell of a headache later."

"Thomas," Madraeus warned, but Thomas ignored him. They both knew it was the only way.

Realizing he was serious, Whitney closed her eyes and sighed, "All right."

She took off Philtzer's jacket and handed it to Thomas. Carefully, she stepped into the coffin and tried to sit. Madraeus turned on his side and tried to make more room. It was a tight fit. Finally, she ended up on her side, facing him.

"Wait!" she sat up suddenly. Thomas almost whacked her head with the lid.

"What's wrong?" Madraeus frowned up at her.

"You've..." She glanced at his blood-stained shirt. "You're not hungry, right?"

"No."

Whitney swallowed hard, then eased herself down into the coffin once more. Lightly, she rested her head on his bent arm, trying not to look him in the eye. The coffin wasn't big enough to allow any space between them.

Thomas closed the lid, and darkness surrounded them. There was a muffled thump as he draped the tarp on top of their hiding place. She heard the engine start. The van rocked as they started moving. Her hand shot out and grabbed the silken lining of the lid.

"Shhh." Madraeus' hand came up to rest on her hip. "You're safe."

Whitney felt his breath on her face. An immediate sense of panic filled her. The complete darkness with a predator so close was too much like the mine. She started breathing faster.

She squirmed as claustrophobia seized her. "How is being locked in a coffin with a vampire safe?"

"Whitney, stay calm," Madraeus grunted as she banged her foot and knees into his legs. "Breathe slower."

"I'm trying," she puffed.

He squeezed her hip lightly. "Think of something else."

"Like what?"

"Somewhere that the dark wouldn't bother you, like camping or your bedroom." His voice trailed away on the last word.

"Right," Whitney whispered. "Like camping or hide and seek." Her breathing evened out a little. Slowly, she let go of the death grip she had on the lid lining. She lowered her hand, and it landed on his chest.

He flinched.

"Sorry," she whispered, snatching her hand back.

"I don't mind." He reached out, grabbed her hand, and pulled it up between them, cradling it to his chest as he had done so many times before when she had been scared. It comforted her more than it should have.

They rode silently for a few moments, feeling the van start and stop as it entered the line to cross the border.

"I'm sorry," he whispered. His thumb moved back and forth over her knuckles.

Whitney's fingers flexed against his chest, feeling the stiff material and remembering that it was dried blood.

"For killing everyone?"

"For everything."

She was prevented from responding by the sound of the door rolling up. Madraeus' grip tensed. They could hear muffled voices from the back of the van. They heard a thumping sound that could have been the tarp being lifted and then dropped. After a few moments, the door rolled closed, and the van lurched into motion once again.

"I think we're across," Madraeus whispered.

"Then why aren't we stopping?" Whitney shifted impatiently.

"We have to get far enough away from the border first."

"Oh."

Once again, they rode in silence, feeling every bump in the road. Madraeus continued to hold her hand as the movement of the van rocked them back and forth.

"Madraeus?" Whitney whispered.

"Yes?"

"What happened in the garden?"

He stopped breathing for a moment and then sighed, "Does it matter?"

"Yes. You ran straight for me. I thought you were going to kill me, but you suddenly stopped."

He remained silent. She felt him move in the darkness.

"You're not going to answer, are you?" Whitney shifted, resettling her head on his arm. She wished she could see his face.

"I... I couldn't..."

Whitney felt him shift away from her. She knew he was still looking at her because she could feel his breath on her face. She wondered if he could see her. She knew his vampire eyesight was so much better than hers in the darkness. His hesitation unnerved her. He was one of the most decisive people she knew.

"Couldn't what?"

He sighed. "When I saw you, the vision took over everything like it had already happened." She felt him shudder. "I thought that I had..." He took a shaky breath. "I saw you die by my hand."

"And that stopped you?"

"I can't live in a world without you."

She froze. His confession shook her to the core. *Was everyone right? Did he love her?*

The van bounced to a stop, jostling them roughly. The door rolled up.

"Damn," Madraeus growled. He shifted forward and kissed her long and deep. It was a kiss of desperation, longing, and frustration.

Whitney jerked backward as the coffin lid opened. Her chest heaved as she stared at Madraeus. She couldn't stand the sadness in his eyes. Without a word, she scrambled backward out of the coffin like a crab, landing in a pile at Thomas' feet.

"Whoa, Whit!" Thomas reached down to help her up. "I told you it wouldn't be that long."

She shoved past Thomas and banged into the door, scrabbling to get it open. Thomas lunged to grab the tarp. He threw it over a ducking Madraeus just before she rolled the door up. Sunlight blazed into the back of the van.

"What the hell!" Thomas growled, but she didn't stop. "Whitney!"

She stumbled away from the van into the grass on the side of the road. Landing on her knees, she wrapped her arms around her head and started to rock. Thoughts raced through her head. *He can't live without me? He just massacred a village! How could he...? How can I..."*

"He can't!" she whispered. "I can't."

Philtzer lifted her out of the grass and guided her back to the van. He settled her in the front seat and covered her up with his jacket again. She heard the door roll shut and the engine start, but the rest of the world was too confusing to think about. She felt the van pull out into traffic once more.

"Get some rest, Whit," Philtzer patted her shoulder. "This story ain't over yet."

Also by Adriana Pridemore

Council of Races Series
This Job Sucks!
Your Job Bites!

Short Stories
(Available on Amazon KDP)
The Apple's Bite
Just a Little Nap
Flaming Fang

CHECK OUT BOOK ONE!

Whitney Martindale's new position as a temp receptionist at InfiniCorp seemed like a blessing. But then she met her new boss, Madraeus Ravilla. He's moody, rude, and blames her for the disaster in the filing cabinet left by her predecessor. Could things get any worse? Yes. Yes, they could.

Whitney's ex-boyfriend turns up at an office party sporting fangs and tries to suck the life out of her! Whitney finds out her boss is a vampire and she works with werewolves, vampires, and a host of supernatural beings called the Races. Now, Whitney is being stalked by her vampire ex, the police are following her, her family and friends are in danger, and she is still responsible for getting the filing cabinet straightened out!

This job sucks!

About the Author

Adriana Pridemore has loved reading and writing all of her life. She has been a journalist, freelance editor/proofreader, and teacher. She currently lives in Montana with her wonderful husband and family, a fuzzy feline queen, and a moose-sized St. Bernard.